Expecting Serendipity

Amy Gelsthorpe

Merry Christmas!

Amy Gelsthorpe
11/17/15

This is a work of fiction. All of the characters, organizations, and events portrayed in this novel are either products of the author's imagination or are used frequently. Any resemblance to actual persons, living or dead, is purely coincidental

ISBN 978-1514628041

This one is for Andrea for giving me best friend material, my Niece Ashley for coming up with the title, my #1 fan Mickey who has been so encouraging, and my family for putting up with my fun attitude while writing!

Chapter 1

I can't believe this is it! It's really happening. We're standing in the middle of Central Park as a few small crowds of people mingle around. I imagine everyone will stop what they are doing and clap happily for us in a few short seconds. As I glance at the crowd, it's surreal, like something out of a movie.

Everything seems perfect! I can barely see straight as my left hand outstretches ready for Josh to slide on my ring. He already is assuming the ceremonial position on one knee. This is exactly how I've always imagined. I can't look at him any longer. I'm so excited…I close my eyes…*My hand is getting tired…* I reopen my eyes and look down at Josh. *He's taking forever,* I think to myself.

I close my eyes again thinking he may feel put on the spot or nervous. All of a sudden, I feel him grab my hand. *Eeek this is really it!* I feel a tug. *This is so strange.* I open my eyes to see what is happening, and Josh is pulling himself up to a standing position using my hand as support. *What the hell? What is going on?* I think to myself.

Josh stands straight up and kisses me once more. Now, I'm so confused. I feel a heat wave come across my body as I try to control my emotions. Josh says, "I need some water. I'm not feeling so well."

Now my face is getting red. I angrily follow him to a nearby water fountain, trying to maintain my dignity. He leans over and takes a short, loud sip. As I look at him hunched over the water fountain, a small part of me is annoyed he could ruin such a once-in-a-lifetime opportunity for a proposal. I try to reason with myself that it may have simply been nerves. Against my better judgment, I'm determined to ignore what's happened and move past my fantasy unravelling.

Josh looks at me compassionately and scared. He's sweating profusely, and it's quite disgusting. *I'm not going to get engaged to a hot mess of a man. This is not how I imagined Josh looking for this Moment…Unacceptable.* I've waited my whole life for this Moment and this is not how it'll happen. I think quickly and say, "How about dessert?" Josh takes my hand. *Ewww…sweaty palms feel so clammy, like holding a damp sponge*, I think as we begin to walk up the block towards Magnolia Bakery.

Walking into the bakery, I'm pleasantly welcomed by the familiar, sweet smelling aroma filling the air. I'm a regular here, often meeting Josh and friends. We're greeted by everyone immediately as we step to the counter. Sasha, my favorite employee, says, "Hi guys! How you two doing today?"

Smiling back at her I mumble a lie, something like, "We're great!" *Although judging by what just happened in the park, I'm not quite sure how great we are.*

I choose the cupcake of the day from the "cupcake calendar". It's always hard to choose from the main menu since everything is so delectable. Usually, I simply go for the cupcake of the day, and today it's banana cake with chocolate butter cream icing which I know is divine. Sasha gives me my cupcake, and I take a quick bite as I walk over to meet Josh sitting at our favorite spot. *Yummy…it tastes great!* Josh has only ordered a cup of water and seems to be acting very strangely.

As I pull my chair out and sit down, Josh barely notices I'm sitting in front of him. Now, I have to imagine he's extremely embarrassed about his failed attempt to propose.

He probably realizes he missed the perfect opportunity and feels stupid, *as he should.* I look at him staring into his glass of water and say, “Is the water making you feeling any better? I bet you’re hungry.”

Josh looks at me with glassy eyes, and I immediately recognize he definitely is not well. He slowly stands up and whispers to me he’s going to catch a cab home. He says, “Kiera, I feel really bad off. I just want to be home.”

“Okay, I’ll go with you?” I say. “I hate for you to go alone not feeling well.”

“NO!” he says, not whispering anymore. “Really, I’m fine. I just need to rest. I think I may be coming down with something. I’ll call you tomorrow.”

What the hell? I think to myself.

Josh awkwardly touches my arm, turns, and heads out the door. Deflated and confused, I sit back down. All of a sudden, my cupcake doesn’t look so appealing. I feel awful. Josh just put me through the worst rollercoaster of emotions ever. Twenty minutes ago, I thought I was getting engaged. Now, I’m sitting here alone because my boyfriend is too damn chicken shit to go through with it. Ever since he stood from his knees, he looked as if he were going to throw up. If that's how I make him feel, maybe he needs to reconsider being with me.

Ugh! I feel so awful thinking about how stupid I must have looked standing there in the park. What was I expecting him to do, just whip out my fancy diamond and slap it on my ring finger. *What an idiot I am.* I wish I'd played things a bit cooler, maybe even pretended to not know what was happening. No wonder he got squirmy. I probably made him uncomfortable.

Josh and I have been dating for two years. We first met at a mutual friend's gala in Upper Manhattan. After a few drinks that night we flirted a little, and before we left we exchanged numbers. I waited three days for him to call thinking he was definitely the type for the "three day rule." When he didn't call after day four, I wrote him off. On day six, he finally called.

He was not exactly what I'd call a charmer, and maybe even shy, but I knew there was something about him I liked and I wanted to get to know him better. When he asked me to dinner for the upcoming weekend, I tried not to sound desperate. I decided to play it cool and hesitated before answering. I told him I would need to clear a couple of things off of my calendar, when really there was nothing.

Finally, I told him yes. I was impressed when he texted me Saturday morning to let me know he'd made reservations at Minetta Tavern, which is known for its epically delicious French cooking.

I remember every detail of the night, exactly what we both ordered, what I was wearing, and what he was wearing. We had a marvelous time together. Josh was school-boy shy, and I found it so sexy. He blushed throughout the night. Once I realized he was easy to make blush, I provoked him by purposefully saying embarrassing things, and we both laughed. We flirted back and forth all through dinner.

After dinner, we went for a walk and talked some more. Josh talked about his job. He's a financial planner for Merrill Lynch. I couldn't help but giggle at the irony, because I'm quite the opposite of a financial planner. I told him maybe he could take a shot at planning my disjointed finances if he liked, and he looked puzzled as I laughed. When he asked why it was so funny, I remember telling him I wasn't the best at managing money (understatement). I told him I pay all of my bills and everything, but I usually play with what's left. I could tell he was unsure about that honesty.

Sitting alone, I think about how Josh has changed me and taught me a great deal about finances. I try much harder to not make "unnecessary" purchases, which is a good thing. Don't get me wrong- I still shop a lot, and have a blast doing so, but now I also save a portion for "rainy days" and as Josh puts it, "For the future." I get a gross feeling in my stomach as I think about what just happened in the park. *How in the hell will I ever get past this?* I feel so rejected. I stand to leave Magnolia's Bakery and my phone buzzes. It's my best friend Danielle.

Danielle: *Hi! Let's meet up. You busy?*

Kiera: *Perfect! I'm leaving Magnolia's. Where?*

Danielle: *Coffee? Starbucks East 87th?*

Kiera: *Yes, give me 5 min.*

Danielle: *K.*

Impeccable timing from Danielle. What an awesome friend! I totally could use a meet-up-with- Danielle after this evening's events. Danielle and I have been friends since grade school, almost 20 years now. We both turned 28 just a few weeks ago. Our birthdays are only three days apart, and that makes things especially fun. We always celebrate together and are inseparable most of the time. After college, we made a pact that no matter what, as long as we were both single, we'd live in New York City as close to each other as possible. We've had our ups and downs and seen our share of differences, but we're BFF'S until the end. We have the type of friendship that people envy. We can be honest as hell with each other and still love one another. We can tell each other we look like shit, and it's perceived as caring for each other. I love her to death.

When I get to Starbucks, Danielle has already ordered our coffees and is sitting at a table. I walk over to her and give her a hug. Already she knows something is up. She puts her hand on her hip and says, "Spill it… NOW!"

"How do you do that? You always know when something is up. We haven't even spoken yet."

"Kiera, we've been friends too long. Besides, your face can't hide anything."

I smile a half smile at her, and feel so grateful to have her as my friend. There is no bull nonsense in this friendship. I say, "Here's the thing… Josh and I just had the most bizarre encounter. We were in the Park after dinner having a lovely walk and talking. I could tell he was trying to be unusually romantic, but I didn't think too much about it until we stopped under one of my favorite trees. I mean, he knows I love this particular tree. He stumbled over himself for a second, and then got down on one knee."

Danielle interjects saying, "Eeek! He asked you to marry him?!"

As she grabs my left hand, her face turns white and contorts in shock as there is no ring. She says, "Where the hell is your ring?"

"Let me finish," I say.

"Okay. Okay…" Danielle says, exaggerated and confused.

"…He got down on one knee, and I was so excited I could barely breathe. I closed my eyes and embarrassingly held out my hand. Why I held it out so sure of myself, I do not know. All of a sudden I felt him tugging on my left hand, and I was so happy thinking this is it! That's when the weirdest thing happened. He began pulling himself back up saying he wasn't feeling well and needed water. We walked over to a fountain, and he got some water."

"What? What in the hell? Oh honey… I always knew there was something about him. He's such a jerk! UGH! What a shitty proposal…well, I mean almost proposal. What happened next? Tell me more."

"I started to feel really crappy, embarrassed, and hated how the night was going. I mean, this is something I've waited for my whole life, and I thought my dream engagement was about to be ruined by him being awkwardly nervous and clearly unsure of what he was doing. That's when I suggested dessert at the Magnolia Bakery. I was hoping he could build up the nerve to finish what he started. We walked over and I ordered a cupcake. All he got was a water. As soon as I sat down, he stood up and told me he wasn't feeling well and needed to go home. He said he thought he was coming down with something."

"Oh shit, Kier! I don't know what to say. That really sucks!"

"Tell me about it."

We finish our coffees and decide to catch a cab to Danielle's place. I didn't really feel like going back to my apartment anyways and was relieved when Danielle suggested I should come hang out. I agreed because wine fests should be partaken in the company of friends, and tonight definitely will require a lot of wine.

We get out of the cab and walk up to her gate box where she enters her code, and we go upstairs. Once inside Danielle says, "Ok, chicka, I want you to go sit down and put your feet up. I'll pour our wine and we're just going to chill and forget our worries."

"Sounds good to me," I say, relieved to be in her company.

As I lean back on her Ethan Allen sofa anticipating my wine buzz, I begin to relax. I love how plush this sofa feels. I helped her pick it out six months ago, and once I saw the brown, distressed leather, I knew it belonged in her apartment. I pull over the ivory chenille throw and place it over my legs.

My cell vibrates indicating a text. I look at the display, and it's Josh. Danielle must have heard it from the kitchen because she's yelling, "Don't you dare respond to him yet! Don't you dare."

I laugh ridiculously hard as I think about Danielle's silly rules of dating. I say back, "Really? It's not like we just started dating you know. We've been dating for two years now. I don't have to play games, and besides I haven't even read the text."

"Well read it…Read it aloud though."

I open the text and begin to read it:

Josh: *feel like an idiot. sorry about tonight. hope you're ok. Let's talk*

Danielle says, "What? Really? I'm so confused. What in the hell is he talking about? I mean it's clear what he's talking about…obviously what he jacked up in the park, but shit, Kier, he really has a lot to learn. You absolutely cannot respond to that text tonight. Let him stir. How random! UGH! Men!"

I laugh at Danielle and say, "Okay. You're right. I won't respond tonight. Give me some wine, pronto!"

I shut my cell phone down, and Danielle and I finish off a bottle and a half of wine. She insists I sleep over, and I agree it's a good idea. Danielle stumbles off to bed after throwing me a pillow and an extra tooth brush.

Lying down on the sofa, I turn my phone back on and have Siri set the alarm for me to wake up in time to go home and shower for work. I live three blocks away so I need to wake up thirty minutes before I normally would to give myself time for the walk home. Before Siri speaks, the text alert vibrates four times. I swipe it off of the screen for a minute and proceed to set the alarm. Then, I look at the texts, and they are all from Josh. *Holy shit!* I wonder why he texted me so much. I read them all, and he basically wants me to meet up with him tonight to talk. He even asked if he could come over in one of them. I decided that I'd text him back.

Kiera: S*orry…missed your txts. At Danielle's and going to bed. Can we meet tomorrow?*

Two seconds later he responds…

Josh: *I really need to talk. I guess it can wait until tomorrow. Text me when you can.*

I close my eyes. *What in the world is going on in his brain?* My mind wonders. I can't seem to get him or his odd behavior off of my mind. I toss around on the couch trying to get comfortable. Finally, I settle into a comfortable spot and just relax. All of the sudden, Danielle's door buzzer goes off so loudly I about jump out of my skin. *What the crap?* Danielle comes out of her bedroom and looks at me puzzled. I say, "Who in the hell would buzz you this late? It's 2:30 in the morning."

Danielle answers the buzz and says, "Yes? Who is it?" A very familiar voice answers back saying, "It's me, Josh." As Danielle buzzes him in she looks at me cross. "You texted him back after we agreed you wouldn't?"

"That's not exactly what happened."

"Oh really? Well what happened and how does he know you're here?"

"I turned my phone on to set my alarm. I saw he'd texted me four times while it was off, they all came through at once. I shot a quick text back just saying I couldn't meet him tonight and that I was sleeping over here."

Danielle rolls her eyes and says, "Smooth move ex-lax!"

"What? I'm sorry. I didn't know he'd come over."

We hear Josh knock at the door and Danielle lets him in. I walk over and can't help but notice how awful he looks. Danielle stands there for a minute looking at us, and then excuses herself. We walk over to the couch. I say, "Why are you here?"

He barely looks me in the eye and says, "I couldn't sleep. After the park I felt so awful. I wanted it to be perfect. I wanted to ask you to marry me. I wanted us to live happily ever after. I'm such an asshole."

"What? No you were just nervous. You're not an asshole. Really, it's no big deal. Let's just put it behind us. We can laugh about it someday. Really, we can forget about it."

Josh stands up and starts pacing around Danielle's living room. He looks at me and says, "Kiera, it's not that easy. Don't you see? I tried, but I couldn't. I just couldn't go through with it. I've been carrying your ring around in my pocket for over a year now. For some reason I've not been able to bring myself to ask you to marry me. I thought for a long time it was nerves, but tonight I finally realized it's not nerves… It's us. We just aren't right for each other. The reason I came here tonight was to let you know I want to break up. It's clear to me that what I thought we had, isn't what we had. It's not the real deal Kiera. If I really loved you enough to marry you, I'd think I would want to propose more than anything. Kiera, that's what you deserve. You deserve someone who wants to propose to you. I hope you can come to accept this as goodbye, and I really do wish you well."

Josh turns to leave. He looks back and says, "We'll need to arrange a time to switch out our stuff in the next few days. I'll be in touch."

Damn it! I'm speechless. I stand there staring at him as he turns to the door and he says, "Goodbye, Kiera."

Chapter 2

I walk down the hallway to Danielle's room as she had excused herself from the living area when Josh came in. I open her bedroom door, and she literally falls out as she was eavesdropping the whole time. I ignore her typical "Danielle" behavior and try to catch my breath. I'm not sure how I'm feeling about what just happened or about this horrible day. I'm not sad, which I sort of find peculiar. I think I'm stunned and possibly taken aback. Danielle pulls herself up from the floor and nonchalantly says, "Is he gone?"

"Yes," I say. "As if you weren't listening the whole time."

"You all talk too quietly; I couldn't hear anything…"

We come out of her bedroom and walk to the living room. Danielle turns for the kitchen, opens the cabinet, gets out two glasses, and pours some more wine. Handing me my glass, she angrily says, "What the hell was so important that he couldn't wait until tomorrow?"

I lean back on the familiar plush sofa sinking my head back to relax. Danielle sits beside me and I say, "He came over to break up with me."

"What?!? What in the hell? I thought he was trying to propose to you a few hours ago? I'm so confused, Kier. I mean seriously confused!"

Staring blankly towards Danielle's T.V. screen I say, "I'm not sad or upset. Don't you think that's a bit odd? I don't know what to think about all of this. I'm not saying that I won't miss him or anything, but I'm not sure why I feel completely numb, really no emotion at all."

Danielle smiles and says, "You know what? I'm not upset either. This is great news! Yep! This needed to happen months ago."

I roll my eyes at her attitude. Ever since Josh and I started dating, Danielle has often whined about losing her best friend to an "unworthy loser." I'm not exactly sure why Danielle ever came to the conclusion Josh is a loser, but maybe her intuition was better than mine. Josh has a great job at Merrill and makes good money. He always treated me nice and is a generous person. I never completely understood Danielle's title for him or why she thought so poorly of him, but I guess it doesn't matter anymore. Needless to say, the two of them never hit it off and it often made things hard for me.

Finally, we both decide we can talk more about things later, and we go to bed since we both have to go to work in the morning. I wake up before Danielle and gather my things for my walk home. When I get to my building, Louie the doorman buzzes me in. He looks at me dubiously as if to say "where have you been all night," probably because I'm wearing the same clothes from yesterday. I ignore his peculiar stare and sprint up the stairs to my apartment. Standing in front of my door I reach in my new Tory Burch Middy to find my keys. *UGH!* Like always, I end up having to sit down and dump everything out. Everything I need always seems to be on the bottom.

Finally, I find my keys, repack my bag, and stand up to unlock the door. My neighbor from across the hallway startles me. He's fourty-ish and extremely, ridiculously, dreamy hot. He's the kind of neighbor every woman wishes and only dreams to have. He's always friendly, yet mysteriously reserved. Often we borrow things from each other and occasionally engage in what I think is casual flirting, but he probably sees it as normal conversation. Chandler is a lawyer at one of the largest firms in New York. He doesn't talk too much about work, but enough for me to know his job is very stressful. He notices me and we greet each other with a friendly smile. I say, "Oh! Good morning, Chandler, you startled me."

"I'm sorry about that. I'm just heading out to work. Have a good day, Kiera. Hopefully I'll see ya later."

As he turns the corner, I feel like I can breathe again. I know it sounds silly, and although I've been in a relationship with Josh for the past two years, every time I run into Chandler I get giddy. It's embarrassing really, but thank God he doesn't seem to notice. Three weeks ago, when I came home after having drinks with Danielle, Chandler and his girlfriend were in the hallway going into his apartment. Being polite, Chandler quickly introduced me to her. Her name was Juliette and I thought the name fit her perfectly. She was poised, refined, and very eloquently dressed. I'm almost positive she was in a Chanel number of some sort. Upon Chandler introducing me to Juliette, I tripped over my laptop bag strap as I was going to shake her hand, but somehow I caught myself on the wall by his door and was able to remain upright. It was anything but graceful. I felt so stupid and embarrassed. I said a quick hello and darted into my apartment. I am certain I looked dumb that day.

I turn my key and continue to walk into my apartment. Closing the heavy wooden door behind me, I realize how exhausted I am. I make my way back to my bedroom to get ready for work.

While in the shower my thoughts are on Josh. I wonder how he's feeling after last night, or if he even cares. Honestly, I truly feel numb about the breakup which seems odd. Sure I want to get married more than anything in the world, and to me the scariest thing is that if he'd have gone through with the proposal I would have said yes. Standing here in the shower with the water streaming down my face, I realize how awful it is to be in such a desperate state that I'd risk happiness just to be married. *How could I have been so driven by the infatuation of marriage to not consider my true feelings about the person I think I want to marry?*

Like most girls, I dreamed of getting married my whole life. Literally, my whole entire life. Ever since I can remember, I've wanted to be married. I used to write my vows and recite them from memory into the mirror over and over. I know it's normal, and most little girls all dream of one day being married, but for me it was constantly on my mind.

Now as an adult it's been my ultimate goal, almost an obsession, to be married. I feel like I've been looking for "the one" forever.

After my 25th birthday the longing to settle down and get married became even stronger than I thought was possible. My biological clock was ticking hard. I was dating two or three different guys, but I definitely could not see myself marrying them. I had fun hanging out with each of them, but my longing and eagerness for marriage grew stronger and stronger.

Finally, when I decided to stop casually dating is when I met Josh. Claire, my co-worker, was the one throwing the gala where we met. It was a 30th birthday party for another co-worker. Claire's husband Richard and Josh were best friends, so of course Josh was at the party. The thought of seeing Claire today at work makes me wonder if Josh has already told Richard about dumping me. I assume if not yet, he would soon.

Claire's desk is adjacent to my cubicle. We're both buyers for Whitaker & Bluff department stores. Since my teen years, I've been intrigued with Whitaker & Bluff. I used to love seeing their displays in the windows at Christmas time…actually, I still do. I can honestly say this is my dream job. Right after college, I quickly discovered how hard it was to get on with Whitaker & Bluff. I had to take a couple of other jobs to get experience prior to landing my current position. Finally, when I turned 26, I got my dream job.

It was awesome how it happened! I was so excited! Talk about being in the right place at the right time. I was a buyer for a discount lower level department store, which will remain nameless, and I went to an open forum to check out new products. I met this lovely woman named Susan Baples. Susan and I hit it off immediately. She gave me her card and told me to give her a call if I was ever interested in changing jobs. As I walked away from her and looked down at her card, I completely freaked out when I saw she was an executive for Whitaker & Bluff. I waited as long as I could wanting to not seem desperate and excited, and then I called her two days later.

I went on one interview and was offered the position as a buyer the same day. I started the job a week after the interview and couldn't have been any happier. Now that I'm here, I literally thank God every day for this incredible dream job and the fun I have while also earning a decent living. I have a lot of fun strategically choosing and projecting new purchases for our stores. It's awesome to have the challenge of picking out the next hot item and always hoping something I choose will take off. A buyer's ultimate satisfaction is picking the next trend.

Claire and I spend a lot of time together. Working on 5th Avenue, we're in the heart of the city, truly the best place to be and work! She and I often venture out for coffee or to grab a quick bite of food. I enjoy spending time with her, but our friendship is definitely not like mine and Danielle's. I guess it's unfair to compare friendships, especially since Danielle and I have been friends for so many years.

Before getting on the subway, I stop at Barney's to grab a latte. I also grab Claire one too. I stir in a pack of sugar against my better judgment imagining the added calories are not what I need. As I sit down on the train, I look around and acknowledge how no one is looking up from their phones or papers. It's a quiet ride in most days, unless there is a city event and then you have the tourists with their maps, kids, and cameras galore. You can always point out a tourist in New York. I try to be friendly to them when they ask for directions unlike most of my New Yorker friends, but at times it can be grueling. Just last week I had an obvious tourist asking me questions about the Statue of Liberty. It's funny how some assume we know more because we live here. I told the lady I knew as much as my history book had taught me. She stopped talking to me and we parted ways, thank God. Most of the time I try to not make eye contact with tourists for that very reason. Once they get you talking, it's all downhill from there.

My phone beeps as I step into the station. I look at the screen. It's a text from Danielle.

Danielle: *I hope you're ok about Josh… I'm sorry if I was insensitive:/ forgives?*

Kiera: *Really… I'm fine. Sure it's a little strange, but I'll manage. Thx for checking on me.*

Danielle: *If you need me let me know. You can come back to my place tonight if you don't feel up to being alone.*

Kiera: *thx*

Danielle: *kk*

I get off the elevator, walk towards my cube, and stop to hand Claire her latte. She stands and hugs me and in an upbeat manner says, "So…How was your weekend?" (Her voice escalating with every syllable)

I'm almost certain by her tone Josh has not told Richard just yet. I debate playing it cool, but then think about how much harder my week would be, especially because it's only Monday. Mondays are slow and Claire and I almost always go out for an extended lunch. I can't possibly keep this from her. I look at Claire and say, "Actually, Claire, I need to tell you something."

She pushes her hair behind her ears, and remaining silent looks me in the eye waiting to hear what I am about to say. I say, "Josh and I aren't seeing each other anymore. That happened this weekend."

Claire's mouth literally drops open. She says, "What do you mean you aren't seeing each other? You said "no"? How could you tell him no? You don't want to marry Josh? Oh Kiera, this is terrible. I hope he's okay, that poor soul. He hasn't even called Richard. I better let Richard know what you've done to him. Oh my goodness, this is terrible."

"What??? What in the hell are you talking about? What do you mean "that poor soul?" You need to get your facts in order! I'm the poor soul. Josh is the one who messed up!"

Claire looks confused and says, "What do you mean Josh messed up? You sound like a spoiled brat! So he didn't propose to your liking? Sorry your fairytale proposal didn't happen for you like you planned. Kiera, Josh has wanted to propose to you for close to a year now. I have a hard time believing he messed this up. If it wasn't perfect, I'm sure he was just nervous."

I can't help feeling pissy and underestimated. Clearly, she doesn't know me too well. I say, "Well you're wrong! You need to get your facts straight. He's the one who couldn't go through with it, not me. He totally crumbled and acted foolish leaving me there to look like an idiot right in the middle of Central Park. So before you keep judging me and think you have it all figured out, I think you should just ask him for the facts!"

Claire looks taken back and says, "What are you talking about Kiera? Just calm down…you're not making a bit of sense. All I know is Josh has been so excited about asking you to marry him for so long now, and what you are saying doesn't add up. He kept telling us he was going to take you to a special spot in Central Park and propose under some tree he knows you love. So you need to understand that nothing you're saying is making any sense to me. He just called Richard Friday morning so up-beat about the weekend, bragging about proposing to you."

I laugh a very sarcastic, maybe even a bit vindictive giggle, and say, "I'm not sure what happened between his call with Richard on Friday and the actual (air quotes) "Moment" he was going to propose, but after the awkward event unfolded, we parted ways at Magnolia Bakery. My night ended with him showing up at Danielle's around 2:00 a.m.

to end our relationship. It was all rather dramatic on his part, if you ask me. I'm just relieved to know his true feelings before we planned a wedding together, or said 'I do'. Better now than later."

Claire looks as if I just stole her puppy and says, "I just can't believe this. It just doesn't add up. Something's missing from this story. I'm not saying I don't believe you. I just don't understand how, or even when, things changed in his mind. It's just so peculiar."

"Look, Claire, no worries really, I'll be fine. Besides, I'm sure it's for the best. Like I said, we're lucky to find out before we got married. I definitely wouldn't want to have to go through all of the hoopla for nothing. Had he gone through with it, I totally would have said "yes" and we'd have gotten married. Then it would have been too late, and we probably would have ended in divorce. Look, I'm glad we had this talk, but I really need to get to work and forget about Josh for a while. Maybe you'll have time to let everything soak in and we can catch back up later."

Claire silently walks over to her cubical. She knows there isn't much work to be done today, but I'm glad she didn't push back. Thank God, she's respecting my space. I glance up at her and I can see her texting. I assume it's Richard.

Claire always tells Richard everything right away, especially good gossip. I suppose it's what she should do since he's her husband and all. She's probably asking him if he knew about Josh and me. I can't help but laugh under my breath as I look at her. She's desperately trying to be secretive, but she's being totally obvious. I turn my monitor on and map out my schedule for the day. My text alert goes off. I look down and it's Josh.

Josh: *Like I said last night… I think we need to arrange a time to get our personal belongings from one another. Think about what works for you.*

I look at the text for a couple of seconds. *Wow!* It's so odd that just yesterday I was thinking we were getting engaged, and now he's texting about claiming our stuff as we part ways. I'm put off at how eager he is to get his stuff. I hadn't actually thought about all of the things Josh has at my place, but after two years things add up. I suppose he's right and we do need to exchange everything back. After all, I have half of my clothes in his closet, and he has his things in mine. I put the phone down and contemplate how long I'll wait before I respond. I decide to play Danielle's waiting game and let him marinate in his thoughts. She'd be so pleased, but I won't tell her.

I turn to my computer monitor to check my e-mail. The first message in my inbox is an email for an upcoming event for buyers. I love Buyer events! They are filled with opportunity for new products, new connections, and there always fabulous parties. I open it immediately. When I see it's in London, I feel like I'm going to completely freak out with excitement.

Generally, I get excited when there is travel involved, but I cannot express how I much I love the idea of getting to visit London. I quickly respond with my RSVP saying I'll attend the event and tradeshow. I have a bubbly butterfly tingle that makes me happy. London will be a great escape! Trying to keep focused on my work, I'm certain that this trip to London couldn't have come at a better time. I debate asking Danielle to go, or perhaps Claire should join me. I am definitely leaning toward taking Danielle.

As I am booking travel with my agent, I feel someone breathing down my neck. I look behind me and Claire is standing over my cube. She says, "So, are we going?"

Shit! She must have gotten the same email. I smile and say, "Of course!"

"Great! I already booked our travel."

"Ha! You're too much!"

I guess that's that, Claire and I will be going to London together. Hopefully, things won't be awkward between us by then, and the whole Josh thing will be history. It's probably best that I will have someone from my company to hang out with in London. I'm sure we'll have a lot of fun together and find some good deals.

When Claire walks away, I pick up my phone again and glance at Josh's message. I decide it's okay now to respond and am happy to include the tid-bit about my upcoming trip to London. I'm not sure why, but it feels good for me to tell him I'm going to London. I imagine him sulking about how he can't believe I'm not upset about the breakup and instead going on with my life and going to London. I hope he is bothered by my lack of worry or care.

Kiera: *Leaving for London soon, so before that*

Josh: *I was thinking maybe Wednesday?*

That was a quick response. Hmmm. I go ahead and shoot back a text.

Kiera: *Sure. 6:00 pm your place. I'll bring your stuff. It's less than mine.*

Josh: *K. See you then.*

This is so weird I think to myself. I put the phone down and look up. Claire is yet again standing over my desk. She says, "Want to go get coffee?"

I hesitate not sure if she wants to talk about Josh or about our upcoming trip to London. I do not want to spend my valuable time trying to explain Claire's confusion about my relationships demise. I decide it will be okay, and say, "Good idea!"

When we sit down in the café, I receive a text from Danielle. I laugh as I think about what Danielle will say about my upcoming trip to London. She will be so jealous. It won't be London she'll be most jealous about either. When she finds out Claire and I are going together, she'll be beyond envious, but she won't overreact. She will act like it's no big deal. I'll play along and pretend I believe she doesn't care. I know at the first opportunity she sees, Danielle will get mad and throw her jealousy in my face. But what are best friends for anyways? I look at the text.

Danielle: *I got you a date for tomorrow night!!!!*

My mouth drops.

Kiera: *What?!? What are you talking about? You're INSANE! A date for what? You're cray cray!*

Danielle: *did you forget? You promised you and Josh would be at the dinner I'm sponsoring Tuesday… you know…tomorrow night right??…*

Shit! Yep, I forgot. Ugh! Tomorrow night. A second text comes through.

Danielle: *tickets are for 2… soooo… there's this really great guy and you'll have fun! Right? You're always so friendly!*

Holy crap! She's always been crazy and eccentric, but this is a lot. I think about all the crazy things she's done for me and decide there is really no choice. I have to do it. I have to go on a blind date with some last-minute guy she found somewhere. Who knows what she's told this guy about me. Who knows what kind of a goober this guy even is. *Shit!* Oh well it won't really hurt anything I suppose. UGH! Feeling apprehensive, I pick up the phone and respond back.

Kiera: *sure. what time?*

She must have had the text ready to send as she knew I'd say "yes" because as quickly as I could hit send her response came through.

Danielle*: great! See ya at my place around 6:45… u won't be sorry! And remember you're welcome to come back tonight if you want company or another wine fest*

The thought of more wine actually makes me queasy feeling right now. Maybe we overdid it last night.

Chapter 3

I can't believe I have agreed to go to the dinner with some random guy Danielle works with. What is wrong with me? *The things we do for each other sometimes.* I guess for me, the part I am looking forward to the most is dressing up for the party. I'm sure I'll find a way to make it a fun night and have good conversations. I always do.

I'm wearing a tight fitting, silky red, crossed strap dress. To complete the outfit, I chose my strappy nude Alexandre Birman stilettos, and carry my new red, patent-leather Alexander Mcqueen clutch. I almost trip in my high-heeled shoes as I get on the elevator. Normally, this would be about the time my hot neighbor, Chandler, would poke his head out of his apartment to see my clumsiness.

Walking to Danielle's, my feet start hurting in the heels, so I take them off. Fortunately, I have my red Tory Burch Mini Travel Ballets rolled up in my clutch for just this reason.

Of course, I will switch back before the party. As I get to Danielle's building I press her code on the call box. She buzzes me up and opens the door. She says, "Wow! Wow! Wow! You look freaking amazing! What the heck was wrong with Josh anyways?"

I give her a smile, and say, "Thanks. Now, I seriously need a drink!"

"Are you nervous about meeting John?"

"Danielle, I'm not nervous… This is just weird. Why does his name have to be so close to Josh? UGH! John, Josh couldn't these 70's and 80's parents come up with something more original? This is so weird. I just got out of a two-year relationship with Josh… Now it's just a couple days later, and here I am going on a blind date with a co-worker of yours, John. It's kind of a lot to digest. Now pour me something! Maybe I should do a couple shots so it kicks in quick."

"I got it. I'll get you something. Don't worry, John is lovely. You'll be pleased. Oh, and he'll be here soon, so just sit down and try to relax."

Danielle starts mixing me up one of her concoctions. Truly she makes the best mixed drinks, especially for times such as this. She extends her hand to give me a beautiful glass with red etching on the rim and says, "This should take the edge off…it's a berry martini." I reach for it and take a huge gulp. "Yum! That is good!" Yet again she's made the best drink.

"Thanks," I say.

We're sitting out on her balcony when we hear the buzz from the call box go off. Danielle gets up to see who it is. I hear a male voice, and assume it must be John. I get up to greet the man, and Danielle says, "Kiera, I'd like you to meet Sam."

"Sam? I say. "I thought you said John was his name?"

"Oh no, this is not your date."

"Um."

I think really hard about who Sam is…I'm sure I have heard his name before, but I'm drawing a blank. Luckily, after a couple of seconds pass, I remember Danielle had mentioned Sam in a passing conversation a few weeks back when she stood me up for dinner. I waited at Tom's Restaurant for an hour before she finally texted me back. I kept texting her, and as I was getting ready to leave, I got a text back from her saying she was so sorry and that she'd explain everything in a bit. She ended up calling me within a few minutes to tell me she'd met this really great guy and had lost track of time. She reiterated her apology, and I just left the restaurant and headed home. I was upset she'd stood me up for a guy. After all I'd left Josh to his own devices for her, and I couldn't quite understand her logic. I ended up eating a Stouffer's when I got home and forgot the whole thing had happened by the next day. I'm not really one to hold a grudge, and if anything, I'm known for being too forgiving at times.

As I approach Sam to shake his hand, I give him a good look over. It's hard to look past the fact that he's very handsome, and I conclude he's very much Danielle's taste. I extend my hand and say, "Hi, Sam, It's nice to meet you." I glare at Danielle and say, "Danielle has told me so much about you." She and I both know I know nothing about him, but I enjoy making her feel uncomfortably squirmy.

As we sit at Danielle's kitchen bar and have some cocktails, there is a light knock at the door. I take in a deep breath and assume it's John. Quickly, I turn my glass up and finish my drink. Danielle looks at me like I'm an alcoholic, but I ignore her. John walks in and, at first glance, I think he's cute. Danielle makes the introduction, and John comes across very easy going. He makes a couple of jokes, and I begin to appreciate his great personality. I can't help but wonder what he thinks of me. Also, I wonder what Danielle has told him about me. There is no telling…

John and I go to sit in the living room and are engaged in a quick "get to know you" as Sam and Danielle come in carrying more drinks. Sam says he has something to toast, but he must first make an announcement. I'm not too sure about this chap. He seems so stiff and bland. His looks may be Danielle's type, but he is definitely too stiff and bland for Danielle for sure.

Sam says, "Danielle, this last month of being with you has been the best thing that's ever happened to me. You've made me the happiest person alive."

I'm starting to feel awkwardly embarrassed for Danielle and Sam, but as I look at Danielle she seems to be hanging on his every word. I'm astonished at how happy she seems. I had no idea she'd been dating this guy for a month. I would think she would have talked about him more.

I tune back in to what Sam is saying. "Danielle, I know we've only known each other for a short time, but I love you so much. I want to be with you every Moment I'm alive."

I'm totally about to gag! He doesn't know her that well. What the HELL is going on here?

Sam places his drink on the table and reaches in his pocket.

OMG! Is this really happening, or have I had too much alcohol?

Sam gets down on one knee, and Danielle is looking at him all googly-eyed. He continues saying, "Danielle Millbanks, will you be my bride and marry me? You will make me the happiest man on the planet."

"Holy-freaking shit!"

I thought I said it under my breath, but it actually came out of my mouth. Danielle is angry as she looks at me. She reaches out her hand and allows Sam to place the ring on her finger. She then begins screeching the loudest "YES!!!" ever, practically screaming it for the people on the streets eight blocks away to hear. I feel bad for my reaction, especially after she says yes, but who in the hell knew she'd agree to such nonsense. John and I just look at each other while Danielle and Sam are kissing deeply, passionately. It's like a scene from a movie where a man proposes and the leading lady says yes. I've never felt more out of place and awkward in all my life; I mean ever. How could Danielle be so serious about Sam, going to marry him, when I, her closest friend, only have heard her mention him one time? This is so weird. I don't know how to act or what to say.

The car ride over to the dinner was extremely uncomfortable. Now, at the venue for Danielle's work event, she and I are sitting at the table under a big white tent. The guys walk out to get drinks from an open bar. A long silence settles between Danielle and me. Finally, I decide to break the silence and start talking about how nice John seems and how the event is lovely. I tell Danielle the evening is not as unpleasant as I had thought it would be, and John has a great personality. The small talk continues, but I can't seem to take it anymore. I look at Danielle and try casually to ask her what has been the proverbial elephant in the room. I say, "Wow! So marriage?"

She cocks her head at me cautiously and says, "Yes, it's so exciting!"

She then goes off on a tangent talking about how beautiful the wedding will be. She asks me if I'd seen her "Dream Wedding" board on Pinterest. As she keeps rambling on, all of the sudden, I can feel my temperature rising. Sweat begins to form as I try to remain calm. *She's my best friend. I have to say something. I can't just sit here and pretend everything is okay. I have to help her in her state of weakness. That is what it has to be. Weakness. She needs me.*

I place my hand on top of Danielle's hand, and I decide to tread lightly. Considering her current state of euphoria, I'm concerned she may not understand the reality. I calmly question, "Danielle, you've only mentioned Sam to me one time? Why's that?"

She finally stops talking for a second. I feel bad having to be the one to point this out. She looks very calm. I think she must see where I'm going with this, and for a minute I feel sorry for her. She places my hand down on the table and says, "Oh no. Oh my God! I'm so sorry Kiera. I just didn't think about it. I keep rambling on and on, I'm being so insensitive. I can't believe I didn't really think about this. I just thought you could be happy for me regardless."

"What are you talking about?" I ask.

Danielle has pity in her eyes. She solemnly stares at me and says, "Kiera, you're jealous! With everything that just happened with you and Josh…I'm so sorry. I didn't even think about how you must feel."

"What?!? Are you kidding me?!?" *Now I am irate. How could she possibly even go there? She's being so stupid.*

Danielle looks at me intently and says, "That's exactly what is going on here. I can't believe it didn't occur to me. You can't be happy for me because you're in your funk of doom and gloom. You've been chasing getting in engaged for so long you're to the point you can't possibly be happy for anyone else. I've told you before, this is not new. You're completely miserable every time someone gets engaged. I'm sure you're going to deny it, but it's the truth and you know it."

I stand up quickly and grab my clutch off my chair. As I turn to walk away, I can see the guys heading back towards the table and it makes the urge to leave even stronger. I turn back to Danielle and say, "You're so off track here. You think you know me so well. You're wrong on this one. I'm not feeling sorry for myself at all. I'm just concerned for my friend who seems to be lacking judgment thinking it's perfectly okay to get married to someone she just met. I'm going home. I don't feel like being here. You're acting ridiculous."

Calmly, I look Danielle in the eyes. With as much sarcasm as I can muster I say, "I hope you have a fun time tonight. I'm out of here."

When I get back to my place, I decide to linger a little longer than normal fiddling with my door to see if by chance I run into Chandler. I pretend to be having some trouble getting into my apartment. After a few minutes pass, I realize how stupid I am, and I finally go inside. *What would I have said to Chandler anyways?*

Once inside I pour myself a large goblet of 40th anniversary Caymus Cabernet. When Danielle bought me the set of large goblets, she said, "Here. Now you can drink your normal amount, but it is only one glass." It's true. It makes me feel justified, like I'm having less wine, even though we all know it's the size of the glass.

I take my wine into my bedroom. Immediately, I see Josh's white Ralph Lauren polo on my night stand. I grab a clothes hamper and begin to place random things that belong to him inside. Tomorrow is Wednesday and I need to make certain I have all of his things together before work.

Surprisingly, as I'm packing away all of his things, I don't feel very sad. It seems strange. I do, however, feel a bit lonely. I assume loneliness is a normal feeling after being with someone for so long and ending it abruptly. I continue searching my apartment for Josh's things.

When I think I've found everything, I undress to get comfortable. I slip into my favorite white tee and short cotton brief-bottom shorts. I take a long look in the mirror. I pull my blonde locks up into a pony tail, and wash my face. Still towel blotting my face, I go back to the kitchen for a second glass of wine. Theoretically, I guess it had to be my fourth, considering the size of the goblet, but who's here to count?

My door buzzes, and I immediately assume its Danielle coming to apologize about earlier. Neither of us is capable of staying mad at each other too long. I walk over thinking I'll just ignore her. I look out the peep hole and I'm shocked to see Chandler standing there.

Of course, I just undressed and look like a complete bum now. Ugh! Why could he have not stopped by two minutes ago before I got all comfy? I quickly run my fingers through my hair and pinch at my cheeks for color. Slowly, I open the door trying to be nonchalant and I say, "Hi Chandler, what's going on?"

He's standing there in my doorway holding a bottle of beer. He smiles the sexiest smile making chills run down my legs. I say, "Come in."

My mind goes back to the awful embarrassment a few weeks ago in the hallway, and me tripping as I met Chandler's girlfriend Juliette. *I wonder if they think about that and laugh?* We're standing awkwardly just looking at each other, and as I start to ask him if he needs something, he also starts talking. We both laugh. I say, "Oh...sorry, you go ahead."

He smiles and says, "Yes. Well, actually, I can't seem to find my bottle opener anywhere and I wanted to see if we can borrow yours?"

I realize by him saying "we" he must be referring to himself and Juliette. I smile back with a flirty smile and say, "Absolutely! Let me grab it."

He's so hot he makes my knees weak. I walk into the kitchen and open up the cabinet looking for the bottle opener. As I stand on my tip-toes reaching to the back of my noticeably tall cabinets, I can't seem to reach the bottle opener, and he notices my struggle. He walks into the kitchen and stands beside me offering to help. Ignoring his offer I grab my short-girl step stool. He says, "Here let me."

I say, "No worries, I use this thing all the time. I hate these high cabinets."

Being only 5'5" can make it hard to reach; but honestly, the only time my height poses a challenge is when I'm working in the kitchen. I climb up on the stool and begin to feel a bit woozy. I guess it's from the wine. I reach up and then my foot slips and I lose my balance. I completely freak out and try to grab onto the refrigerator. Luckily for me, Chandler is beside me waiting on the opener and he catches me before I hit the floor. I feel so stupid yet again. I'm certain he either thinks I'm the biggest klutz or a drunk. So embarrassing!

Chandler is holding me sideways from my clumsy fall. As we look at each other, we burst into laughter. He turns my legs down towards the floor and slowly places my feet on the kitchen hard-wood floor. I decide I'd never seen him so loose and relaxed. I attribute it to the freak show I just demonstrated. He says, "Kiera, are you alright?"

I laugh some more and say, "Yes. I'm so sorry about that."

Chandler says, "Are you kidding me? I haven't laughed this hard in a long time!"

Smiling a big toothy smile at him, I hand him the bottle opener and say, "You know where to find me and I'm always up for a good laugh."

As we make our way to the hallway between our apartment doors, we say goodnight. I tell him he can leave the bottle opener by my door when he's done, or I'll get it from him later. He says, "Thanks Kiera! I better get back to Juliette. I'll catch you later."

He turns back to his apartment and I watch him inside. I go back to my door and close the door behind me. Smiling the whole way back I roll my eyes at myself for being such a flirt. I mimic myself in my foyer mirror saying, "I'm always up for a good laugh." *I'm such a total DORK!* I imagine what he and Juliette are talking about and how they treat each other.

It's hard to get Chandler off my mind the rest of the evening. Finally, I decide to go to bed. All night long I toss and turn waking up every hour on the hour. Around 5 a.m. I give up and get up frustrated with my lack of sleep. I make some coffee and hear the low battery alert beeping on my cell phone. I go to my bedroom to grab my charger and plug in my phone. I check my notifications, and see I missed a text from Danielle and Josh last night. Curious, I open Josh's first.

Josh: *Can u look and c if any if my tools r in your storage rm out on your balcony?*

I hadn't thought about it, but I'm sure he does have some things out there. Although, Josh was not a "Mr. Fix it," he could definitely do minor things like fix cabinet doors or hang things on the wall. I quickly send him a text back.

Kiera: *Absolutely. C ya around 6.*

I immediately go out to the storage room and fight through the mess and spider webs as I look for his tools. I move my bike out and pull out a couple of boxes. Finally, I see a little red tool box sitting beside an old half-deflated Ab Ball I bought a few years back, which has gotten little to no use. As I reach to pull it out I hear someone yawning. I lean over the balcony and see Chandler having a cup of coffee reading something on his iPad. He sees me and says, "Good morning Kiera! You're up early?"

"You too!" I say.

He says, "Do you always wake up this early?"

"No. I didn't sleep well."

"What are you doing?" he asks.

I think about making something up, but what the hell, I say, "Josh and I broke up. I'm packing all of his things up to take him after work."

Chandler leans over and says, "I'm sorry, Kiera. I had no idea."

"Really, it's no big deal. I'll be fine. It's for the best. These things happen you know…"

"Trust me, I do. Luckily though, for now things seem to be going in a positive direction with Juliette. I hope we can advance our relationship soon."

Advance. I immediately fixate on what he means by this terminology. Noticing that he's still looking at me I quickly say, "That would be wonderful for you. I am glad things are going so well."

I try to sound genuine although I'm still quite confused about the meaning of "advance," and I'm not too sold on Juliette being Chandler's type at all. Chandler says, "Wait here a minute."

He goes inside and comes back out holding my bottle opener. Reaching across the balconies that are not side-by-side, but rather cornered from each other, I can't seem to reach it. We both laugh, and I tell him I have plenty of bottle openers, and really it's not a big deal.

He says, "No. No. No. When I borrow something, I like to give it back. You stand right there and I'll toss it to you. You ready?"

I giggle a little under my breath and say, "Why don't we just meet in the hall?"

He says, "This is way more fun, right?"

I shrug back at him, and feeling ever so flirty, I say, "You're right. This would be more fun! Go ahead toss it to me!"

He slings the bottle opener up in the air, and I somehow clamp onto it catching it cleanly. I'm so excited that I didn't look clumsy, until all of a sudden I lose my grip. The bottle opener falls out of my hand, and it's too late. Chandler and I can hear it hit the pavement eight stories below. We both burst into uncontrollable laughter. We're trying to re-live the whole scenario laughing in between our words re-telling how it had all happened. Chandler gets quiet, and I can hear a female voice saying, "What are you laughing at?"

I realize it's Juliette. I don't want her to see me, so I go inside and close the door.

Chapter 4

When I get back inside my apartment, I see my phone is blinking with a notification. I pick it up and remember it's the text from Danielle that I haven't read from last night.

Danielle: *I'm sorry. I didn't mean what I said. Maybe a little of what I said, but not all of it. Forgives? I need you… You're my maid-of-honor!*

Ugh! I'm a little frustrated by her, but I know it won't last too long no matter what. I decide to text her back.

Kiera: *you r right. I'm a little bitter about everyone around me getting married. It's now you, a friend at work, and all of our sorority sisters. Always a bridesmaid never a bride…sorry im being selfish! I'll shut up about it and be the best Maid of Honor ever!*

I put the phone down and realize I'm not done.

Kiera: *maybe I am jealous. I'm just so stuck on meeting my one and settling down. It's hard to understand why it's not happening. Also you getting engaged to someone after only dating one month is weird for me. I just met him, too! But I'll try. If you're happy, I'm happy. Let's do dinner; maybe after I drop off Josh's things tonight?*

I hit send and go into my bedroom to get ready. I get out of the shower and get dressed. I hear my text go off.

Danielle: *Great idea! John and Sam can come right? He thought you were so hot!!!!*

OMG! She's crazy! Why'd she think I'd want to ever see this guy again after leaving them last night? I text her back immediately:

Kiera: *WHAT?!? No. just us.*

She comes back again, so quickly, before I can un-wrap my towel from my head.

Danielle: *Come on, u can do it. How do u ever expect to find what you're looking for not putting yourself out there? He thinks you're sooooo hot!!! Don't mess it up Kiera! Great guy!*

It really is no use. She always wins. I might as well do whatever she says. I text back.

Kiera: *Whatever. I can meet around 7ish.*

Danielle: *Perfect!! You won't be sorry! Feeling determined…We're going to find your 1 if it's the last thing we do! We're on a mission! Remember before we're 30!*

I don't know why, but for some reason I like the sound of this determination. Call me crazy, but I'm drinking the

"Danielle Kool-Aid," and it tastes great. This is a mission that I'm set to win. I laugh as I think about the silly pact Danielle and I made as kids, to be married by 25. It didn't work out too well for either of us. After 25 came and went, we reconvened and amended the terms of the pact to 30. Let's see if this works. Danielle is right. This is a mission! I feel silly as I look in the mirror on the way out of my apartment and proclaim to myself that I will be married before I'm 30, but it makes me giddy anyways.

When I get to the lobby in my building, I check my mail and say a quick good morning to Louie the doorman. He smiles and says, "Good morning to you kiddo! You seem to be mighty chipper today. It wouldn't have anything to do with your neighbor Chandler would it?"

"I'm sorry? What do you mean?"

Louie reaches in his pocket and hands me my bottle opener still intact. I giggle at him and say, "Louie you little sneak! However did you get that, and how do you know it belongs to me?" Louie winks at me and says, "Us doormen have our ways."

I laugh and say, "I bet you do…and to answer your question, my mood has nothing to do with the bottle opener."

I shake my head at him and smile as I take the bottle opener. I say, "Have a good day, Louie!"

I'm in such a good mood I can hardly wait to get to the office. I stop for my morning cup of coffee, and grab a quick bagel with walnut raisin cream cheese at Absolute Bagels. I finish up my bagel on the subway, and check in on all of my social media websites. Not much on Facebook. I look at my favorite blog, peekingpines.com, and see a really cute dress I have to have. I look the dress up on Pinterest and immediately see that Danielle has gone nuts with her bridal boards. I almost gasp when I see this ugly bubblegum pink bridesmaid dress she just pinned. Of course it would be typical of her to pick an ugly shade ensuring she looks better than her bridesmaids for her wedding. Thinking about Danielle's shortcomings makes me giggle.

When I tap on Instagram, I almost drop my phone. I see a picture of Josh with his red-headed co-worker Gina whom I had met previously. The picture is posted on Gina's feed as Josh doesn't have an Instagram account. I met Gina when a group of Josh's coworkers and I went out for drinks one night. She and I connected and started following each other after that to share pictures. In the picture, she had her arm around him and was kissing his cheek. Surprisingly, I was overwhelmed by a fiery jealous feeling. *What the hell is this? It's been less than a week and he's already messing around with this thing? Unbelievable!*

I get off at my stop still holding my phone and staring at the picture of the two of them. A text comes through and I switch out of my Instagram app to look. It's Danielle.

Danielle: *Have you been on Instagram?*

Oh great! Everyone who's connected with her and knows me is seeing this… How embarrassing!

Kiera*: I saw it:/*

Danielle: *What the hell?*

I decide not to reply and walk into my office building. I go straight to my desk avoiding conversations with anyone. Claire walks over to my cube looking at me perplexed. I assume she's staring at me funny because I just walked past her without saying anything at all. I look at her and say, "What?"

She sits down on my cubicle desk and cocks her head quizzically. I can tell she saw the picture too. She finally says, "I'm sure it was nothing. They probably went to dinner as a group and had a few drinks."

I stop Claire by putting my hand up and say, "I don't really want to talk about it."

She says, "I understand. How about we talk about our trip to London?"

"Great idea! Well, if I know you well, which I do, you've already mapped it out for us… What are you thinking?"

"Since two days will be total business, if we leave on Wednesday, we can do our work on Thursday and Friday. I was thinking we should take Monday off and sight see on Saturday and Sunday. Thoughts?"

"Umm, let me think about it… Heck yeah! So is that an itinerary you're holding?"

"Girl, you know it is!"

"Let me see what it says," I say.

Claire hands me the itinerary. I look over it, and it looks perfect. I love how she is so organized. We're staying at St. Pancras Renaissance London Hotel. The name sounds so regal.

<u>London Itinerary</u>

Wednesday: Travel

Thursday: Event for Buyers 8:00 a.m.- 3:30 p.m.

Sightseeing/shopping nearby- dinner- drinks

Friday: Event for Buyers 8:00 a.m.- 3:30 p.m.

Sight seeing/shopping nearby- dinner- drinks

Saturday: Windsor Castle/ Tour

The museum of Brands, Packaging and Advertising-

Afternoon; Soho, Cinema and dinner- evening

Sunday: Kensington Palace and Hyde Park- morning

Jason's Canal Boat Trip along Regents Canal-

Afternoon; St. Katherine Docks- dinner

I say, "Claire this is awesome! I'm so glad we can go together."

"We don't have to stick to it, but I thought it would be nice to have."

"You're amazing! I truly love it, and I really am so grateful we can do this together!"

After lunch I start dreading my upcoming 6 o'clock exchange with Josh. I can't help but think about what I might say to him about the picture of him and Gina on Instagram. I decide I can't bring it up no matter what, and that I must maintain my dignity. Claire and I go and grab a coffee for our break. It's about 3:30 p.m., and I get off in an hour and a half. She asks me what I'm going to do until 6 o'clock. I tell her I'm going to go to the bar close to Josh's apartment and have a couple of drinks. I also mention meeting up with Danielle later. She says, "That'll be good for you. Not a good day to be alone."

I agreed. Then I tell her about John and all of the details from last night, including Chandler. She smiles big and says, "Sounds like Josh isn't the only one on the rebound."

"Ha! If Danielle has anything to do with it, I'll totally be on the rebound full force. John seemed nice enough. I'm not expecting much, but we'll see."

The last hour of work seemed to drag by slowly. Finally at a quarter till 5, I head out of the office. Waving goodbye to Claire, she asks if I want her to join me for "before" drinks. I tell her no, it's fine. I go home first to grab Josh's things placing them in a large laundry basket. As I head towards his place, my stomach is in knots. I stop into the bar around the corner from Josh's and have a cocktail. My first drink is an Apple Martini. I finish it rather quickly and decide it isn't enough. For my second drink, I order a Jolly Rancher Martini. Both drinks are very fruity and end up being just what I need. I now feel relaxed and capable of facing Josh.

I pay the bill and head to Josh's with the heavy laundry basket in tow. Several people have stared at me strangely as I've been carrying this overflowing basket of Josh's things. I knock on the door and wait. Taking in a deep breath, I'm relieved I had the drinks before. *I feel pretty tame actually.*

He hasn't come to the door yet, so I knock three more times. Finally, I hear him on the other side opening the door. As he opens the door and I see his face, I calmly say, "Hi."

"Hey, come on in."

I feel very awkward, yet calm. I walk in and see my things lying on the sofa. I think about the many memories we've shared in this apartment. Looking at the sofa with my things hanging over the luggage makes the break-up seem real. *This is it.* Josh takes the basket from me and I go to pick up my things. He says I can keep the luggage since he just got the new luggage a few weeks back. *This is so weird.* I tell him thank you and walk over by the door. He follows closely behind me and places his hand on the back of my shoulder. I turn to face him and he says, "Kiera, I hope you do know I'll miss you and us. I want you to take good care of yourself and please know I wish you well always."

All I can seem to muster out is, "You too, Josh."

I turn and walk away without looking back.

I push my stuff out into the hallway of Josh's building. Leaning up against the wall, I slowly fall to the floor in a seated position. I place my head in my hands and let my feelings marinate a few moments. I'm not sad. I simply feel alone. My phone buzzes. It's Danielle.

Danielle: *are you done yet? On the way yet?*

Oh shit! I really don't feel like the sound of going anywhere. I decide to try to get out of my plans. I text her back.

Kiera: *leaving Josh's now. I may call it a night…*

I wait, and again she must have known what I was going to say because as soon as I sent it she shoots back.

Danielle: *Don't even try to skate out on plans tonight. You simply can't be alone! Be here in less than 45!*

UGH! I put my phone in my purse and head out to grab a cab with all of my belongings from Josh's in tow.

I pay the cab driver and head up to Danielle's apartment. When I get to her place I notice the door is propped open with a shoe. I scoot by with all of my things in my hands and enter calling out Danielle's name. She answers from the bedroom and says, "Just a minute."

I sit my things down in a corner of the living room by the couch. I glance at myself in the mirror hanging over the mantle. I need some touching up. I pull my makeup bag out of my Tory Burch Cross Bag and touch up my face in Danielle's guest bathroom. I can hear a shuffling sound coming from Danielle's bedroom. I call out her name again and finally she peeks her head in the guest bathroom at me and says, "Hi-ya sweets!"

"Hi-ya yourself. What are you so happy about?"

I realize what is going on when I hear Sam say, "Hi Kiera". *Oh nice.* I think to myself. My face blushes and Danielle starts giggling. I say, "Were you two?"

We both burst into big laughs. Danielle turns the fan on in the bathroom and starts telling me how amazing Sam is in bed. She says, "Kier, he's amazing!"

I roll my eyes at her and continue on with my lip gloss. I notice how obnoxiously happy she looks. I can't help but feel happy for her. She flushes the toilet and as she walks out of the room says, "Want a cocktail before we leave?"

Immediately I say, "Yes!" emphatically as I need something to take the edge off.

I finish fixing myself, and I walk into the living room where Danielle and Sam are kissing all over each other. I take two big sips of the drink Danielle made as she hands it to me. It's nice and strong. I feel a bit woozy and a little nauseated. Danielle must notice because she says, "Kiera, are you okay? You don't look so well."

I walk over to the kitchen and pour a glass of water. "I'm fine I think. Really, I'm okay. I think I must be hungry. I probably just need some food. I haven't eaten since lunch."

Danielle grabs me some crackers and pours a little Sprite into a yellow Solo cup. I drink the Sprite and eat two crackers pretty quickly. Immediately, it starts to make me feel a lot better. Just as I'm finishing my Sprite, the call box buzzes. I assume it's John. Danielle smiles at me and goes over to let him in. On her walk over she says, "This ought to make you feel better."

Two seconds later she walks into the kitchen and says, "Kiera, I'd like for you to meet Seth Gresham."

Confused, I say, "Hello, Seth! Nice to meet you!"

I cautiously look at Danielle in hopes of a follow up on who exactly Seth is, and perhaps a reason why he's here. She says nothing to answer my questions. Instead, Danielle pours Seth a drink and he follows her into the living room. Sam walks over to Seth and they shake hands followed by the "man hug" back patting bit, like old buddies. Obviously, these two know each other well. Sam drinks down the rest of his cocktail making an annoying slurping noise while doing so. He walks over to set his glass down on the bar and says, "Well, we should probably get going!"

I say, "Shouldn't we wait for John?"

Sam laughs and says, "Danielle, did you not tell Kiera?"

"Tell me what?"

Danielle says, "Kiera, can you come here? Boys, you go on down. We'll follow."

"What's going on, Danielle?"

"I'm so sorry. I totally forgot to mention that something came up, and John is busy tonight. Seth is Sam's best friend. He just got out of a nasty relationship so we just thought a second go with someone new would be just what the doctor ordered."

Feeling extremely side-swiped, and increasingly annoyed, I say, "I'm not a charity case, Dan! I don't need a man to be happy. I'd have been perfectly fine just hanging out with you and Sam alone, or perhaps even the two of us would be a nice thought."

"I'm so sorry, Keira. I didn't mean anything by it."

"Let's just go." I say, rolling my eyes. We close up the door and walk to meet the guys in the lodge. As we turn the corner, I feel a wave of nausea overcome me again. I grab a hold of Danielle's arm and throw up all in the hallway. She says, "Oh my God! Kiera, honey are you okay?"

"No, I'm not okay! Clearly I'm not okay! I feel like a bag of crap. I must be coming down with something. I'm going home. I'm so sorry Danielle. Please give Seth my wishes. I'll call you tomorrow."

I hug Danielle. As I turn to walk out the back entrance to avoid seeing Seth and Sam, Danielle says, "Kiera, wait! There isn't any chance you could be pregnant is there? This is not like you. As a matter of fact you've been feeling weird a lot lately. I remember you said you were late for your period a while back."

Holy shit! My heart falls to the floor, and I feel like I can't breathe. I feel my face flush and the reality hits me. "Oh no! Oh no, Danielle, I can't even remember my last period, but I just thought… I just thought I was stressed. You don't really think? Oh my God! No way."

"Holy crap, Kiera, wait here. I'm going to tell Sam and Seth to go on without us. They can go and have a guy's night. I'll tell them I need to be with you and you're not feeling well."

"Seth and Sam will just think I don't like Seth. It'll be so awkward."

"Who cares what they think? We have to find out if you're pregnant, and I'm not leaving you alone. Wait outside for me."

Chapter 5

Danielle and I stop by Windsor pharmacy to pick up a pregnancy test. Once inside, we walk back to the "Family Planning" aisle. Overwhelmed at all of the different options and test kits to choose from, I reach for the E.P.T. kit since it seems to be the most popular. Danielle can act so crazy and silly at the most awkward times, and it is easy to see there is no exception to that rule tonight. She puts on her "serious infomercial" voice and begins to read the boxes. I can't control my giggling as I watch Danielle read aloud. Honestly, there is no one else in the world who can make me laugh during such a potentially stressful time like she can. I'm so thankful she's with me.

Danielle is pretending she's in a commercial for E.P.T. She's holding the box up next to her face. She says, "For a result you can trust, go with E.P.T. for your family planning solutions." I burst into laughter! She takes the box and straddles it, as if she's going pee, and says, "Place absorbent tip pointing downward in your urine stream for five seconds"! Tears are literally streaming down my face as I am laughing so hard.

"You're so freaking funny! Shhhhh! Stop it people are looking at you like you've lost it."

Just then, an older gentleman passes the aisle. He turns around to get a second look, and then he rolls his eyes and keeps moving. Again I say, "Okay enough. Seriously, knock it off Danielle!" Why do I even bother? Danielle could care less about what people think of her. I guess that's one of the things I cherish about her. She puts the box down and looks at her watch as if to act out she's waiting five minutes. She's completely nuts! As embarrassing as this is, I can't stop laughing at her. Finally, she screeches, "EEEEK!! Negative! FALSE ALARM!"

"You're completely insane!"

At check-out, the older gentlemen from earlier is ahead of us staring daggers at Danielle. Little does this man know, this kind of attention will only make her act worse. He has no idea who he's dealing with. She looks at him and back at me. In a loud exaggerated voice she says, "Kiera, I'm gonna go grab you a HUGE box of CONDOMS in case this PREGNANCY TEST is NEGATIVE which it most likely will be! I'm gonna make sure this kinda of thing won't happen again CRAZY girl. I told you to ALWAYS USE PROTECTION! Do you want your usual, EXTRA LUBRICATED and RIDGES, or not? How LARGE should I go?" She's desperately trying to make this gentleman feel uncomfortable and enjoying every minute.

At this point, leaving the pregnancy test in the checkout line and bolting for the door seems like the best escape, but instead I can't help but laugh. Funniest part is, she's not kidding and is trekking to the back of store to grab the condoms. I place the E.P.T. test up on the counter and quickly glance to see the face of the person behind me in line. I feel so ashamed and embarrassed, yet ironically entertained. I'm actually hoping Danielle will hurry up so we don't get the line backed up. Finally, I hear her voice coming and she's loudly proclaiming, "I got 'em. I got you some CONDOMS!!!"

Oh my… that's my best friend (sarcastic), and oddly enough, I'm relieved to see her face. To her amusement the older gentleman is still in the store making his way to the exit, but he looks back and his face is priceless. I can tell Danielle was immensely pleased the older gentleman had seen and heard her. We both burst into uncontrollable laughter.

Back at my apartment, Danielle orders me to take the test. I say, "Don't you think maybe I should wait until tomorrow morning to take the test because I read it's more accurate in the morning?"

She immediately yells, "HELL NO! You're taking it right now. What are you thinking? Now get in that bathroom and start peeing!"

She can be so bossy, but I concur and head to the toilet with Danielle hot on my heels. The toilet seat is cold and I can't seem to pee under all of the pressure, not to mention my tiny New York bathroom is not big enough for two people. I ask her to wait outside, and again she says, "HELL NO! I'm not leaving. Now pee!"

"UGH! Okay, well you can at least look away. You're making me anxious, and it's hard to pee."

Finally, after what seems like forever, I'm peeing on the stick. I place the cap back on the tip and sit it down on my counter. It's already working and we both are staring intently at it. Although, it's cliché to say in this very moment I feel as though the world has stopped and time is standing still. I turn away and tell Danielle I can't look. She says, "Kiera, it's ready."

I'm imagining what my life is about to be like. Either way, I feel like it'll be changed. If I'm not pregnant it'll be good. I'll always remember just the break up with Josh. But if I am pregnant, life will certainly be different, and life with Josh may not be over completely. I'm so scared. I turn and look down at the stick sitting on the white counter top and the bright blue plus sign is predominant and bold. I'm pregnant.

"Holy shit!"

"Oh my God, Kiera, you're PREGNANT!"

"Oh no. I need to sit down. I don't feel well. I'm so dizzy. What the hell am I going to do?"

Danielle says, "You're going to have a baby! That's what you're going to do."

Danielle and I both have always said if we had an unplanned pregnancy, we'd carry on with the pregnancy and have the baby. We promised we'd be there for each other the whole way through. I'm definitely not questioning whether or not I'm going to have the baby, and she knows this, but I am questioning how this is going to work with Josh. I'm having a "What am I going to do? How could this have happened?" Moment.

What I can't imagine is being a single mom. Alone is not how I planned to experience my first pregnancy. I hate Josh so much right now. Everything could have been perfect if he could have gone through with the engagement. Things didn't have to be like this. I totally would have said yes, and we'd be celebrating this new baby right now. Instead, he chickened out and we're not together anymore. Danielle must know my thoughts. She says, "Kier, it's not going to change things between you and Josh, you know that right? I'll be with you. I promise we've got this. We're gonna get through this fine. Stop thinking about him. He screwed up, and you can't change that. Look, I'm sleeping over tonight and we can talk about how you'll tell Josh. I'll do some research and help you find a doctor. You also need prenatal vitamins quick! I just texted Sam and told him we're having a crisis and I'm staying here tonight. I'll order some Chinese food. Go rest on the couch and try to relax."

Danielle is acting so responsible and calm. It's hard for me to take her seriously because so much of the time she's silly, but I have no choice right now, and besides she's doing a great job making me feel better. I don't really feel like being teased, and she's certainly not being silly. She has stepped-up for me in a serious way. *Thank God she can be here for me right now.*

The room is spinning like crazy, but lying here on the couch, I finally feel safe and calm. Things are soaking in, and I feel consumed with many racing thoughts. My mind is going 100 miles an hour as I try to contemplate how I'll tell people this news. This is not how I'd envisioned things going for my life. *How will people respond? What will everyone think of me? My Mom! Oh no… I'll have to tell her. I'm sure people at work will talk about me. Oh shit, this is going to be so freaking hard. How did this happen? I was so careful with my pills. I really don't want to tell Josh. What about Josh's Mom? Oh shit! This sucks!*

There's a knock at my door. Danielle says, "I'll get it." She hangs up from ordering the Chinese food and walks over to the door. She looks out the peephole and says, "Ohhh! Ohhh la la!"

"What? Who's it?"

"It's hottie, hot pants from across the hall. What's his name? Oh yeah, Chandler."

"What? Oh no! I look terrible. Don't you dare let him in." *He always comes to the door when I'm at my worst.*

She cracks opens the door and I can see his bare feet. He asks her if I'm around. She says actually she's not feeling too well and I'm here hanging out, taking care of her. Danielle then says, "What cha need?"

Chandler says, "Nothing really. It's okay, I'll stop back by later. Tell her I said I hope she feels better soon."

Danielle closes the door and glances over at me. She says, "I don't know how you contain yourself around that one. He seems amazing! I love how shy he acts. I think he has a thing for you."

Oh shit, here we go… Danielle thinks any man who says one word to a woman has a thing for her. She's so outlandish about her theory. Once she had a meeting about one of her co-workers making her feel uncomfortable because he'd put smiley faces on work emails to her. She claimed it was "clearly flirting."

"You're crazy! You should see his girlfriend. She's perfect…beautifully and remarkably perfect in every way. It's quite sickening. He told me the other day he was ready to "advance" their relationship. Not sure what he means. Her move in or get married, I guess. I just told him Josh and I broke up. It's crazy, but I feel so wobbly-legged around him. Honestly, I know he's way out of my league. Besides, none of it matters, he's just a hot neighbor I occasionally flirt with who has a beautiful un-pregnant girlfriend with which he's "advancing", so he's way off limits. Not to mention, he's quite a bit older too. So, if you don't mind, please just let it go!" *I do wonder what he wanted though.*

"Well, Kier, you're not exactly chopped liver in the looks department. I can't imagine that his girlfriend has anything on you. Besides I bet you're younger too!"

"All right, enough about my neighbor. When's the food coming?"

"They said 15-20 min. Just lie back and relax. Today has been a very stressful day for you, and stress-plus-pregnancy is not a good thing, I do know that much."

I place my head back down on my couch and try to calm my thoughts. It doesn't really work too well, and my mind starts wandering again. I can't stop thinking about this baby, this tiny little human baby, that's forming in my body right now. *I'm not sure what kind of a mom I'm going to be, but one thing is for sure, I'm pregnant and the rest is small details.* These thoughts actually give me a bit of solitude. Sure the situation sucks and is not at all what I'd planned for, but it's not the end of the world.

The doorbell buzzes again, which I assume this time it'll be the Chinese food. Danielle says, "I got it…just lie still and don't get up."

She's back at the door, and looks back at me very surprised as she opens the door wider. I hear a familiar voice questionably say, "Someone order Chinese?"

Danielle says, "All right, you can come in. Especially since you have our food, and I'm assuming you paid for it too? Or, did you knock the guy out and snag the bag?" They both laugh.

I sit up and say, "Hi Chandler." *I wonder why he came back?*

I must look puzzled because he says, "I guess you're wondering why I'm here…"

"No, it's fine…no worries, come on in. I've not been feeling too well, but its fine to come in. I feel a little better."

Chandler walks over and puts the food bag down on the table. Danielle looks at me with a sneaky smile and is pointing at me silently mouthing behind his back, "I told you so. He likes you!"

I roll my eyes at her and invite Chandler to have a seat. He sits down in the chair next to the couch, and I can tell something is on his mind. It's also hard to ignore the smell of alcohol permeating off of him. This is definitely a bit awkward. We haven't really spent too much time together over the years, especially to the point of having him sit in my living room, so I try to make casual talk. I can tell something is up right away. I say, "What's going on? Are you okay?"

Chandler scoots up to the edge of the chair, closer to the proximity of the couch where I'm sitting. He opens a packet of soy sauce and pours it on top of my rice. He stops, looks into my eyes, and says, "Juliette just broke up with me. I'm feeling pretty shitty actually. I'm sorry for barging in and wouldn't have normally bothered you, but I knew you and your guy just broke up and thought maybe misery would like company?"

"Awe, Chandler, I'm so sorry."

In the background, Danielle is making yes gestures with her hands and smiling while jumping up and down. Luckily Chandler's back is to her so he can't see her shenanigans. She then writes on a napkin that she's going to leave us alone. *Oh my God! She wouldn't dare.* Danielle grabs her oversized LV bag and says she has to get going. Chandler stands up and says, "Oh gosh, you don't have to leave. I hope you're not leaving because of me?" I can't help but notice how sincere and polite he is, even after he's clearly had a sizable amount of alcohol.

Danielle says, "Oh no, don't be silly, no worries. I was leaving anyways. I need to run home to take care of things there. I hope you two have a great evening. Oh, and there is plenty of Chinese food for you both! See ya later, Kier!"

Holy shit. She really is leaving me here. Unbelievable! She puts her hand "air phone" up to her ear and mouths, "Call me."

This is seriously weird. I sit back down next to Chandler not really knowing what to say to him. There is a long, uncomfortable silence as I try to situate myself on the sofa. I can't seem to figure out what do with my feet. Should I put them on the couch or on the floor? Finally, I rest them on the floor. *Ugh! This is so strange.* As I begin to say something, he also starts talking at the same time. This seems to happen with him frequently, and we both laugh. The laughter breaks up the awkwardness a bit. I say, "How about I grab us a couple plates and we share this food? I'm starving."

"Great idea. I'm pretty hungry myself. I hope I'm not intruding, though? I mean, I didn't mean to run Danielle off."

I walk into the kitchen, grab some plates, and carry it all over to the living room. I say, "Don't be silly. She was leaving anyways." Changing the subject I say, "Would you like a beer?"

He says, "Yes."

I grab him a beer out of the fridge, and pour myself a glass of water. What I really want is wine, or at this point, liquor, but of course I wouldn't. When I get back into the living room I notice Chandler has moved over to the couch. He's dividing the food equally onto the plates. I hear my cell phone buzz. I reach down onto the coffee table to look to see who is calling. Lo and behold, it's a message from Danielle.

Danielle: *have fun!! Call me later☺ prrrrrrr!*

What the hell does she mean by "prrrrrr"?

I decide to turn my phone to silent. I'm not sure if I love or hate her at the moment. I'm kind of shocked she'd leave me after the news I just got, but at the same time I guess she felt a bit like the third wheel, if that's possible for her. I know she knows Chandler is strictly my neighbor, but something about him here tonight does seem different. Either way, I'm not exactly sure what to expect with

Chandler being here, and I guess I can always call her back over in a bit when he leaves if I need to.

I sit down next to Chandler and we start eating. I flip through the T.V. channels and surprisingly, I don't feel nervous like I usually do around him. Maybe it's because he's had alcohol and seems very relaxed, or maybe because I'm too exhausted to care. I haven't even peeped into a mirror to see how I look, and strangely that doesn't seem to bother me too much right now either.

Finally, I ask Chandler if he wants to talk about his breakup. He tells me no, so I change the subject as quickly as I can. Luckily, I thought of something to say pretty fast and tell him I'm going on a trip to London with my co-worker Claire in a couple weeks. I can see right away that he's impressed, and I ask him if he's ever been. He says he loves London and that I'll have so much fun exploring. He tells me his family visited London every other summer. Then he mentions several spots that are "must sees," but I can't seem to concentrate on too much of what he's saying because I find myself lost in his dark blue eyes and gorgeously long eyelashes. I feel woozy just looking at him. I can't fathom how Juliette could end things with him. He seems so honest and sincere and well, just perfect.

He must feel my unconscious staring, because he catches my attention and says, "Kiera?"

I snap out of it and say, "Yes. I'm sorry. What did you say?"

"Oh, I was asking where you're staying in London."

"Umm, I can't recall the name precisely. I think it was something like Pancreas… St. Pancre something."

He stops me and says, "Oh, St. Pancras Renaissance London Hotel."

"Yes, that's it!"

"I know exactly where that is. You'll love it! It's a great location. Make sure to have some sort of plan because time really slips away and you get busy and overloaded wanting to sightsee. You want to make sure you get a lot in."

"Oh believe, me that's already taken care of. My co-worker is super organized, and since it's a business trip, we're traveling together. She's really awesome. I reach into my laptop bag sitting next to the couch and pull out the schedule Claire printed. Here is what she came up with. We read the itinerary together while I hold it in my hand.

London Itinerary

Wednesday: Travel

Thursday: Event for Buyers 8:00 a.m.- 3:30 p.m.

Sightseeing/shopping nearby- dinner- drinks

Friday: Event for Buyers 8:00 a.m.- 3:30 p.m.

Sight seeing/shopping nearby- dinner- drinks

Saturday: Windsor Castle/ Tour

The museum of Brands, Packaging and Advertising-

Afternoon; Soho, Cinema and dinner- evening

Sunday: Kensington Palace and Hyde Park- morning

Jason's Canal Boat Trip along Regents Canal-

Afternoon; St. Katherine Docks- dinner

Chandler seems impressed. He says, "Wow! Okay, I'll bow out with my ideas. You were right. Sounds like you're in good hands and don't need any pointers from me. Your co-worker is a pro! Seriously, I think all of it sounds like a great plan, and like she thought of everything. Believe me you'll really enjoy the trip."

"Really?!? That's wonderful to hear you say. I mean with your world travel experiences and everything. I can't wait to go, but I've definitely had some apprehensions. Hearing you think this is a good itinerary makes me feel a little better."

I notice as I'm finishing my sentence Chandler's facial expression has changed. He reaches out his hand towards my face and lightly touches my cheek. Slowly he's moving closer to me and before I know it our lips are interlocked in a long, passionate kiss. I feel as though I'm floating on air. *Holy cow this is really hot!*

Chapter 6

I don't want this moment to end. We continue to kiss ever so passionately as we move to my bedroom. He feels so good next to me. I love how he's taking charge of me, yet being so gentle as he guides me. I can't believe this is happening. I can just hear Danielle and what she'd say. I envision her giving me a thumbs up and a golf clap. She'll never let this rest. I'm so glad she left. What an awesome friend she is to have considered tonight's events.

Finally, we're on the bed peeling our clothes off of each other, panting. Our bodies are touching and he's caressing my back so lightly. The desire is so strong for each other we can't take it any longer, and we give into our impulses.

As we lie next to each other, I feel so natural and beautiful. I've never felt this confident with anyone before. Maybe it's the age difference. I consider the things that would cause me to feel this way, but no matter what it is, he's made me feel more sexy and powerful than ever before. I can't stop smiling. *This has turned out to be a great night.* He wraps his arm around me tight. Just as I close my eyes and feel my body melting into his so peacefully, I remember… *OH NO! I'm pregnant. Ugh!!!! OH NO!* I must have jolted because Chandler says, "Oh my, is everything alright? Are you okay?"

All I can muster out is "Oh no! Oh crap what have I done?"

Chandler quickly stands up and is squandering around for his clothes saying how sorry he is. He keeps saying it's his fault for coming over and letting things get out of hand. He says, "I don't have to stay. I'm leaving. I'll go."

He keeps rambling on-and-on blaming himself. Finally, I can't take it anymore and I say, "No, this is not about what just happened, believe me please, it's really not. Well, maybe it kind of is, but not directly. Crap, I really know how to get myself into trouble."

Chandler looks so confused with my rambling. He says, "Should I go, or do you want to talk about it? I'm sorry if I over stepped my bounds. You are just so beautiful and I think I…we both felt so fragile and vulnerable. Kiera, you made me feel amazing and alive tonight, and I think about you a lot, not just tonight. I mean it. Please don't think I was looking for a rebound. I came here to see you because you make me laugh, and the total truth is that I've always had a thing for you. I couldn't help but feel like maybe the feeling might be mutual. After a few drinks, I worked up the nerve to come see you. I didn't plan on anything else, honest. You were just so beautiful. I'm sorry if I messed up by coming. I should go."

I'm at a loss for words. How can I tell this man I just slept with, oh by the way I'm pregnant? Chandler inches to the door and turns one last time. Without saying a word he nods at me and leaves for his apartment.

I slide down to the ground on the wall I was leaning on, and bang my head up against it several times. *I'm such a freaking idiot! I should have never let that happen. I'm pregnant! Freaking pregnant…and Josh doesn't even know yet. I just slept with my neighbor! UGH! I'm a total mess!*

A couple of days have passed since I slept with Chandler, and I haven't been to work all week. I called in sick without offering much of an explanation. Besides, it's not a lie, I have been throwing up like crazy every morning this week. Claire has been calling me daily, but I haven't felt in the mood to speak to anyone except Danielle. She keeps saying I need to get out of the house and go back to work. I know she's right, and I really want to get out of this apartment, but I still feel like one more day could do me good. I watch Chandler come and go from his apartment through my peephole throughout the day. Honestly, I'm not sure if I'm more bothered by the way the other night ended and my not offering him an explanation, or by my being pregnant. I can't seem to get him off my mind no matter how much I try. I find myself day- dreaming about him all day long. I actually think about him more than this pregnancy, which is sort of peculiar. Yesterday morning when I saw him leaving for work, it looked as if he wanted to come and knock on my door, but he resisted and went on about his day. Maybe I was simply hoping.

When I told Danielle about what happened between Chandler and me the other night, she was elated. I don't quite understand her excitement, or where she thinks this could lead, but I just let her have her thrill. I may have even played off of it a bit too much leaving nothing to the imagination. Danielle loves details and I made sure I was explicit in giving it to her. I don't know what she expects from this whole thing since I'm pregnant with Josh's baby and it'll certainly pose a problem with my chance of anything with Chandler. I mean, I have to tell him. I have to explain the big blow up right after our rendezvous. I can't leave him thinking he did something wrong, or that I wasn't interested, because clearly I am. The fact is, I'd love to pursue him but why would he want me? There is no way in hell he wants to get involved with a woman carrying someone else's baby. Why would he want that drama? I had no business sleeping with him. I can't bear the thought of him thinking any of this, and I have had such a hard time imagining myself facing him with the truth.

I glance at the clock and see it's only 5:00 a.m. I already texted Claire last night to tell her I'd be back the day after tomorrow, and that I just needed one more day to recover. *Ha! Little does she know. I'll need more like 9 months, or how about the next 18 years to recover.*

My mind goes back to Chandler. I recall the other morning when I discovered him out on the balcony around this time, and I'm curious if he's there now. I put my K-cup on, press the button, and wait for the ready light. I put in a Café Escapes Chai Latte hoping there is not too much caffeine, since unfortunately this is something I now have to consider. I walk over to my balcony door and open it as quietly as I can, trying not to draw attention to myself in case he's there. I sit down and listen for his breathing, or any sign he's there. I hear nothing. I decide to shuffle my chair around and set my mug down on the glass top table a bit loudly to see if he will hear and respond, but nothing happens. I glance over the corner and confirm he's not there.

Disappointed, I look down over the balcony and see Louie looking up at me waving. That crazy doorman must never sleep, and he's right about one thing, there is not much that can get past him, even if it's only 5:00 a.m. I smile, wave back at him, and giggle under my breath at how awkward he can be at times. As I sit back in my chair, I can feel a slight breeze and morning chill. I'm glad I thought to bring my cashmere throw out with me and I wrap up in it a little tighter. Although there is some street noise, it's quieter than usual outside. This is the best time to hangout out on the balcony when living in New York.

Sipping on my Chai Latte, I lean back and relax enjoying how peaceful it feels just being in the Moment. I close my eyes to try to focus on how relaxed I feel, not Chandler nor my pregnancy. I'm jolted as I hear a door slide open. I realize its Chandler. I look over, and he's standing at the edge staring at me. *I wonder how he knew I was here.* I say, "Good morning."

He smiles and says, "Good morning".

There is a brief silence before I say, "How are you?"

Emotionless he says, "Well, and you?"

He's making it hard for me to get a read on him, or a read on where we stand after the other night. The conversation seems cold and unnerving. I feel I have no choice but to bring up what happened. I can't imagine there will ever be a perfect time, so I go for it. I say, "Look, Chandler we need to talk about the other night."

He places his finger up and says, "One second."

For a brief moment I'm curious by what he's doing, but then I can hear that he's at my door. He knocks and I go to let him in. I smile and he says, "Okay, this is better. I want to see you face-to-face. May I come in?"

I don't know why, but him saying this gives me high school girl chills and butterflies all over. *God he's so hot.* I tell him to come in and I walk over towards the sofa inviting him over to have a seat. My legs are wobbly, and I feel the same school girl giddiness rushing over me again. He makes me feel tingly in places I never knew existed. I had wondered if those feelings would go away since we've now been together, but apparently not, and that makes me even giddier. For the first time I consider what I look like. I'm wearing cotton, baby blue pajama shorts and a white tee without a bra. My long blonde hair is loosely pulled back in a top bun, and I'm so thankful I washed and moisturized my face first thing this morning. The more I think about it, I actually start feeling quite confident of my early morning appearance and less concerned. It probably helps that I've often been told I wake up beautiful, even by Danielle, who

I know is an honest soul. I decide to let it go as we make small talk. My phone buzzes, and I look down trying to stay in the moment with Chandler and not be rude. It's a text from Danielle. I glance at it.

Danielle: *Please go out to dinner with Sam and me tonight. I know you need to get out of the house. Let me know?*

I put my phone down and try to focus back on the conversation with Chandler. He's talking about how comfortable my sofa is, weird. I decide to cut the pleasantries of small talk, and I jump on the elephant in the room. I say, "Chandler, look…about the other night, I need to explain." Before I could go any further he says, "No. Just stop. No need for an explanation. I feel terrible about everything. Kiera, I'm so sorry that I let myself get out of hand. We were both in a vulnerable state with our previous relationships ending, and things just got carried away. Really and truly, I'm so sorry Kiera. Really, really, sorry. I've felt awful about the whole thing. I shouldn't have come back over here like that, especially after the first time, and Danielle telling me you were not feeling well. I don't know what came over me. It was highly inappropriate. I hope you'll forgive my judgment."

Oh crap. He's sorry… Regretful? Really?!? I feel awful maybe even insulted. How could he be sorry? It was so magical. Right? He made me feel amazing! Finally, I tell him to just stop and listen. I actually feel hurt, like I might cry. I assume the tears would be due to my pregnancy hormones. *Ugh these pregnancy hormones!*

"Chandler, listen, I didn't blow up the other night over regret from what happened between us. Damn it, I actually felt like it was long overdue. I'm sorry and shamed to hear that you clearly have some regrets. For me there is so much more to what happened. It doesn't really have anything to do with you. Reasons that are more personal on my end." I pause because I can see he's processing. I love how he's taking time to respond. It's as if he's formulating his thoughts before saying them aloud, again a very sexy trait. One that guys my own age need to learn.

Finally, he says, "Well that's a relief! I've been worrying myself to death over the past couple days. I thought I overstepped boundaries and offended you. Frankly, I've just felt terrible. So bad that I wished I could have had a redo, but hearing you say this makes me feel so much better and relieved. I am glad I don't have to feel regretful because I don't ever want to forget how you made me feel. I want you to know I'm not the kind of guy who typically shows up for a quickie and then disappears into oblivion. The other night meant a lot to me, and I hope it did to you as well."

I feel light-headed and whimsical, as if I'm floating on air. "Really, you have no regrets?" Chandler cups my face in between both of his hands and says, "Hell no! I have no regrets."

He leans in and begins passionately kissing me like I've never been kissed before. I feel amazing and euphoric. Again, we're lost into each other and peeling each other's clothes off as fast as we can. This time we're not moving towards the bedroom. The desire is too strong to waste time, and we can't contain ourselves very long. Chandler pulls me on top of him and we enjoy each other even more than the first time. I feel so invigorated with him, so alive and sexy.

When it's over, he lies down on the sofa. He holds me tight next to him and we spoon. It's amazing how safe I feel in his arms. He's holding me so passionately, and I can tell he doesn't want to let me go. I can't help but think how long Josh and I were together, and how he never made me feel this way. Josh always hated spooning. Chandler whispers in my ear, "Do you know you're amazing?"

I don't answer as it seems rhetorical, and we fall to sleep. I awaken with Chandler reaching over me to grab his beeping cell phone. He says, "Are you going into work today?"

I tell him no and he says, "Hmmm. Me either."

He sends a quick text and says, "Want to go back to bed for a while since I'm not gonna go in today either?"

He smiles that sexy smile, and I nod my head yes as we go back to my bedroom. I pull the blankets back, much like a turn down service would do, and we both climb in. I can't help but think about the last time we were in my room together and the thought gives me happy chills. We both lie down and cuddle as we both fall back to sleep.

When I wake up, I notice that Chandler is still sleeping. I gently move his arm off from around me, and I'm able to sneak out from under him. I slip away to the bathroom for a relaxing shower. When I'm finally dressed and my hair is dry, I open the bathroom door and see that Chandler is up. P*robably my blow-dryer woke him.*

I walk out into the living area, but realize he's not there. He must have gone across the hall maybe to shower himself. My cell phone buzzes and it's Danielle again. I realize I never answered her last text.

Danielle: *Hello? I hope u r ok? So do u want 2?*

I start typing but another text from her comes through:

Danielle: *u know… dinner tonight?*

I shoot back a text.

Kiera: *Yeah. Maybe. Probably. I guess.*

Danielle: *Have u talked to him yet?*

I'm not exactly sure who she's talking about. Josh or Chandler. *Oh shit…Josh!* Somehow I had magically put him and the baby out of my mind again. *How can I keep screwing up like this? I have to tell Chandler about this baby. He has to know. But more importantly, I have to tell Josh.* Another text beeps through from Danielle:

Danielle: *Hello??? Have u? I'll go with if u want… I can see u r reading these messages…y aren't u responding?!?*

I definitely now know she's talking about Josh. Oh crap! Josh…

Suddenly, I hear my front door open, and I see its Chandler. He flashes his teeth with his sexy smile and says, "Room service!"

"Wow!" I say. He's carrying a tray full of an assortment of breakfast goodies. *Why does he have to be so freaking amazing?*

Chapter 7

Chandler and I seem to lose track of time as this day has flown by. Definitely the "time flies when you're having fun." This morning we ate our breakfast and watched some daytime television. Mostly we just relaxed on the sofa and talked about our lives, sort of a "getting to know you better" time. I learned Chandler grew up in New York City, and as a child he knew he wanted to be an attorney. He comes from a long line of attorneys. His dad, uncles, and grandfather all practiced law.

I tell him more about my job as a buyer for Whitaker & Bluff. Chandler seems so interested in everything I have to say. I love how he has so many follow-up questions and listens intently. He is so different from other guys I've dated, including Josh. With Josh, most everything he said and was interested in was about him.

Things with Chandler just feel natural. I feel like we've always been together. It's odd really, and hard to explain, but it just feels so natural. I look at the clock and it's almost 4:00 p.m. Chandler sees me look and asks if I have plans for dinner. He said he doesn't want to interrupt my plans. I tell him no, he is not interrupting at all, and I would love him to stay if he's free. We decide we'll order in and continue on with our day, the same as we had. I decide I need to text Danielle so she'll not worry or bother me anymore. Ignoring the text about Josh, and deciding to live in the moment and try to put him and this baby out of my mind, I shoot her a text back.

Kiera: *2 tired for dinner. Have fun. I'll call tomorrow.*

Danielle: *But I wanted u to meet someone.*

Are you freaking kidding me? Surely she isn't trying to set me up again. I text back.

Kiera: *WTH?*

Danielle: *Oh never mind! Fine see u tomorrow.*

That crazy girl was going to try to set me up with someone else. Unbelievable! She clearly cannot be trusted. UGH! I laugh under my breath, and Chandler asks what's so funny. I tell him Danielle is crazy, like he wouldn't believe. He admitted that he already kind of figured, which I thought was even funnier. We both laugh, and since we're already on the subject of her, I decide it is a good time to tell him the story of her quick engagement. I give him the whole story, but decide he can't fully understand the level of her insanity without seeing her Pinterest page and her "Dream Wedding" board. I grab my phone, pull up the app, and show him the awful pink dresses I'm almost certain she's picked for us to wear. In the middle of me showing him the dress, and me imagining that I'll have to wear this horrible dress, it occurs to me yet again that I'm pregnant. *Oh no!!! I can't have a pregnant belly in Danielle's wedding?!? I wonder if she's thought of this… Knowing Danielle, I'm sure she has and she probably has some sort of crazy plan too. The thought scares me.*

Now I have three things I do not want to think about, being pregnant, telling Josh, and Danielle's wedding. I push the thoughts as far out of my mind as I can. Unfortunately though, I start feeling nauseated and it makes it hard to completely forget my situation with the baby growing inside of my belly. I really want to enjoy my time with Chandler, and I've pretty much decided I'm not going to tell him about the pregnancy right now, so I manage to suppress the nausea as best as possible. As I justify in my mind, I really don't see a need for him to know. I mean why should it matter right now? We're just casually hanging out. I mean, yes, it feels like so much more, but I'm not in any place to rock this boat. It's too early, and I'm not sure where things are going. With this justification, I'm able to enjoy the rest of my night with Chandler for the most part and the nausea seems to subside after a while.

After dinner, we talk about my trip to London more, and Chandler offers some suggestions to add to Claire's itinerary. I jot them down real quick, but I make sure to tell him I can't promise Claire will consider anything out of what she has already planned. He smiles and says, "Claire seems like quite the character!"

I smile back and say, "You could say that for sure."

Then I tell him Claire's husband, Richard, is Josh's best friend. I explain things might be sticky now with Claire and me, but nothing that I can't get past, just awkward maybe. He tells me he understands because Juliette's older brother is one of his partners at his law firm. I interrupt him and ask him if he's interested in having dessert. He flashes me a flirty look and I throw a pillow at him and smile. I say, "Not that kind of dessert."

He almost looks like he's blushing, which I think is ridiculously cute. I say, "Let's go for a walk and get some ice-cream, want to? Then, when we get back, we can maybe have seconds!"

He stands up and says, "I think I like the sound of seconds, but ice-cream is good too."

I grab my Tory Burch bag, and we head out the door for our walk. As I'm locking up I hear Danielle calling my name. "Kiera? Hey!"
I turn from my door and look at her puzzled "Danielle? What are you doing here?"
"I came to check on you."
"Oh. Well, I'm fine. We were actually about to go out for a walk."
"I'm sorry. I can just call you later."

Chandler pipes in and says, "Kiera, I'll give you two a second and go over to my place and grab a jacket. Just knock when you're ready to go. Sound good?"

"Yes, that works."

I re-open my apartment and Danielle and I go in. She's staring at me not saying a word. Finally, once the door is closed completely, she squeals, "You little liar!!"

"I'm not a liar."

"How long has he been here you sneak?"

I don't answer her right away, but instead look in the mirror. I start primping, but decide that I really look pretty good for just laying around all day. I also feel incredibly happy. Danielle points it out. She says, "Kier, you look better than you've ever looked. Honest. You look so happy."

"I am. I feel great. I really need to get back to him. We were going out for ice-cream."

"Ok. I'll go. But just tell me one thing. Have you told him about the baby?"

She can tell by the look on my face that the answer is "no." She says, "No big deal. I'm sure you want to tell Josh first anyway. Let's schedule that and I'll go with you. Sam will go, too, if you want. When can you do it?"

"I'm not sure. I forgot to tell you I have a last minute work trip to London the week after next. It's only a few days, so hopefully before I leave."

"How could you forget to tell me about a trip to London?"

"Really, it's no biggie only 4 or 5 days."

"By yourself?"

Oh no… I have to tell her Claire is going.

"Claire is going, too."

"Oh shit, Kier. Does she know yet?"

"No, but hopefully she will by then. I can't keep it from her, especially if I tell Josh. He'll definitely tell Richard."

"Ok. Just schedule a time with Josh and let me know. I'll figure it out to be there no matter what."

Danielle heads toward the door, stops, and kisses my cheek. She says, "Everything is going to be alright, Kier. I know it is." She leaves and I lock the door as I step out too.

I knock on Chandler's door to let him know I'm ready. He opens immediately and invites me in. I notice his apartment is a lot larger than mine and definitely screams a man lives here. I don't mean that in a bachelor pad-dirty disaster way either. It's just plain, with no decorations at all. The more I think about it, it would be kind of strange if it were decorated. He says he wants to show me around his place because it didn't seem right that I had not been over. I liked that he seemed to be very clean and tidy. There were no dishes in the sink, and the counter was clear and clean. His bathrooms were neat and fresh, and his bed was made. I'm extremely impressed. After my tour we decide to go for our walk and ice-cream.

Once in the lobby, we both check our mailboxes for mail. Louie is at the door, and I glance over at him. I see he's pointing his pointer finger and middle finger towards his eyes, and then turns them back at me as if to say he's watching me. I smile, and he smiles back. I'm pretty sure he knows something is going on between Chandler and me.

As we walk outside, we can immediately feel how amazing and crisp the weather is. I love New York City in early September. I look over at the bank next to my building, and the temperature reads 63 degrees. It feels amazing. We walk about three blocks over to one of my favorite ice-cream food trucks called "Izzy's Flavors." I'm not sure why, but ice-cream sounds so divine at this very second. I order black raspberry pecan caramel truffle, and Chandler orders dark chocolate turtle. We sit down on a bench nearby and people watch for a few minutes. I have a cold chill, and Chandler gives me his coat. I apologize for not thinking to grab one for myself. He smiles and says, "Kiera, you're just simply beautiful. I mean just really beautiful in every way. I have had so much fun being with you today. I feel like I've known you forever. I hope you don't think I'm weird for saying this, but I hope you feel the same."

I feel so happy inside. Butterflies are flittering all around my stomach, and I feel as though I could scream for 20 minutes from a mountain top. Finally, after staring at him for a few moments, I lean and place my head on his strong, solid shoulder. I say, "Just so you know, I feel the same."

Chapter 8

Chandler stayed the night last night, and now he's back at his place showering for work. He said we'd meet up again tonight for dinner, and I know I'll be counting down the minutes all day. I can't stop humming; I feel so incredibly happy, as though nothing could take this feeling away. I'm going back to work today, and I actually am not dreading it as much as I thought I would.

I grab my purse and immediately a wave of nausea overwhelms me. I charge to the bathroom. I throw up what feels like fourteen times and feel utterly horrible. I go to the kitchen, pour myself some Ginger ale, and start to cry. *Shit! Why me? Why does everything have to be so complicated? Why did I have to have a failed relationship and find out I'm pregnant? Better yet why does it have to be Josh's baby? How will I ever tell Chandler?* I eat some saltine crackers, chug down the Ginger ale, and then grab my keys to lock up. I head out for the day.

On the subway, I try to fight through the nausea. I continue to sip on some Ginger ale. It would be completely mortifying if I spew my guts out in front of all of these people. Although I know for certain it wouldn't be the first time someone threw-up on the train, I don't want to be one of "those" people. I try to focus on keeping my eyes shut and concentrate on telling myself I feel well, only it's so hard! *Holy crap! I feel like I have the flu. I feel like a total bag of dog crap.*

As I'm looking down towards the ground, I feel someone tap me on the shoulder. I look up and literally almost barf my guts out. It's Josh! He questionably says, "Kiera"?

"Hi, Josh."

"Are you okay?"

Oh shit! I'm certain, as I stare at him waiting and hoping for my words to come out, he's definitely thinking I look like this because of the breakup. I can see the pity in his eyes as he stares me down. *How can he be so self-centered and sure of himself?* Finally, I feel like I can muster out a sentence. I say, "Not really. I've been under the weather…sort of sick for about a week or so."

"Have you gone to the doctor?"

"Not yet." *If only you knew what was really wrong… you sack of shit!*

"Are you okay to go to work? Maybe you should have called in."

"No. I'll be fine. I haven't been to work for a few days, and I have a lot to do before my trip to London."

"Oh yeah, I forgot about that. Richard said you and Claire are going together. I'm sure you two will have a great time. Listen if you're sure you're okay, I need to get off. I'm running a bit behind schedule this morning."

"Oh, I'm fine. No worries here. Have a great day!" *Asshole…*

"You too, Kier! See ya around."

Yep… you certainly will be seeing me around. More than you know. God, I really can't stand the very sight of him at this moment.

A part of me so badly wants to scream "I'M PREGNANT, ASSHOLE!" to him as he turns to walk away so carelessly. *Are you freaking kidding me? "See ya around"… UGH! I'm utterly sickened by his presence.*

As I walk into the office I immediately see Claire. She's talking to another co-worker, but she spots me. Before I get to my desk, she's already darting her way towards me. "Kiera, honey, you look awful. Are you okay? I mean, you just look terrible." *Lovely*, I think to myself, and then realize I have to respond as she's continually staring at me awkwardly.

"I'm fine. Still a little sick, but I'll be okay."

Desperately wanting to change the subject and get all of the attention off of me, I quickly ask Claire if there is anything new I should know about. Clearly she doesn't realize I'm talking about work, because she looks at me so strangely and says, "Kiera, I'm so sorry. I honestly had no idea that it was happening, and I swear to you, if I knew I'd have told you. I swear I would have… please believe me."

What the hell is she talking about? My face must have looked confused because she says, "Even Richard didn't know until recently."

I finally think I'm connecting the dots, and I realize this has to have something to do with Josh and his red headed co-worker, Gina, since I just saw their picture on Instagram a couple days after our break-up. I decide to play along with Claire in order to get all of the facts straight. Oddly enough, I am unfazed by the prospect of his shenanigans.

"Claire, it's nothing to do with that. I mean, I think it's crazy and all, but whatever."

Just as I suspect, Claire begins to divulge every last thing she knows. I know I can only get the info from Claire if I act like I know exactly what she's talking about.

"I had no idea he'd been going out to drinks with her all of those nights. I mean, what was he thinking? Richard and I can't believe he was even planning to propose to you knowing he was being unfaithful. It's no wonder he crumbled when he tried to propose. I'm sure he felt so shitty about the way he was doing you. He swore to Richard he and Gina had not done anything until he broke it off with you."

There you have it. Just as I suspected, it's about Gina. I knew there was something to the Instagram picture and something fishy about the way the picture looked.

Claire continues talking and says, "Oh sweetie, I hope you'll be okay. We've been so worried about you."

"Claire, I'm fine. Really, I promise, I'm fine."

What I really want to say is, "Oh by the way, I'm sleeping with my hot neighbor." I refrain mostly because of the overwhelming nausea that's taking me over.

I'm now leaning over my desk trash can vomiting up everything, including the saltines I was hoping to keep down. Claire is holding my hair for me and rubbing my back. She takes me to the bathroom when finally I get some relief between heaves. As we walk into the bathroom, I can feel it coming up again. *Am I really this sick from pregnancy, or is it possible I'm bothered by Josh and Gina?*

After throwing up for a bit longer, I finally feel like everything is out and the nausea is subsiding. Claire rubs my back as we sit in the lounge area attached to the bathroom. She's patting me and looking at me like I'm a poor soul. I can't contain myself any longer. I look into Claire's eyes, "I'm pregnant, and Josh doesn't know."

"Oh my goodness! You poor thing. Here, sit here and lay your head on me."

Claire is being so comforting. Even though Danielle would be upset at me for telling her, I'm glad I told her. She really is making me feel better, and as I let her hug me, all of my discomfort and nausea from the morning seems to pass. After a while, I collect myself and we head back to our desks. Just as we're stepping back, my cell phone vibrates and I look down to see it's my Mom. *Oh crap! I'll have to eventually tell her*. I let the phone go to voicemail. It's so funny, but she's one of the few people in my life that still chooses to call instead of text. I guess that's true for most of her generation.

I check my voicemail as it beeps in a new message. "Hi, Kier! I hope everything is going well with you and I hope you'll call me soon. Tell Danielle and Josh I said hello. I really wish I could talk to you. Please call me. I hope you're okay. Bye now."

My Mom lives in California. Being a single woman, not dating at all most of my childhood, she's certainly made up for it in recent years. My dad left us when I was three, and I haven't seen him since. I have no memories of him, and he never kept in touch. My Mom has always said I'm better off, and I tend to believe her. Sometimes I wonder what he's like from time-to-time, or if he ever thinks about me.

Thinking about growing up without a father and how well I turned out, makes me question if I should tell Josh about the baby. I quickly dismiss the thought as I know it wouldn't be the right thing to do. It is hard for me to picture life in a few months having to share my baby with Josh. All I know is, telling my Mom is the last thing I want to do right now. She preached to me my whole life about the importance of finding the right man, and not wasting time on the wrong ones. She also has been conscientious, teaching me about practicing safe sex to ensure there were no un-planned pregnancies. I hate feeling like I'm going to let her down. Truly, I never want to tell her.

I'm back at my cubicle, and Claire is walking over. She says, "A penny for your thoughts."

I lean my head up against my hands, and place my elbow on the desk. I say, "I know this is awful of me to say Claire, but there have been so many times the past couple days where I've hoped I'll miscarry and never have to mention this to anyone else. Isn't that terrible?"

"Oh, honey, no it's not terrible. You're just scared. Listen, don't say that, just try to relax. Everything will be okay, I know it will. You'll make a perfect Mommy and it will all work out. You'll see. Who cares about you and Josh not being together? This baby will be loved by a lot of people, and you and Josh are grown adults who can figure the rest out. But honestly, Kier, You really need to tell him soon."

"I know. I'm going to schedule a doctor's appointment first. I need to confirm it's viable, and then I'll tell him. Please don't tell Richard yet in case he feels like as Josh's best friend, he should tell him. I really want to be the one to tell him."

"This is your business. I won't say a word."

Claire looks at her phone and gives me her OBGYN's phone number. I can't believe I have to do this. I take the number and tell Claire I'll call it after lunch, but she insists I need to call now. I tell her I think I'm about 7 weeks, and that I have plenty of time. I can't finish my rebuttal as she's already dialed the number and is pushing the phone up to my ear. Immediately a voice comes on saying, "Gynecology appointments. May I help you?"

I stutter and say, "Umm…Yes, hi, I need to schedule an appointment. I recently took a pregnancy test and it was positive. I'd like to confirm it's viable."

The lady pauses and finally says, "How far along do you think you are?"

"Seven weeks."

"We have Friday and Monday open."

I start to schedule an appointment for Friday, and I feel my stomach turn into knots as I realize that is only a couple days away. I feel so anxious and nervous. I say, "Actually, I can't that day. I'll need to call you back."

I hang up the phone. Claire looks concerned, but doesn't lecture me. Instead she says, "Let's go to the café and relax."

In different circumstances I might laugh that we're already taking a break when neither of us has accomplished any sort of work but not this morning. Besides, she was right. I needed a break or at least a change of scenery.

On the walk over, I realize I missed a text from Chandler. I remembered that last night he asked for my number by saying, "What if I want to text you tomorrow? I don't even have your number." I gave it to him, and he said, "What if you want to text me?" I said, "Then I guess you better text me first." I think it's really cute he's already texted me, and it's only 9:05 a.m.

Chandler: *Can't wipe this smile off my face. I hope u have a good day!*

I must have let out a giggle because Claire looks at me and says, "What? What's so funny?"

I say, "Oh, its nothing. I think I'll just have some water and a banana. What are you having?"

That seemed to get her mind off of my giggle, and as she was ordering her items, I quick texted Chandler back.

Kiera: *I know how u feel! See u around dinner time.*

I must have smiled again because Claire is in my face saying, "What's so funny that you keep smiling?"

"Just a text from Danielle."

"Oh, okay. It must be funny. I know how funny that one can be."

Claire asks me if Danielle knows about the pregnancy. I tell her yes. We make small talk about Danielle and her wedding. I tell Claire about how terrified I am about the dress choice I'm almost positive Danielle will choose. Claire starts laughing and wants to see the dress. Feeling a little guilty to be bashing Danielle's dress choice, I still look up her Pinterest board, "Dream Wedding," to show Claire. As I hold up my phone to show Claire the awful pink dress, we both burst into a teary laughter. Claire totally understands how Danielle is, and she says, "Classic Danielle. She is going to make sure she outshines you while you all look like blown up pieces of bubblegum."

"It's true, but I love her anyways! The one thing I've always loved about Danielle is her ability to make herself outshine the world. I guess I sort of always knew I'd be stuck in a moderately ugly bridesmaid dress in her wedding. Just the cost of being her best friend. I'm trying to keep a sense of humor about it, and it seems to be working. The only real concern I have is that now with me being pregnant, I might actually end up literally looking like a blown up piece of bubblegum, especially if she goes through with this wedding anytime soon."

Claire says, "Enough about Danielle's wedding… You don't think the pregnancy will interfere with our London trip, right?"

"No. No way! Not at all. Really, I think I'll be fine. I do hope the morning sickness goes away soon, especially for the plane ride. Most people say it doesn't usually last too long, so we will keep our fingers crossed. Why?"

"I just don't want you to be miserable on the plane or the trip for that matter."

"Claire, I promise I'll not ruin our trip to London. Besides I can always ask for nausea medicine. I think I'm feeling off today because yesterday was not nearly as bad as today. I'm just stressed."

When we get back to the office I sit down at my desk and stare at the pile of work. I'm behind. As I'm thumbing a brochure for a new line of clothes for one of the major sellers, I'm startled to hear a male voice behind me asking if I'm Kiera. I turn to face the man who's dressed in khaki pants, a white polo shirt, and a baseball cap that says Flowers.com. He's holding the largest, and most beautiful, bouquet of white roses, at least two and a half dozen, with a lime-green ribbon tied around the stems. I say, "Yes, can I help you?"

He hands me a clipboard and asks me to sign by the "X." Butterflies start flittering in my stomach, and I feel happy, yet nervous. I notice Claire is staring at me perplexed. I feel a little shy and embarrassed to be creating such a scene around the office. I think about all the times in the past when various women in the office have received deliveries, and how envious I was to watch. Now that it's my turn, I feel like I'm making a spectacle of myself. I question if this is how most of the other women feel. I sign the paper and he places the flowers on my desk. I'm pretty sure I know who sent them.

Claire comes running over and says, "Awe!!! Kiera, dear Josh must have thought things through and he's probably waiting outside. Go ahead open the card. I bet he ended things with Gina. I hope you'll forgive him. It's just what needs to happen you know, now with the baby and all. This is your destiny! A happy ending…"

I can't open this card in front of her. I say, "Claire, if this is truly what you think, then I really feel like this is a private moment. I should read the card without worrying about what others think. Do you mind giving me a minute?"

She looks disappointed, but she honors my request and walks back over to her desk. When she sits down, I open the card. I glance up and can still see her peering over at me, but I look down to read the card anyways.

Kiera,

I can't wait for dinner tonight… I feel amazing knowing that I'll get to be with you in a few short hours. I'll knock on your door around 6:00 p.m. I am taking you out for a nice dinner. Already made reservations.

Chandler

Chapter 9

Wow! I can feel myself smiling from ear-to-ear. This is insane how incredible he's made me feel in such a short time. It's completely amazing, and it's invigorating. This is so cliché; but honestly, I can't recall a time where I ever felt this way about someone. It's crazy really. As I look up, Claire is standing over me.

She says, "Well, Kier? Was I right? What did Josh say?"

The cat has my tongue. I don't know what to say. She continues to stare at me. *Oh no… what to say… I can't lie to her.* Again she says, "Come on, Kier, what did the card say? Don't leave me hanging? Is he apologizing? This seems so romantic. Is he waiting outside? Oh, I bet he's downstairs awaiting your response. This is so exciting! You can tell him about the baby and everything will be amazingly perfect."

Oh, this is awful. I really don't know what to say to her. I feel speechless. She seems so hopeful. It's almost sick.

Finally, I try to stall. I say, "Listen, I really need to work. We can talk about it later."

The look on her face tells me that I am fooling myself thinking I can stall. Claire's expressions make it clear she's becoming agitated. Eventually, after Claire continuously makes several exaggerated huffs and puffs, she stomps toward her desk in such a dramatic way making the building seem like it might collapse, I say, "Claire, it's really complicated."

She says, "Kiera, I'm married to Richard. I can do complicated. Tell me what he said in the freaking card!"

Clearly she has no idea of what is going on, and the flowers are not from Josh. I say, "I don't really expect you to understand any of what I'm about to say, but the answer is no, they're not from Josh. The roses are from my neighbor Chandler."

She's now sitting on my desk. Determined to see what the card says, she grabs it from my hand and silently looks down reading it. Cocking her head, she looks at me and says, "Why are you going to dinner with your neighbor? And why is he so excited to see you? And reservations? Kier, what's going on? Are you dating your neighbor? Does he know you're pregnant? Oh, Kier, what the hell have you gotten yourself into now?"

Oddly enough, I feel like this is the same conversation I'll have with my Mom sooner or later. I feel a mixture of emotions, mostly embarrassed although I don't feel like it is Claire's place to judge me. I'm a grown adult, and I'm not the one who ended the relationship with Josh. I'm free to move on. I'm not sure why it's such a big deal. It's clear that Claire is determined for me to answer her, and she certainly isn't going to drop it until I do. It's funny really, the differences between Claire and Danielle. Danielle thinks it's awesome that I'm seeing Chandler, and Claire acts as if she's simply mortified I'd do this to Josh. I can't seem to respect the one-sidedness she shows towards him; after all, he's the one who ended things, not me. I suppose it is her loyalty as Josh is Richard's best friend and all, but what about me? What about my happiness? And hello! News flash! Josh seems to have moved on to Gina. When I finally have enough, I tell Claire I really need to get some work done, and she walks away a bit defeated.

Who really cares if she's mad at me anyway? She can't tell me what to do. I'm a grown woman, and I can date whomever I please. When Claire is in her seat, I position my roses to cover my view of her so we don't have to look at each other. I'm sure it's perceived well, as she probably doesn't want to see me either. Call it rude, but I'm no longer in the mood to see her or deal with her nonsense.

We manage to avoid having lunch together today because Claire had to go out with a client. She made sure to tell me she was unavailable before she walked away from my desk. I suppose she thought to mention it so it wouldn't seem like she was avoiding me. Funny thing is it's a mutual client, and normally she would've invited me along, so clearly she's trying to avoid me. At the moment, this is fine by me.

As soon as she walks away, I'm able to put her out of my mind. I decide to work through lunch at my desk to catch up on my work. I make sure not to spend my entire lunch working. I decide to spend at least half of my lunch hour on peekingpines.com looking for cute ideas on an outfit for dinner tonight with Chandler. I'm so excited to see him, I keep staring at the clock and the flowers. The flowers are a nice touch as they permeate the whole area by my desk with a lavishing, rich smell. Unfortunately, after focusing on the smell a few too many minutes, I'm starting to feel nauseated. I tolerate them a while longer and then place them down on the floor. Claire is gone anyway, so now is a good time to move them. Besides the smell, they are definitely a mood lifter for me even if my pregnant belly can't stand the smell. The same thing keeps happening with my perfume. I can't tolerate much in the way of any fragrances. I decide to send Chandler a quick text to thank him for the flowers.

Kiera: *They're beautiful!!! I love them… Thx*☺

Chandler: *beautiful flowers for a beautiful girl. Glad u like! See you soon…*

As I place my phone down, I'm overwhelmed by guilt. *How terrible can any one person be?* I'm pregnant with another man's baby and going on a date with someone who has no idea. Shame keeps percolating in me. I hope I am not blindly leading him on. *It's true he certainly is in the dark about my being pregnant and all. I simply have to tell him. He has to know because this just isn't right.*

This really sucks! I feel knots in my tummy, or maybe it's another twinge of sickness. The knots feel more intense when I notice Claire is back from her client lunch. I can't decide if I'll ask her any questions about how it went. From the looks of her face, I think I'll wait. *How dare she be upset with me! This is Josh's fault.* If he wouldn't have chickened out on the proposal and started dating Gina, we could have been planning our lives together - wedding, baby and all. *Screw her!* I ignore her for the rest of the day which doesn't seem to be a problem. I can see she's doing the same to me. I'm more than confident she phoned Richard, and they probably had a good long talk about me, but I really don't care. Before she notices I've moved them, I pick the flowers back up quickly and place them where I can't see her.

Finally, it's as close to five o'clock as its going to be for me, and I decide to hit the door running. On my way out, I glance back to see Claire. She also notices me. I roll my eyes at the thought of her, and continue out the door. Back at my apartment I place my roses on my white granite countertop and admire how beautiful they really are. I feel like a high school girl all giddy inside about my date tonight. As I'm getting freshened up for our dinner, I contemplate how I might bring up the news of the pregnancy.

I look at myself in the mirror. My tummy is as flat as ever, maybe even smaller from all of the morning sickness I suppose. There are no physical signs of pregnancy at all. Feeling confident I pull out my new Herve Leger Marina Foiled Rose Gold dress I recently wore to a buyer's event. I love the way I look in it! It got so many compliments at the event, and I feel confident it still looks great on me. *I'm so happy it still fits.* The top is halter cut and backless with only an x-strap. Form fitting, the dress sits about 6 inches above my knees. I decide to wear my Jimmy Choo black, strappy heels. My straight hair is down, but I've added a few curls for body. As I put in the diamond earrings Josh gave me for Christmas last year, I feel strange. Thinking about him makes me sad. Honestly, this is the first time I've felt sad at the thought of him in a while now.

My thoughts go back to the baby, and how I think my life should be. I try not to cry. It may be hopeless with all of these hormones flooding my body. Determined not to ruin my makeup, I take in a few deep breaths and roll some Mac Angel lipstick and gloss on my lips. I blot and smile as big as I can in the mirror. I hear the doorbell buzz, and all of my fears vanish away. I feel hopeful as I go to let him in.

I say, "Just a min." My phone is beeping as I walk over to the door to open it. I swing the door open and he lets out a whistle. He says, "My, my, my. You look incredible, Kiera! Utterly, incredible!"

I smile back at him and say, "Thank you! You look pretty hot yourself."

Chandler places his right hand behind my head and pulls me in closer with his left hand. We passionately kiss as he holds me tightly to him. Not wanting the moment to end, I close my eyes and feel so safe. My phone beeps again, and we both release.

I look down to see who it is. I have three texts. One from Danielle, one from Claire, and one from my Mom. *I have to tell my Mom. I've been avoiding her calls for weeks now, and she's beginning to worry*. I did text her a brief message a couple days ago to ensure she wouldn't file a missing persons report or anything crazy like that. Claire's text says she wants to talk about everything, and that she's sorry for the way she acted today. She said she's hopeful we can still swing the London trip, and ended it with a smiley emoticon. Danielle simply wants to know what I'm wearing on my date tonight, and asks if my belly is interfering with choices. She said, if so I can come to her closet. Danielle is about 2 sizes up from me, and I contemplate how well that could work for keeping me out of maternity clothes as long as possible. *UGH! The thought of maternity clothes make me cringe.*

Chandler looks at me while I'm staring at my phone and he says, "Everything alright?"

I must have a strange facial expression, so I make sure to smile and say, "It's great! Shall we go?"

He nods "yes," and clutches my arm in his. We head out the door. As I'm locking up, I have that yucky gut wrenching feeling again, and know I have to tell him about the baby. Downstairs, I see Louie staring at us with a big smile. I smile back and say, "Hi, Louie! Having a good day?"

He returns the smile and says, "I absolutely am."

I can't help but smile as I feel like he knew things might happen between Chandler and me. *What a funny, friendly doorman he is.* As we walk out, a cab is already parked waiting for us. We get in and Chandler gives the address to the restaurant. I tell him I'm so hungry and can't wait to see where we're going. Chandler stretches his arm around me and I scoot in close to him. His cologne smells so sexy. I'm relieved it seems subtle, and surprisingly it's not making me nauseated. I was delighted when the cab stopped on Downing St. in front of a restaurant I've wanted to try for some time called Mas (Farmstyle). Inside, I am very impressed with the intimate ambiance, and the romantically quaint and cozy atmosphere. As the host walks us to our table, I'm shocked to see Danielle and Sam. Of all of the restaurants in New York, what are the odds we'd be at the same one?

She waves, and I wave back. She winks and motions at my dress choice in a way that lets me know she thinks I look amazing. Luckily, she stays seated as we proceed to our table. I'm sure Sam made her stay put, and I certainly appreciate him for that.

Looking around, I feel a bit overdressed, but Chandler is in a tie so, I try not to make a big deal about it. I feel confident and love this dress, so I make it work. He asks if I'd like to order a bottle of wine. *Oh shit, I'm not sure what to say!* I tell him I'm not really in the mood for alcohol. He says, "That's fine, no worries, in that case I'll order by the glass."

I order a glass of water, and ask Chandler to pick out the appetizer. The waiter suggests the Marinated Octopus with Watermelon and Tomato Salad, Pickled Red Pearl Onions, Anise Hyssop, and Micro Basil. The thought of watermelon, much less octopus, is enough to make me feel sick right now, but I smile as Chandler looks at me and says, "Oh that sounds lovely. We'll have that."

I manage to keep a pretty face, although my gut feels like it's about to spew, and my eyes are feeling watery. *I hope I don't barf!* My cell phone buzzes. I look at it and see it's Danielle.

Danielle: *Can we stop by table and say hi?*

I text her back since Chandler is busy staring at the menu and say:

Kiera: *sure*

Chandler asks me what I'm thinking about having, and I glance down and point to the first thing I see. I say, "I'm having Roasted Monkfish with Huitlacoche Purée Chorizo-Apple Ragout, Chanterelles & Maple Gastrique. What about you?"

He says, "Yum, that does look good, but I'm going to try their Roasted Goffle Road Farm Chicken with Peach Compote Smoked Cipollini Onions, Goat Cheese Tart, & Swiss Chard. Usually, I wouldn't order chicken, but it just sounds so good tonight."

The waiter takes our order and brings the appetizer. I nibble around the octopus and watermelon trying not to eat very much as I feel like I may throw up out at the sight of it. These hormones are crazy. I seem to feel more nauseated at nighttime as opposed to the traditional morning sickness I had in the beginning. All I can do right now is keep swallowing and telling myself I will not throw up over-and-over in my head. As I drink a long sip of water I feel a bit of relief from the nausea wave. I tell Chandler I can't eat anymore of the appetizer because I need to save room for my dinner. When I sit my glass down, I catch a glimpse of Danielle and Sam coming towards our table. I try to act like I don't see them.

She and Sam walk up. Danielle says, "Hi you two!"

Trying to act surprised I say, "Hey! What a surprise! Did you already eat?"

Danielle says, "Yes, the food is amazing!"

After a quick introduction of Sam and Chandler, the waiter comes in behind where Sam is trying to stand forcing Sam to quickly tell us to have a great evening. He quickly excuses himself. We say goodbye to Sam, but Danielle is still standing over us. As the waiter delivers our food he relays the names of the courses we chose. Danielle begins acting strangely. I notice she keeps looking at the trays of food and looks worried. I can't seem to get a read on what the problem is. Maybe she sees a hair or something. The waiter places my food in front of me and says, "For you the Roasted Monkfish with Huitlacoche Purée Chorizo- Apple Ragout, Chanterelles & Maple Gastrique an excellent choice!"

Then he retrieves Chandler's food from the tray and says, "For you, the Roasted Goffle Road Farm Chicken with

Peach Compote Smoked Cipollini Onions, Goat Cheese Tart, & Swiss Chard. Another excellent choice!" The waiter asks us if we'll need anything else, and Chandler asks for another glass of wine. I tell him I'm fine. The only thing I can think of that I might need at this time is for Danielle to excuse herself. *I'm not too sure why she's still lingering.* I can tell Chandler is feeling awkward with her just standing there, so I say, "Thanks for stopping by and saying hi! Can I call you later?"

Danielle seems to be ok with this and leans in to hug me bye. She tells Chandler it was nice to see him. As she begins to walk away she quickly turns back around. I've just started to place a forkful of my monkfish entrée into my mouth and Danielle knocks the fork flying into the air.

Chapter 10

"Danielle, what the hell are you doing? What was that for?" Chandler is now standing and trying to find the fork, looking so confused by Danielle's actions.

I say, "Danielle? What in the hell is your problem?"

Finally, she blurts out, "You can't eat monkfish because of the mercury!"

I must look confused, because she says, "Shit, Kiera, do your research! If you're going to be stupid enough to get yourself into this mess, at least be smart enough to deal with it responsibly!" I'm thinking she's a complete nut job right now, and everyone in the restaurant seems to be staring. Danielle, looks at me and says, "Kiera, you're PREGNANT, and pregnant people shouldn't have fish with that much mercury in it!"

My mouth drops wide open. *Oh shit, oh shit!* I want to crawl under the table! I'm feeling nauseated again, like I might throw up at that moment. It's evident in Danielle's expression that she did not mean to get as carried away as she did, and I certainly don't think she intended on spilling the beans at all. Clearly, she's right, I need to research all of the ends and outs of pregnancy. I knew about alcohol, but I had no idea mercury was a no-no. Hell, I'm not really even sure what mercury is other than the pretty mercury vases I collect from Pottery Barn. I guess in some ways I haven't really accepted the pregnancy and not really cared or wanted to know much just yet. Things are still so new and I haven't given much thought to what I can and can't have.

I study Chandler's face. It goes without saying, he knows the baby isn't his since we just slept together for the first time this week. I feel like a major bag of ass, and want to go home. Danielle looks at me and says, "Oh, Kier, I'm sorry. I'm really sorry…I'll go now. I should just leave." She walks away and my stomach feels like it's turned completely upside down. I manage to tell her bye all the while, inside, I want to slap the shit out of her for ruining my night. Chandler remains calm and respectable. He hesitantly tells her to have a good evening.

After she's walked away, and I look down at the table, I see that without saying a word Chandler had switched entrée's with me. I tell him he really didn't have to do that, and I could just eat around it, but he insists saying, "No, go ahead."

No matter how hard we both try to recover from the night's events, the whole incident with Danielle has certainly put a damper on our dinner date. We don't discuss it any further as we eat. After dinner, we grab a cab and go back to our building. Chandler still has not mentioned anything about Danielle or the baby. When we get to the building, and as we're walking up, I say, "Dinner was really good!"

I feel stupid immediately after saying it, but I know it's the nice thing to say. I ask Chandler to come in for a few minutes, and much to my surprise he agrees. I grab him a beer from the fridge and a bottle of water for myself. When I walk into the living room, I see him holding an old picture of Josh and me. It's in a Tiffany frame Josh's mom got me a few years ago. It was always my favorite picture of us. We were at my work Christmas party and Josh was wearing a red bow tie that matched my shoes perfectly. I love the bow tie look. The picture was when our relationship was at the highest level, and we were genuinely happy. It was when things were new. I feel pained looking at it, but for some reason, I haven't been able to put it away just yet. Seeing Chandler holding it makes me wish I'd put it away.

Chandler places it down lightly and takes his beer from my grip. We sit down on the sofa. I know what is about to come, so I decide to let him speak first. I'm probably a coward for not fessing up without him prompting, but I don't know how to start, and I kind of want to know his thoughts first. Chandler says, "So…you're really pregnant?"

I nod and say, "Yes. I'm pregnant."

I tell him that the other night when he came over and we had Chinese food together was the night I found out. I say, "I should not have slept with you. I should have been up front and honest, but you were so irresistible. I've had a crush on you for so long."

Chandler says, "How far along are you?"

I hesitate, "I really can't be too sure. I'm going to go to the doctor soon, but I think about 6-7 weeks."

I can see him contemplating something, before he asks I say, "Josh is the dad, but I haven't told him. Listen, Chandler, I realize I've done wrong by not telling you sooner. Instead, I've allowed us to carry on as if everything was okay. I hope you can understand, I've just been so…so clouded, with mixed feelings and emotions. I've been enjoying my time with you so much. I guess I've been selfish. I'm sorry, Chandler, truly sorry."

Chandler takes my hand and says, "Listen, don't be sorry. It's clear you've got a lot on your mind. Let's just try to relax and not worry about this for now."

He seems so nonchalant and calm, I'm utterly amazed. He's looking at me sincerely and he says, "Just relax."

As I sit back on the couch next to him he continues to stroke my hand and says, "When are you going to tell Josh?"

"I haven't decided. I'm not sure how he'll react, and I'm scared as hell."

Chandler stays over long enough to finish his beer, and we chit chat a little bit more about my plans. I tell him where my thoughts are and explain how I'll raise the baby without Josh. I tell him as long as Josh wants to be involved, we'll work it out. I can't imagine Josh not wanting anything to do with the baby. Chandler says, "Kiera, for the record, I like where things are going between us. I know it's early, and there are some curves and bumps, but please know I'm not really all that scared by this baby situation. I never imagined myself saying that to anyone and I know whatever this is between us is new, but I care a lot about you and I want to be here for you. However you want to perceive what I'm saying is up to you. Please talk to Josh. You both have a lot to discuss. In the meantime, I'm here if you need anything."

Chandler hugs me, kisses me on the cheek, and says goodnight. I watch him into his apartment and gasp for breath as he so often leaves me with a lightheaded feeling.

I walk over to my sofa and see my phone blinking. Of course, I've missed seven text messages from Danielle. Honestly, I'm relieved tonight happened because I'm not sure I'd have ever worked up the nerve, and now at least it's early on, and not weeks or months into whatever this is with Chandler. All of the texts are her saying how sorry she is, that she hopes I'll forgive her, and yada-yada. I can't really be mad at her. Instead of letting her feel awful all night, I decide to send her a text and tell her no worries.

Kiera: *Honestly, it's fine. Everything is ok. I'm not mad. Ly*

She immediately beeps back…

Danielle: *Oh thank God! Let's talk tomorrow. BTW when u make your doc appt I want to come. I need to know the due date. No way in hell will I make you wear a bridesmaid dress pregnant! We'll plan wedding around you…*

Ahh! That's some good news. I lie and say…

Kiera: *Hadn't thought about that but u r the best to wait till baby is born! Night!*

Danielle: *Promise no hard feelings?*

Kiera: *I promise.. now not another word about it!*

Danielle: *U R the best!*

Kiera: *ik*

I put my phone down and flip through the channels on the TV. Nothing looks good. After watching one and a half old re-runs of Friends, I decide it's time to contact Josh. I send him a text.

Kiera: *We need to talk. Any time this week?*

I set the phone down again and go to wash my face and brush my teeth. When I come back, I can see my blue notification light blinking. I pick it up and see it's from Josh. Seeing his name makes my heart skip a beat.

Josh: *sure what's up?*

Kiera: *Can we meet at Magnolia's… maybe tomorrow morning or afternoon?*

I stare at my phone for ten minutes and finally he responds.

Josh: *sure around 10:45 a.m. good?*

Kiera: *perfect thanks*

He doesn't respond, and if I'm being honest with myself it bothers me. I'm glad tomorrow is a Saturday because after my night's events, it'll be nice to sleep in. I feel so nervous about seeing and telling him tomorrow. I can tell it's going to be one of those nights where my mind races a million miles an hour consumed by thoughts. I curl up on my couch and watch TV to fall asleep since I'm pretty sure it'll be a rough night for sleeping.

I wake up around 9:00 a.m. and get in the shower. As soon as I get out, I hear a knock at the door. I wrap my white towel around my body as best I can and run to look out the peephole. I see Chandler. I quickly open the door. He's already seen me nude, besides I'm covered up. I say, "Hi!"

He says, "May I come in?"

"Sure!"

He's holding a to-go bag and two to-go cups. He says, "I brought breakfast."

I smile. I can't believe he's here after everything, and with breakfast on top of that. I say, "Wow! What a lovely surprise."

I tell him I need to get dressed, but for him to go set it up by the couch. I really quickly throw on my favorite J. Brand jeans and a white tee. I twist my hair into the towel, and head back to the living room. "Wow, Chandler! Everything looks and smells delicious."

He pats his hand on the sofa for me to sit next to him. I walk over and sit down. He leans over and kisses my cheek. He says, "Good morning beautiful."

Ahhh! My heart literally skips a beat. He makes me feel so happy and tingly inside. "Good morning," I say back. "Wow, what a spread you have here!"

He says, "I know pregnant people can be picky, so I thought I'd bring variety. Surely you'll be able to pick something you like."

"I'm impressed, and actually, it all looks tasty to me today believe it or not!"

We eat and I enjoy every moment of us being together. I look at the clock and see its 10:15 a.m. Chandler notices me checking the clock and says, "I'm sorry. Do you need to be somewhere?"

I nod "yes" and say, "Actually, I'm going to meet Josh at 10:45 to tell him about the baby. I texted him after you left last night. I know it's the right thing to do. I just really don't want to."

"Oh, I see," Chandler says. "Well, I should probably get out so you can finish up. I'm glad you were able to eat so well. Maybe we can hang out later when you're back, if you feel up to company. If not, I'll understand."

I stand up and say, "I'm not sure why you're being so incredibly awesome to me, but I appreciate it, and breakfast was marvelous!"

He leans down and kisses my lips. He then turns to the door and I close it as he walks out. Again, I feel lightheaded and happy. *What an awesome man he is.* I can't seem to wipe the silly smile from my face while I finish getting ready to meet up with Josh. I'm so happy Chandler came by this morning. He really lifted my spirits, and God knows I needed that today. It seems silly, but after seeing him and knowing he says he's here for me if I need him, helps me feel as though I can face whatever comes my way today.

On the way to the bakery, I text Danielle to let her know I'm going to tell Josh about the baby. She wastes no time in texting me back. She says:

Danielle: *I'm proud of u. It might be hard, but it's the right thing to do.*

Kiera: *thx I'll let u know. Going to Magnolia's…*

Danielle: *want me to come and wait outside for u?*

Kiera: *no I'll txt if I need u.*

Danielle*: how bad was last night with Chandler? Did I screw it up?*

Kiera: *No. it was awkward but he brought over breakfast this a.m. so I think strangely enough its fine… or whatever?!? I'm confused but we'll see. I gotta get life straight first anyways:/*

As I walk into the bakery, I immediately am haunted by the last time we were in here. *Why in the hell would I choose this place?* I suppose it was familiar, and a place where we frequented, so it just felt natural to suggest it. I sit down and see Josh is ordering a coffee. He sees me and holds up his finger as if to say he'll be over in a second. The usual week shift staff must be off because I hardly recognize anyone. I choose a table by a window and sit down. As Josh gets closer to the table, my heart feels as though it may pound completely out of my chest. I take in a deep breath. He casually sits down and quietly whispers, "How are you?"

I semi shrug and feel as though I may crumble into a million pieces all at once. *What was I thinking? This is going to be so hard.* I answer him and say, "I'm okay. How about you?"

He says, "I'm doing pretty good. I guess I can't complain."

We small talk a few moments longer, and then the inevitable happens. He asks me what I need to talk to him about. My head feels so unbearably heavy, I place my elbows up on the table to hold it up.

I stare at him for a moment, and then I say, "Josh, I'm pregnant."

He doesn't say anything. Nothing. He is just staring at me blankly. I can't get a read at all. Finally, after a long silence I say, "Josh? Say something please."

He continues to stare at me. He pushes his hair back with his hands. This is something I've seen him do many times before when he's been frustrated. Again I say, "Please say something?!?"

He begins to speak, "Wow! Kiera. Just wow!"

He laughs and pauses for an uncomfortable amount of time still staring at me. I feel as though I may throw up. Finally, he breaks his silence and says, "Of all of the lowly stunts you could pull, this is the one you choose. You brought me here to tell me you're pregnant? Really? Really, Kier? That's really funny."

I'm in utter shock and disbelief. "Is this about Gina? Are you trying to salvage our relationship, because what a shitty ploy to pull!"

Holy crap! He thinks I'm making this up! You've got to be kidding me?!? I'm practically biting my tongue in half, and when it's to the point it might bleed I say, "You lowly piece of shit! You think I'm making this up?"

I feel enraged, and before I know it I reach across the table and slap him on the face as hard as I can. Boy does it make me feel so good!

I stand up and walk out noticing many spectators in the midst. I'm so angry I can feel the blood boiling in my face. I feel as though my face is as red as a beet. I'm sweating profusely. I sit down on the bench outside, and see Josh coming towards me. He stops and stands in front of me and says, "Kiera, you slapped me. What in the hell was that for? I'm so sick of your behavior. I don't know why you can't just let it go. Let go, Kiera. It's over between us. We've got nothing left. It's over, and there is nothing left to talk about."

I stand up and say, "That's where you're wrong, asshole! You go on believing what you want. I could care less about you and your sorry excuse for a life. This has nothing to do with you dating Gina! I'm pregnant, and I'm doing this with you, or without you! You can think whatever you like but I don't have time for your shit."

I pull myself up off of the bench and walk away. A part of me thought Josh would call for me to wait. I'd hope he'd handle the situation like an adult, say he was sorry, and that I'm right we do need to talk, but instead when I turned around, all I could see was him walking away in the opposite direction.

Chapter 11

By the time I get back to my apartment, I feel defeated and beaten down. I'm so tired I go inside and wash my face. I tried to hold back the tears all the way home, but as soon as I saw my building, I released them in a major way. I can't explain how I feel. Maybe a little offended that Josh would think I could be so desperate for him that I would lie or fake a pregnancy. Certainly, I am hurt and scared for my baby's future. I stop and think for a second considering how all this time I thought Josh knew me, but then the realization hit and I can see he doesn't know me at all.

I lay back on my couch and try to rest my eyes as I feel a headache coming on, probably from all of the tears. I must have fallen asleep, because I'm startled and roll off the sofa when I hear a knock at the door. Luckily, I catch myself and stand up quickly. I'm assuming its Chandler, and I'm surprised when I see it's actually Claire. I open the door and say, "Hi, Claire, please come in."

She takes one step in and says, "Kier, you look awful."

I am a bit taken back and I say, "Well, tell me what you really think."

I let out a small giggle. She kindly smiles back and says, "From one friend to another, I'm just being honest, my love. Look, I came over because I felt terrible about the way I acted at work over your flowers, and your moving on so to speak. It's just hard for all of us to be friends with you both now leading separate lives. Richard says Josh is fine, and he seems to be holding up well."

I put my hand up and say, "Please, just stop. Really. I don't want to hear any more about what you and Richard think about poor Josh. Truly it makes me nauseas."

Claire looks so confused, so I continue to speak. "Listen Claire, Josh made the decision not to be together anymore. I'm not at fault. I'm tired of constantly having to tell you he's the one who completely crumbled the proposal and ended things. I'm finally reaching a peaceful state about the way things are going, and I really wish you two could leave it alone. Josh has wasted no time moving on to Gina, as you can see on social media, and I'm trying to move on, too. The only problem is with the baby. My battle is going to be a bit more challenging than Josh's as he doesn't even believe there is a baby. Ha! He thinks I made it up."

Just as I suspected. Claire looks at me with her head cocked sideways with intentional meaning in her eyes and says, "I'm so sorry. Truly, I'm so sorry you're facing all of this. I honestly just thought you'd like to know how he's doing. Should Richard and I talk to him?"

All I can do is shake my head and sit down on the couch. I feel the all too familiar dizziness returning. Maybe I am a being a bit harsh to Claire, but I feel angry. Claire sits down beside me and places her hand on my knee. Feeling vulnerable to the familiarity of Claire I say, "So, he thinks I'm a liar. I told him this morning. We met at Magnolia's. He wasn't very supportive. Not supportive at all, actually. How could he think I'm making the pregnancy up as a ploy to get him back? I'm not that desperate. And how could he be so conceited? I don't even want him back. The way he acted towards me was so hurtful. This is our baby, our blood. I guess I'm on my own, and honestly I'm okay with that. Truly I am. Maybe, more than I should be. Besides it doesn't really matter, it doesn't change anything. This baby is real with him or without him.

Claire says, "Kier, I'm here for you."

I could detect coldness in her voice as she said it, and I was too familiar with how this sort of thing would play out. Everyone knows she's on Josh's side as Richard and Josh have been friends for a very long time. It was just the nice thing for her to say. I say, "Listen, I appreciate you coming by, but I really need some alone time and rest. If you don't mind maybe we can catch up Monday at work."

"Ok. I don't mind at all. What about the London trip?"

"I haven't thought about it. I'm not sure. I'm going to my first appointment soon. Maybe I'll know then."

Claire patted my back with motherly concern, and for a moment I almost thought she meant it until I could see the pity in her eyes. She says, "Kier, don't worry about London. Richard really wants to go along, and I'm not sure it would be the best decision for you to come feeling the way you do about Josh and with the pregnancy and all. I'm afraid things would just be awkward between you and Richard."

She stops speaking, I suppose because she doesn't like the eat shit look I'm giving her, and she says her goodbyes.

I close the door behind her without much of a word and immediately pick up the phone to text Danielle everything. I'm mystified by Claire's behavior, although I'm not sure why. It's very much her character to behave like this. I can't believe she said, "I'm not sure it would be the best decision for you to come feeling the way you do about Josh and with the pregnancy and all." *What in the hell is wrong with people?!? Was she for real?* I'm having a baby with a man who believes I'm making it up as a stratagem to get him back. *UNBELIEVABLE! I'm pissed.*

I pick up my phone for Danielle. I dial her number feeling too jittery to text; besides, there is too much to say. She doesn't answer. *UGH!* I psycho dial her number three more times, all going to voicemail. Finally, she texts me back.

Danielle: *paying at SB I'll be over in a few. Want a latte? I can get decaf…*

Kiera: *no thx. Just HURRY!*

Danielle: *911?*

Kiera: *No. a lot going on*

Danielle: *you told your Mom?*

I'm beginning to lose my patience with her. *Why's it that she can text, but can't talk?*

I don't answer the last text to try to provoke her to call me back. It works because my phone is ringing. I answer and hear, "What the hell do you need, psycho dialer?"

"Just get over here. It's too much to explain in text or phone."

"I'm on the way. You told your Mom, didn't you?"

"No. just hurry. It's nothing to do with my Mom."

"Oh shit! I forgot. Josh. It's Josh, right?"

"Are you close?"

"I'll be there in about 15 min."

"K. See ya soon. Bye."

We hang up the phone, and I go splash more water on my face as I feel flush again. I can't make it to the bathroom, my breakfast comes back up. At least I make it to the trashcan. I tie up the trash bag and put it out on the balcony. I'm very quiet because I'm almost positive Chandler is sitting out there with coffee. I need to have some time with Danielle before I see Chandler. I'm not sure how long I'll avoid him. I want to see him, but right now I just need some friend time.

I unlock my door in case Danielle comes and head back to my bathroom to freshen up. I re-apply some of my favorite moisturizer by Benefit, "Total Moisture." Then I put some Tory Burch "Cats Meow" lip & cheek tint on my cheeks and lips; however, as red as my face is from the recent spew of my guts, I don't need very much color. If Claire didn't hold back saying how awful I looked, I know for sure Danielle would make me cry. Freshening up is a good thing. I pick up my bottle of J'Adore by Dior and spray it all over in case I reek of vomit. My hair is in a ponytail, and luckily not in harm's way of the spewing coming out of my mouth. I've learned with the pregnancy, ponies are my best friend. I can't wait for this stage to pass.

I hear Danielle come in, and I am so excited to see her. I practically skip- hop to the door. She must notice I seem happy to see her because she says, "Wow! I wish I had that effect on everyone!"

I smile back and feel the tears forming. *I'm going to cry. I feel it coming.* It's that feeling you get with the familiarity a best friend can give. The comfort of knowing they won't judge you. The history you both have, all the times she's held you before, and you her. I know she understands, and it makes the tears flow even more. No words are spoken. No words are needed. She wraps her arms around me and lets me cry.

She says, "There, there, cry as long as you need. No need to explain right now. Just let it out."

After a few moments pass, my tears turn into bursting into laughter, and she's staring at me like I'm a crazy person. Then she starts laughing. She says, "What? What's so funny?"

I continue laughing. I'm sorry, you just made me laugh the way you said, "No need to explain right now." It was just funny.

"Of course, I want you to explain! Silly!"

"Thank you, Danielle. I needed a laugh."

She smiles at me and says, "I'm so happy to help. Now spill it! EVERYTHING!"

I begin by telling her about Josh. I say, "Josh thinks it's a ploy. He doesn't believe there is a baby. He's convinced I'm saying this to get him back. Ha! It's kind of arrogant don't you think?"

Danielle says, "Arrogant is one word. So he's just going to ignore the whole thing or what? What was the conclusion of the conversation?"

"I slapped the shit out of him. Told him he was a sorry excuse and left."

"Well, at least you played nicely. I think it's awesome you slapped him! The only thing that would have been better would have been a good kick in the nuts if you ask me. What a freaking jerk-off. You should call his mom."

"Nah, not worth my time. I'm hurt, but not for me. It's hard to explain really. I honestly, don't have any emotional attachment to Josh anymore, and I'm certainly not going to force this on him. I make plenty of money. Honestly, I don't need him. I'm not sure I ever needed him. I just can't believe he thinks I'm capable of making this up, or that he'd deny this is his child. It hurts me for the baby. I know I haven't given being a mom too much thought, and honestly for the most part I've tried to put it out of my mind, but today his behavior has allowed me to face some things. This is real. There is a real human being growing inside me. Josh's behavior is a bit unfortunate for the baby, but it doesn't really bother me. I'll be okay. The baby will be okay one way or another."

"Kier, you sound so sure of yourself, so grownup and mature. I mean it. I'm for real. You're sounding more mature than I've ever thought before. I believe in you Kier, and I've no doubt that you can handle this 100%. This baby is one lucky boy or girl! Plus you have me, and whether you want me to say it or not… I'm going to say it anyways… wait for it… You also have your mom. Time to tell her, friend. You should call while I'm here."

I'm not so sure this is a phone call conversation, but here goes. Holding my phone I become a bit more untroubled. Perhaps it'll be easier telling her over the phone. At least I won't have to see the disappointment on her face. I'm dialing the number and I realize I haven't yet told her Josh and I broke up. Ahh. This will be great… Two surprises in one day. This is too much. Hopefully, Gage isn't there.

Gage is Mom's "friend boy." They have been dating for about a year now. He's fine, I suppose, if you like his type. His type meaning flamboyantly rich. He loves to tell of his numerous present and future purchases. Sometimes I question if that's why my mom dates him. For the past few years, as well as past few men, this tends to be her thing, leaning on the gold digger side. Oh well, as long as she's happy, I try to be supportive of her and whomever she decides to be with. Gage often answers her phone for her, and honestly it annoys me to no end when I hear him say "hello." I take in a deep breath just in case he answers and prepare myself for the worst. I'm relieved to hear my Mom say, "Hello darling! I've been waiting for you to return my calls. I've been worried sick." *I HATE when she does this…*

I hesitate and Danielle taps me on my shoulder as sort of a push. I say, "Hi Mom."

I wait for her to respond again. *Oh how extremely grueling this is.* I feel like a child. When she doesn't respond to the, "Hi, Mom," I say, "I'm so sorry for not returning your calls. Work has been crazy, and I have hardly had anytime to myself for anything, let alone returning calls. I did text you. Please forgive me, Mom, I'm sorry."

We both start to talk at the same time, and I interrupt her to say, "Listen, Mom are you in a place where we can chat? I sort of need to talk to you about some important things."

"Do you need money?" *I love how that's always her initial response to everything.*

"No. I don't need any money, I make plenty of money to take care of myself. That's not what I need to talk to you about. Are you where you can talk a few minutes, though?"

She says, "Well sure. I'm free, just sitting here in the kitchen having a cup of mint tea. What cha got? What's going on?"

Here goes… and instead of giving any backstory I just blurt it out, "Mom, I'm pregnant."

Dead silence falls on the other end of the phone. "Mom? Hello? Did you hear me?"

I could hear the phone shuffling, so I know she is still there. Finally, she answers me and says, "Yes. Yes dear, I heard what you said. I'm sorry, I'm just a bit taken back. I'm assuming Josh knows, and you two are well, you know, going to make right by this."

She's waiting for a response from me, and I feel numb. I know exactly what she means by, "make right by this." How in the hell do I tell her we broke up, he doesn't believe I'm pregnant and thinks I'm lying about the baby to get him back? Oh this is so hard. Shit! I feel just like a child fessing up to trouble I got into. I feel like I'm six and broke my mother's vase, hid it, and now I'm having to tell her about it. I look at Danielle for support. She looks at me and says, "Say something, Kier. Tell her the truth."

I take in a deep breath, and my mom says, "Hello? Kier you there?"

"Yes, Mom, I'm here." And then I do what I do best. I blurt it out.

"Mom, listen, Josh and I broke up."

"WHAT? What do you mean broke up? You're having a baby. You can't just break up. Kier you did tell him right?"

"Mom, yes, of course I told him. We broke up a few weeks ago, and he's sort of already seeing someone else. He ended it with me. Look, he thinks I'm making up the pregnancy to get him back."

Mom surprises me and says, "What a BASTARD!"

I can't help but agree with her. I say, "I am relieved you know, and I agree with you. Josh is a total jerk. I don't want you to worry about me. I'm fine really. Danielle is here with me and I have friends. Everything is going to be okay really."

"Is Danielle with you now?"

"Yes. She's here with me now, and honestly I'm fine. Truly, Mom, I'm fine."

"Kier, if it's any consolation, you turned out fine and I raised you without your dad. Although, this isn't ideal, you'll make it work. I mean it. You're doing the right thing having this baby. That's it! I'm coming to visit. I won't be able to be there until Monday. There are lots of flights from

LAX to New York to choose from. I'm already on-line looking. I need an early one, but I'm coming nonetheless."

My heart falls, and as much as I love my Mom, I really don't need her to come just yet. I quickly say, "Mom, please not this week. I want to see you, I really do, but I need just a little time to figure everything out. How about you give me two weeks so I can arrange a couple days off?"

She hesitates and says, "I have a good mind to call Josh's Mom and give her a piece of my mind."

"NO! No way Mom, don't do that. Besides, I doubt she even knows. What do you say? A couple weeks? Send me the dates, and I'll work it out at work."

"Alright, honey, maybe you could call me a bit more often though and keep me up to date on what's going on."

"You got it! I love you, Mom."

Chapter 12

As soon as we are off the phone, I actually am relieved to have I told my mom. Danielle doesn't have to ask any questions because she was sitting so close to me on the sofa, she could hear the whole conversation. She says, "I think it went well."

I agree with her and say, "I need a nap. It's been a long day, but can you stay a while, I don't really want to be alone."

"Absolutely! Now, get some rest, and I'll be here when you wake up."

I must have slept at least an hour or more. When I wake up, I am refreshed and smell the aroma of delicious food. I walk out into my living area and am surprised to see Chandler sitting on the sofa with a bag of take-out, and Danielle was nowhere in sight.

“Hi, beautiful!” Chandler says.

“Hi!”

“I hope it’s okay I’m here. Danielle let me in, and I brought food for us. She said since I was here she’d leave and that you should wake soon. She was right, I have only been waiting for you to wake for about 10 minutes. I brought some food. Do you feel like a burger? If not a burger, what about a chicken sandwich?” He smiles and says, “I brought both!”

I can’t help smiling back. “Actually, I’m starved! Thank you for this. I’m getting spoiled by all of your deliveries, but honestly, I kind of like it.”

“Great, because honestly, I kind of like it, too!”

He flashes me the most sexy and enticing smile ever and pulls me down onto the sofa next to him. He begins nibbling on my ear. Chills and shivers are shooting down my spine. He cups my cheeks with his palms, and leads me towards his cleanly-shaven face for a long, slow kiss. I can barely breathe. I pull back to catch my breath. He stands up, pulls me up with him, and we kiss all the way to my bedroom. Slowly he undresses me and I undress him as we lay back on my mahogany sleigh bed. He’s passionately kissing me while he caresses my body gently with his hands. I feel so fragile in his arms with the way he looks at me and the way he handles my body so gently. I've never been touched like this, and I never want to forget the way he makes me feel, so special.

Whispering how beautiful I am in my ear, we give in to each other. Once again, all is forgotten. When it's over, we just lay there holding each other. My head is on his chest, and he's running his fingers through my hair. After a few more minutes pass, we get up and go eat our food in the living room.

Things seem so comfortable between us. Chandler, being twelve years older, certainly is a plus on a relationship level. He constantly talks about settling down and having a family which is way different than guys in their twenties. Aside from the advantage of his age difference, Chandler is a major turn on, and I hope whatever we're trying to achieve progresses quickly in the right direction. It's extremely sexy the way Chandler seems to know what he wants, and I love how much he shows that he wants me. Sure, I often think about his recent break up with what's-her- name… but, for the majority of the time he makes me feel as though we've been together a very long time. I think this is the reason why the conversation between Josh and me seemed less about me and more about the baby. I don't miss Josh at all. I may miss the idea of settling down, and the baby definitely makes things more complicated, but I am happy and that's all I need right now. One more benefit of unofficially dating Chandler is Danielle loves him, and she hasn't tried to set me up with anyone in a while. *Whew! Thank God!*

Chandler arranges our lunch on the coffee table. He asks me choose to what sandwich I want to eat first? I go for the chicken sandwich and hope it stays in my stomach, unlike my breakfast. For the most part with my pregnancy, the sickness has been in the morning and at night. The morning time sickness has been especially hard on workdays, having to ride the subway into work. I'm hoping it all passes soon.

I sit down next to him on the sofa, and he pours me a glass of Ginger Ale. I smile. He smiles, too. He kisses my cheek, then we eat our food. Chandler asks if everything is alright, and I say, "No, everything is not alright… Everything is actually perfect!"

We finish our lunch and curl up on the couch. Chandler turns on the Cooking Network. "30 Minute Meals" is on, but I'm not sure if either of us really care. I'm impressed with his choice of shows, as I too love to sleep to the Cooking channel. We fall asleep for a few hours.

I open my eyes and look at the clock. It's almost 6:30 p.m. I try to get up without waking Chandler, but he begins to stir. He asks if I'm hungry. I laugh and say, "I know as long as you're here, I won't go hungry."

He laughs, too. It's so funny how he constantly shows up at meal time with food–in-hand. He says, "What? I like to eat, and I like to feed you. You're eating for two you know?!?!"

I don't know if I'm imagining things, but I feel like he may be taking a bit of an interest in this baby thing. I've heard of a woman's biological clock ticking, but I suppose after 40 for a man, maybe they think family time too. Anyhow, hearing him say, "You're eating for two," gives me a tingling sensation that I kind of like. For the first time, I feel excited about being pregnant, and he makes the moment seem special by acknowledging the baby. I don't know. All I can say is it makes me feel happy.

I decide to take a shower, and as I'm undressing, I glance back in the mirror to see Chandler undressing. I cackle, and he does too. We enjoy ourselves a while in the hot, steamy shower. When we're finished, he says he's going to wrap up in the towel and run across the hall for some clothes.

On his way out the door he says, "We're going out for dinner, and then back to my place."

I say, "Are we?"

He kisses my lips ever so lightly and says, "I'll be back in ten minutes."

I'm hoping he isn't expecting me to be ready in ten minutes. I can do twenty or thirty, but not ten. I decide since I'm not sure where we're going, I'll wait to get dressed until I see what he's wearing. As soon as I hear the door open for him to go across the hall, I hear him talking, and I wonder who he's talking to in his towel. I step out of the bathroom and walk towards the entry way. The door is shut. I glance out my peep hole and about fall out when I see Chandler standing in his towel talking to Louie the doorman. I'm laughing so hard, my abs (or baby) start hurting. *How awkward! How awkward he's talking to Louie in a towel outside my door, and how awkward I'm pregnant and can feel my abs.*

About ten minutes later, I hear Chandler knock once. I say, "Come on in," and he does. He's wearing nice jeans and a collared shirt with a frontal, college-boy styled tuck. He looks very hot, yet casual. I decide jeans are a good choice. I tell him I need a couple minutes, then I'll be out. He shouts back towards my room that it's no problem, and for me to take my time. I grab my favorite Paige brand skinny jeans, and begin to put them on. *Oh shit! They don't fit…ugh!*

I pull, tug, and stretch as much as I can, but nothing. Finally, feeling defeated I take them off and opt for a boyfriend fit. My old faithful Rag & Bone Dre's will do the trick. I always have room in them. Sure enough, I pull them straight up no problem and I still have room to grow. *I really don't want maternity clothes.* I dress the jeans up by cuffing them and putting on a heel. I reach for my Jimmy Choo off-white, leather pumps and look in the mirror. They are perfect!

Now, I need a shirt. I choose a Teal "Kimono Basic Top" similar to the one I saw on peekingpines.com. I like the top because it is stylish, flowy, and loose fitting to hide my pregnant tummy. I feel great in it! I empty my bag into my Givenchy Antigona bag and spray some J'Ador on my neck. Finally, I apply mascara and Mac Angel lipstick. Feeling prettier than I had in a while, I head for the living room.

Chandler stands up to greet me and says, "You look beautiful!"

Goose bumps form on my arms as he pulls me into a deep embrace. He kisses me on my forehead. He makes me feel amazing. He asks me where he should put his towel, and I start to giggle uncontrollably. He looks at me questionably and says, "What? What are you laughing at, crazy girl?"

I'd almost forgotten about the towel incident with Louie until he handed me the towel. Laughing so hard to the point I can barely speak, I say, "So… Have you seen Louie lately?"

Now Chandler's laughing. He says, "Wait. You saw that?"

"Did I ever?!?"

Not knowing where we are going quite yet, we head out to get dinner. Of course we would have to pass Louie, and trying not to laugh is impossible. We both snicker, squeezing each other as hard as we can to try to keep our composure.

As soon as we get outside, we hail a cab. Chandler knows where we're going and says, " 420 West 13th St."

The cab driver says, "Am I taking you to Fig & Olive?"

"Yes," Chandler replies. Then he turns to me and says, "Ever been there?"

I'd not ever been. I know there are several locations, and I've heard good things about it. I'm excited because I always enjoy a new place. I say, "Nope, I've never been but sounds yummy! It's French right?"

He smiles and says, "Some of it, but they've got a great menu. I'm sure you'll love it!"

I'm just happy to be out of the house and I know I'll love whatever. I take Chandler's hand and say, "Thank you so much for getting me out of my apartment. This is just what I needed tonight."

He rubs my hand and kisses my cheek. "Kiera," he says. "There is no place else I'd rather be. The truth is I've wanted to be with you for a very long time, and I'm so pleased with the way things are turning out."

The cab stops and we get out. I really want to hear more.

We walk inside the restaurant, and immediately they seat us. It smells so good. The hostess sits us in a cozy corner by a window. There are beautiful plants surrounding the table, and the ambiance is superb. It's a shame I've never been in here. I ask Chandler to pick me out something yummy since I know he's such a "foodie." I tell him I need to step back to the ladies room.

Damn urine! I'm constantly peeing.

He says, "Sure, I'll pick you out something spectacular!"

I love the way he says that. Who says spectacular? He truly is amazing. I'm totally smitten.

I almost hit my head in the tiny bathroom stall when I hear my text alert go off. I pull up my jeans, glance at my phone, and I see it's Danielle. I'd forgotten about her leaving me this morning and now wonder why she hadn't checked in. I look at what she sent. Without her being able to see it was "read," I decide to just peek at the preview of the message, but I accidently click the text… too late…

Danielle: *Chandler still with u? I hope u were ok with me leaving… he wanted to stay and I thought it'd be fine…*

Great! Now that she's seen I've read it I have to respond.

Kiera: *No, its fine. He's taking amazing care of me. We're at Fig & Olive! Smells yummy!*

Danielle: *Fun! And I bet he's taking care of u!!! Call me tomorrow. Did u tell him about Josh this a.m.?*

Kiera: *No. I thought maybe u did.*

Danielle: *tell him*

Kiera: *maybe later having too much fun! Don't be such a spoiler!*

As I leave the bathroom, I almost fall over when I see who is in the restaurant. I look around to see if there is a route I can take back to my table without being seen. There really is no way I can find. *Holy shit! I feel faint and sick…* Chandler sees me looking around, and must be able to tell something isn't right. I'm just standing here like a frog on a log staring at Josh and Gina.

Chandler motions for me to come on. Suddenly I am not feeling so pretty anymore. Even though I am here with Chandler, the perfect man, I feel so rejected and replaced as I pass the table. Gina is facing me, and I know she sees me, because I can't help but look at her. She's not very pretty, and though some might think that should help, it doesn't. I'm not sure why I care they're here. I don't want Josh, so why do I care? I think it's just too soon to see my replacement and him together. Somehow, I manage to walk straight past their table keeping my gaze on Chandler. *Whew! I made it.* I sit down in, or somewhat stumble down, and once I feel settled, I notice I am now directly facing Josh. *Ugh! This sucks!*

It's clear to Chandler something is up, so I explain what's going on. I tell him about this morning's conversation with

Josh and he says, "Why in the hell would he not believe you? Who does he think he is?"

I say, "I'm not sure. All I know is there's a real baby inside me, and I'm going to raise it with all the love I can give. I can do it with him or without him. My mom did a pretty good job with me when my dad left, so I'm not too scared to try myself. Sure, it's not ideal, but I'm pretty sure I'll manage just fine. Anyways, I want to forget about him and focus on us tonight. By the way, my mom is planning a visit in a few weeks."

He says, "Oh, how nice! Umm, does she know about us?"

I laugh and say, "Not exactly. I actually didn't want to send her to the hospital with a heart attack. With the news of the break-up and pregnancy, I didn't think it would be a good time to share my dating my really hot neighbor. Oh, and by the way, he's 12 years older than me too!"

We both laugh. He says he understands, but he hopes to meet her. Then he asks, "Will she mind I'm a little older?"

I say, "No, I'm sure she won't when she meets you."

Chandler apologizes but says he has to take a work call. I tell him no worries and go ahead. When he comes back to the table we finish up our dessert.

Somehow I've made it through dinner facing Josh, and as we stand up, Chandler puts my bag on my shoulder for me and takes me by the arm. I can see Josh staring at me. I'm happy he sees me with Chandler. He knows who he is, and that we're neighbors. Josh also knows I've always thought Chandler is hot. I'm finding great pleasure in this moment. I hear my text alert and look down.

Josh: *very classy Kier… very classy*

What in the hell?

I put the phone back down in my bag and ignore whatever the implications of his text are. Chandler is also in a text conversation with the client who called during dinner. He has to spend a great deal of time on his phone with clients, but he's always respectful about it. I don't mind at all. I wonder why Josh is calling me "classy"? *What a jerk!* I try to forget about it.

When we get back to our building, we walk into the lobby. Chandler says, "Remember, you're coming over to my place tonight?"

"I remember! What are we going to be doing at your apartment?" I say with a silly smile.

He grabs me and pulls me in close to him caressing my neck with his hand. The elevator dings and the door opens to our floor. We don't even make it inside his apartment before our hands are all over each other.

He has me up against his door, running his hands all over every inch that matters on my body. His hands are undoing my bra. He whispers in my ear, "I want you now. I want you right now, right here."

Finally, his door is unlocked and he leads me to his bed. Each time I'm with him, I feel like it's a new, enchanting experience. Our bedroom life is more than sex. It's like nothing I've ever experienced before. I know it's early to say, but I feel like its love, passion, romance, and everything happy all in one. I feel I love him.

Chapter 13

My text goes off, and I get up out of bed to get dressed. Chandler says, "You're not leaving right?"

"No, I'll stay till you make me leave."

"Then you may be here forever." He smiles.

Gosh he's so sexy! So incredibly sexy!

I pick up my phone, and see another text from Josh.

Josh: *First, u say u r preggo, and then u follow me on my date… very classy lady u r. It's over Kier! Over!*

OMG! Are you kidding me? He thinks we followed them there? You've got to be kidding.

Chandler looks at me. My face can be so telling I'm sure I look shocked. He says, "Everything okay?"

"Not exactly! Josh has been texting me since the restaurant. He seems to think we followed them there. Unbelievable!"

Chandler is appalled. He says, "I'll say he's a freaking piece of work. Give me your phone. I'm turning it off. No more distractions for you tonight. I want you to be able to relax."

So he did. He took my phone, then he took his phone, and turned them both off. He placed them on the counter in his kitchen.

His apartment was much nicer than mine, but I suppose he makes quite a bit more as a partner at the law firm. I glance around. I count three bedrooms and definitely more living space than I have. I tell him how nice his apartment is. He says, "You've been in before."

I say, "I know, but I never really paid attention. It's a good bit bigger than I thought."

"Yeah, I like to have extra room."

Looking around, I notice there are no pictures of Juliette. He must have already stashed them away, which is quite reassuring to me. I should probably do the same with my pictures of Josh. I make a mental note to tackle that as soon as I get home. I don't really want to put my clothes back on, but I certainly can't stay wrapped in his blanket, so I tell him I am running across the hall to grab something comfortable. He insists I wear some sweats of his, and so I do.

As I put the ash gray oversized hoodie on, I notice the softness of it and I imagine it to be one of his favorites. It's probably been washed a million times. There is nothing better than a broken in sweatshirt. When I come out of his bedroom, he whistles and says, "Now that's just plain hot."

We curl up next to each other on his couch. I doze off without realizing, and when I wake up I can see the sun peering through the white drapes next to his bed. I don't even remember walking back to his bed. He rolls over and kisses me so gentle. He says, "Are you wondering how you got to the bed?"

"I must have sleep walked…"

"You were resting so well I didn't want to bother you. I scooped you up and put you to bed. I must say, I loved having you here, lying next to you all night was a dream come true."

"You're too kind to me. I must say…waking up here next to you feels so natural and comforting. You're such a wonderful man, and I'm falling very fast for you."

"I feel the same about you. I know there are some curves with the baby and all, but Kier, I'm not scared of that at all. I just want to be with you and see where this goes. Now enough serious talk. You stay here. I'm going to cook us up some breakfast."

"You're amazing! I'm going to get up and put my jeans on at least. Also, I need to check my phone."

This is turning out to be one of the best Sundays I've ever had. Chandler has made Grecian Florentine omelets, Belgian waffles topped with whipped cream and strawberries, and freshly squeezed orange juice. When we sit down to eat, I turn my cell phone on and immediately my text alert buzzes six times. I look at the screen and see Danielle had sent a text around 10:45p.m., but the rest were from Josh. I'm still disgusted by Josh, so I decide I'll look later.

Chandler and I finish our breakfast. After we are done, I help him clean up the kitchen. While we pre-wash the dishes, we keep splashing each other with water and laughing. He's so much fun. I'm having the time of my life with him. I'm enjoying every minute of being with him.

There is a loud startling knock at the door. I look at Chandler and say, "Are you expecting anyone?"

"Not that I'm aware of."

Chandler goes over to the door and opens it. I think I might pass out. I can't manage to say anything, but Chandler says, "Hey man is there something I can help you with?"

Ignoring Chandler completely, Josh says, "I figured you were here when I knocked at your place and there was no answer. I want to talk…I just want to talk. I know I'm a jerk and have acted like a complete bastard, but I'm here now and would like to know if you'll at least talk to me. When you didn't answer my texts, I went a little nuts. I needed to see you."

I'm still stunned, and not sure why he's here. Chandler looks at me and says, "Are you okay?"

I manage to nod my head in an unsure manner. I let out a whisper and say, "I probably should talk to him at my place…so, we'll just go over now."

"Are you sure?" Chandler asks concerned.

"Yes. Really. It's fine."

I grab my Givenchy bag and walk towards the door searching to find my keys. The way Josh is staring at me makes me feel like a child who was just caught by her dad making out with a boyfriend. We walk across the hall, and after I unlock the door, I motion for Josh to come inside my apartment. I look back and notice Chandler is standing in his doorway watching the whole time. Once Josh is inside, I lean my head out the door and tell Chandler it'll just be a minute. He seems unsure as he cocks his head sideways and whispers, "I'm right here if you need me."

I shake my head and fake a courageous smile. I mutter, "Thank you."

I close the door behind me and turn around to see Josh sitting on my sofa holding my favorite picture of the two of us. The picture in the Tiffany frame. I now wish rather than making a mental note of putting them away when I thought of it earlier, I would have just gone and done it. I notice his eyes have softened since the last few encounters we've had. Feeling a bit annoyed by his intrusion, I walk over and say, "What do you want to talk about? Or better yet, what are you doing here?"

Josh stares out for a few moments too long. I say, "Josh? Are you going to say something?" Finally, he says, "Kier, I'm a jerk. What can I say." He stares at the picture a few minutes longer and says, "Look how happy we were here…"

Without saying a word, I sit down in the chair next to the sofa. He looks at me and halfway smiles. He says, "How far along are you?"

I am so pissed at him, yet the softness in his face and kindness in his voice somehow makes me feel sorry for him. I want to scream at him or hit him over the head with a frying pan, but for some reason the anger turns to mush. I say, "I can't be sure until my appointment, but I think probably around 8, maybe 9 weeks." After I answer him, a little fire begins to overwhelm me and I am outraged. I say, "What the hell, Josh? According to you, I'm making this up to try to get you back. Why are you here now, and why in the hell are you asking about a hypothetical baby that you don't even believe exists? You hurt me. I can't believe you thought I'd make up a pregnancy to try to get you back. Crap, I don't even want you back. I'm doing just fine without you."

Instead of addressing me on the pregnancy Josh says, "I see you're doing just fine playing house with Chandler the hot neighbor. Really Kiera? He's not right for you. He isn't even your type. Plus he's too old. He's old enough to be your dad."

The outrage is back and I say, "Stop it right now! Why do you care anyways? It's over with us."

Josh looks at me and says, "No Kier, you're wrong. It's not over...You're carrying my baby, remember."

I say, "Since when do you believe I'm carrying your baby anyways, and why all of the sudden the change of heart? You put me through a living hell yesterday morning. I don't really appreciate your waltzing in like this and interrupting my day. You should have called."

He says, "Kier, I know you're mad. I understand. I was just shocked. This consumed my thoughts all day yesterday. Last night, when I saw you with Chandler, I realized I do love you. It pained me to see you so happy with someone else. I've really screwed up, Kier. I know I don't deserve you to listen to me, and I know you'll question my being here a million times over, but I screwed up."

Feeling unwanted pity towards him I ask, "What about Gina?"

"Last night at the restaurant, we split up. I met her there to talk about you and the baby. I told her I wanted to tell her first, but all day long I couldn't get you off of my mind…and the baby sealed the deal. I want us to be together. I want us to be a family. I don't expect you to accept me right now, and I certainly don't expect an answer. I had to tell you my feelings. I'm sorry about the texts, me challenging your class, and acting like a jerk last night. I suck! Truly, I hate the way I've acted."

I stand up and peer out the window. This conversation is making me nauseous. My head is spinning. I think about all of the times I wanted nothing more than to marry Josh, and how excited I was in Central Park when he almost purposed. I'm so pissed at him. I look at him and tell him I need him to leave. I say, "Get out. I need you to go right now. I can't even formulate words to tell you how I feel right now. Please just go."

He stands up and says, "I'm so sorry, Kier. I'm sorry. I hope you take time to think. All I know is I want to be with you now. I want us to be a family. I want to be this child's father if you'll have me. I want to be your husband. I don't care about what we've done over the past few weeks, or who we're seeing. I want you, and I'll wait as long as I have to. Please think about everything I've said."

I say, "Just go."

He shuts the door behind him and fall out on the sofa as tears fill my eyes. I feel awful and so confused. I'm embarrassed that I feel sorry for him. How on earth do I have pity for him after all he's put me through? It is beyond me, but I do.

I hear a noise in the hall. I think it must be Chandler's door closing. There is a knock on my door. I look out the peep hole and see its Chandler. I open the door to let him in. As soon as he's inside, he embraces me with a hug. My head is full of everything that just happened between Josh and me. I can't contain my tears at all. With the raging hormones in my body and the drama in my life, that seems to be the case all too often right now. Chandler holds me. I cry on him for what seems like forever. Finally, when I feel like the tears are letting up, I sit up and say, "I'm so sorry you have to see me like this."

Chandler says, "Are you serious? Kier, I don't know what just happened here, but I have good mind to go after him for upsetting you like this. Please just rest. You don't have to talk about it anymore right now."

I'm so relieved to hear him say that because right now I don't know what I'd say to him, and oddly enough, I really just want to be alone. He must be able to tell because he says, "Would you like a little time alone?"

I nod my head and say, "I think it might be a good idea. I'll probably take a nap and rest."

Chandler kisses my forehead and says, "Okay then. I'm going back next door, and I'll be there all day. If you need anything, or you're ready to see me, you come knock. If not today, then I'll be by after work tomorrow. Rest well."

I say, "Thank you. I promise I'll let you know." I'm not sure why I notice, but he closes the door much gentler than Josh did when he was leaving.

Am I crazy or what? Danielle will kill me when she realizes I even gave Josh the time of day. I can't believe what's happened, or that he came here to Chandler's like that. My text alert goes off. It's Danielle. *Shit!*

Danielle: *U didn't respond to my text last night… Still with Chan? Stay the night?*

I respond back.

Kiera: *Sorry. No. Yes.*

Danielle: *Shit, Kier… no details? That's pretty cut and dry???*

Kiera: *Sorry I'm sleepy*

Danielle: *Can I come by later?*

I really don't want her to, but if I say no she'll come anyways. She knows that too, she's not really asking. I might as well say yes.

Kiera: *sure.*

Immediately she shoots back…

Danielle*: Awesome! I hope its okay, Sam is with me. Be there in about 2 hours. Wedding stuff.*

Oh shit! Sam? Two hours… ugh… damn it Danielle.

Keira: *alright.*

I haven't seen much of Sam since the engagement, but I suppose I haven't really made any effort. Danielle has certainly attempted to include me in every detail, but I've managed to skip most of it except for her compulsive and obnoxious wedding pinning of her wedding board on *Pinterest.* I hop in the shower although all I really want to do is hop in the bed. My stomach is in knots as I can't seem to get Josh's visit out of my head. I don't want to see Chandler tonight, and since Danielle is stopping by, I see it as a good excuse to text him I won't be able to see him tonight, but maybe tomorrow. Immediately I feel better, which I sort of find strange. I suppose it's one less thing to worry about today. I actually am excited tomorrow is Monday, and I get to be at work. Work is such a great life distraction sometimes, and I need all of the life distractions I can get right now.

Danielle and Sam arrive about an hour earlier than I expect, but I guess that's not too unusual for Danielle. Thank God I fixed myself up because it's hard enough to try to convince Danielle everything is fine when I look good, I can't imagine what she'd have thought of my appearance an hour ago. I ran the curling iron over my hair, put on my favorite lip color, added light mascara, and I even put a cute flowing plum dress from Revolve on. I was certain to fool even Danielle. She will think everything is just dandy.

Upon entering my apartment Danielle immediately, says, "Oh no… what's wrong Kier?"
Shit! I really can't get things past her no matter what. I say, "What do you mean? I'm fine. Just really tired." Then, quickly trying to change the subject, I say, "I'm going to make my appointment tomorrow. I guess I've waited long enough. Besides, I'm starting to feel a little excited about being a Mommy!" *There I think it worked…and I even like using the word Mommy!*

Danielle seems to have forgotten she thought there was a problem. She says, "Yeah!! Kier, I'm so happy you're getting out of your funk, and I can't wait to go to doctor with you. I think Chandler might be just what you needed! You've really livened up. I knew once you two figured things out, you'd hit it off quick! That's really awesome, Kier! I just knew it had to be awesome, and I'm happy the baby news doesn't seem to scare him, right?"

I shake my head and say, "No, not at all actually."

See this is terrific! Just awesome really! Now, the reason we came by if you don't mind ummm. I just need to ummm…to… I just need to talk to you about the wedding…"

Chapter 14

I must look confused because she says, "Oh no, it's nothing bad, it's just we need to talk."

"Okay, well what is it?"

Danielle places her hand on my shoulder and says, "I know I promised to wait to get married so you wouldn't be pregnant and all, but we can't wait Kier! We honestly can't wait to be married. Like, we want to do it sooner!"

I look over at Sam and he's wearing the goofiest expression on his face. In that moment, I want to turn Danielle's head towards him and show her, just so she can see how weird he seems at times. I realize after a few quiet moments that Danielle is waiting for me to say something, so I say, "Oh wow! That's great! So when were you thinking?"

She says, "You're really going to love this because we're doing it the weekend after next. Just some place local. I'm taking next week off to plan everything, but the best part is you won't be showing much, and it's just perfect! It's exactly what needs to happen. Aren't you so happy?"

Holy shit! I'm not sure what I should say… Danielle seems so excited. I finally say, "Wow! Umm, are you rushing because of me or what?"

"No, silly, although you're a factor. Honestly, we just can't wait, that's all."

I take in a deep breath. It's not that I dislike Sam, it's just weird that my best friend will be married to someone I don't know…Like being *married to a stranger*.

With everything else going on in my brain right now, I decide to put this in the back of my head and give Danielle what she wants. I say, "Danielle…Sam, I think this is wonderful news! I'll help you as much as I can, but unfortunately I can't take too much time off right now."

Danielle says, "Oh, Kier!!! Thank you so much! No worries about help. I got it all under control. I hope you can arrange your mom's visit to be in time for the wedding though. She's like my second mom, and I really want her there."

I say, "I'm sure I can. She can't wait to come."

Once I look at the calendar, I realize the weekend Danielle is planning to get married is the weekend I am supposed to be in London. I resolve that I won't be going after all, Besides I'm pretty sure Claire doesn't want me to go now as she is concerned about it being awkward for Richard. It'll be for the best, really. I pick up my phone and send a quick text letting Claire know I won't be able to make London, and I decided it's for the best. I tell her I'll see her tomorrow. Then, I tune back into Danielle's and Sam's excitement. They really do each seem equally excited.

I say, "I'm so excited, truly for you both!"
Danielle says, "Oh thank you, Kier. I'm so happy."

"I know you are. I can tell. Honestly Danielle, you both seem so perfect for each other."

Funny thing is, over the course of the last couple of minutes seeing them interact all giddy, I felt bad for all of the judgmental moments I've had towards Sam. They truly do seem happy, and I can't really argue with happiness.

We hug, and I start crying. *Damn pregnancy hormones again!* After a minute, Danielle pulls my head up and says, "Okay time to spill. Something is wrong, and don't feed me hormone garbage. I know you, and I've known you forever. I know something is off. Tell me what it is."

Sam says, "Girls, how about I run out and get us an early dinner?"

I don't answer, but Danielle says, "Perfect, honey! Surprise us."

Sam leaves, and we're all alone. Danielle grabs herself a beer and sits on the kitchen barstool. She says, "Alright, dear, let's talk. What's gotcha all in the dumps?"

I'm not sure where to start, but I sit down on the sofa and say, "I spent the night with Chandler."

"Well, I figured that," Danielle say. "He's so awesome for you, Kier. I'm seriously stoked about the two of you, and the fact he's cool with the baby is beyond me, but let's go with it!"

She's literally going to kill me when she finds out I gave Josh the time of day and talked to him.

I say, "Last night, Josh and Gina were at the same restaurant as Chandler and I. We saw each other, but didn't speak. Josh sent me several texts through the night, but I didn't get them because Chandler turned our phones off. This morning after breakfast at Chandler's, there was a knock at the door. It was none other than Josh."

Danielle says, "You're shitting me! He really had the nerve

to come to Chandler's place? How did he know you were there?"

"I guess he must have knocked on my door and when I didn't answer, he knocked on Chandler's. Besides after he saw us together last night, it didn't take a genius to figure it out."

"Well, we both know he's no genius, so it must have been obvious between you two!"
She really hates him with a passion!!

I ignore her "no genius" statement and continue, but before I can get much out, she says, "Oh no! Wait a minute, Kier. Did you talk to him?"

I nod my head "yes" and wait for her to respond. There really is no use in my continuing until she gets out her peace of mind. Danielle continues on, "Holy cow, Kier, why'd you talk to him? Please tell me you didn't talk to him in your apartment, or like invite him in?"

I think she's done so I say, "Danielle, I'm pregnant with his baby. I have to talk to him and if you must know, yes, I invited him in and yes, I listened to what he had to say."

Sitting here on the sofa I feel like I'm in an interrogation. I wait for her next round of questions. I can tell she's pissed, but I'm kind of pissed too. She has no right to be pissed at me for talking to the father of my child. For some weird reason, I feel extremely defensive of Josh right now regardless of if he deserves it or not.

Danielle stands up and walks into the kitchen to get some water. I can't believe she's being quiet. I don't know why, but finally I break the awkward silence. "Look, he feels bad for the way he's acted, and he's sorry. The crazy thing is, I believe him. He seemed sincere. He says he's sorry about the way he acted about the news of the baby, and that he doesn't deserve to be forgiven. Honestly, it isn't right for me to not give him an opportunity. This baby is his no matter how he acts."

Danielle laughs at me. I'm quite taken aback at her behavior and confused why she's laughing at me. She says, "You accepted that ass's apology didn't you? Kier, what a freaking sucker! What about his Gina girl? Is she okay with the baby?"

I quietly say, "They broke up."

Danielle laughs more and says, "I see. How convenient is that? I know you well enough to know exactly where the conversation went from there. You actually don't even need to share more. Let me see if I can elaborate for you…"

Dramatically, Danielle begins mocking Josh, "Kier, I've been such a jerk. I'm so sorry. I know I don't deserve to be forgiven, and I hate the way I've acted. I hope you'll please find a way to forgive me. I want to be a family and I hate the way I treated you. Am I on the right track here?"

I hate her! I hate that she's pretty much 100% on point as to how the conversation went, and I'm not sure what to say. All I know is best friends know too much about each other, and I'm feeling rather irritated with mine.

Sam comes in the door with food. For the first time ever, I'm ecstatic to see him. We eat our takeout fairly quietly. I can tell Sam realizes he may be in the way. He finally says, "I'm thinking about heading over to John's to watch Sunday night football. Do you mind?"

Danielle answers, "No, not at all. I'll see you later at home."

Hearing her refer to her apartment as "home," as in mutual home, seems rather strange to me, but I guess they are getting married. I might as well get used to these phrases. I guess I just didn't realize they settled on her place being "home."

When Sam closes the door, Danielle wastes no time in picking up from our conversation. "Was I right? Is that about how the conversation went?"

"As a matter of fact, it did sort of sound a bit like you mentioned, but so what? What if he truly just didn't know how to react?"

Danielle looks at me and says, "Oh my God! You're not thinking of getting back together are you? What about Chandler? He's laid everything down, even willing to stick by you pregnant and all. Kier, please tell me you're not thinking about working this out with Josh after everything he put you through?"

I say, "Look Danielle, the truth is I don't know what I'm doing from one minute to the next. He caught me off guard, that's all. Damn it, we were together for two years. That's a long time. For him to waltz in here and dump all of this onto me is hard. This is just not a good time for that. I'm so consumed and fragile with the pregnancy. I just don't know what I want. Well, except for my best friend to not be so judgmental and maybe give me a break. I mean it's not like I haven't let you make some crazy choices."

Immediately after I said that, I regretted it. Danielle immediately reacts like a bomb exploding into a million pieces… she slams her drink glass down hard on my counter and stomps over to the living area where I'm sitting. She says, "What do you mean by that? What in the hell is that supposed to mean, Kier? Whatever are you referring to? Are you talking about Sam? It's him isn't it? I thought you were over that by now. Who cares that we got engaged so quickly? When you know, you know. If anyone should be able to accept that, it should be you. Oh, wait a minute, you dated Josh for two years and he chicken-shitted out of the proposal. You must not know the feeling."

I can't believe this is happening. We sound like a bunch of two year olds. I say, "We're getting carried away. This just needs to stop. I shouldn't have said that to you. I just wish that you could be a bit more understanding."

"You're right, we do sound stupid, but sometimes it's nice to know how you really feel. I hate that you can't just leave the whole "Sam and I barely know each other thing" alone though. I need your approval."

I say, "Danielle, I feel the same way. Just let me be, and figure this out on my own. I just need to be able to talk to you and you not freak out about Josh. Look, I honestly don't know what I'm going to do. Josh hurt me badly. I don't know if I can recover from that kind of hurt. I really like how I feel with Chandler, but I just need time. I need to go to the doctor to see what they say, but I feel like Josh has a right to go, too. Please try to understand. I'm not saying we're getting back together. I'm just saying I can't shut him out of this baby's life."

Danielle's face seems to soften. She says, "I'm sorry. I hate that we had to get so angry with one another, but I guess these things need to happen. You're so important to me Kier. That's why I want your approval on my life."

"I feel the same way. I guess we can agree to disagree. Look, it's not that I don't like Sam. I'm sure I'll even grow to love him, it's just hard for me to understand why the hurry. I'm going to try to jump over that hurdle because I want you to be happy."

Danielle, says, "Kier, that means a lot, and I promise to try not to be too bossy on how I think you should run your life, especially regarding Josh seeing the baby. I have to be honest, though, I know he's wrong for you on every other level, aside from the baby. You need to trust me on this. So, as far as him being more than a father, I'm not sure I can contain my thoughts or advice. You have to respect that."

I decide not to argue with her because this conversation has got to end, and I need rest. I would really like her to leave. I say, "I'm glad we've reached some sort of resolve."

She says, "Me too!"

She must be over the visit as much as I am, because she grabs her LV bag, comes in for a hug, and says, "I'll call you tomorrow. Or better yet, call me after you schedule the doctor appointment. Okay?"

I say, "Sure! That sounds perfect. I'll call you then."

She closes the door, and I lock up after her. I change into my pajamas and settle down on the couch. I must have dozed off because I'm startled when I hear my text alert sound. At first I thought it was my morning alarm, but then saw my phone blinking. I looked up to see HGTV's House Hunter's International was on, and was surprised how early it still was. I look down at my phone to see it's a text from Chandler.

Chandler: *Hi! Hope you're doing ok*

My heart literally skips a beat for a second. I smile at how girlish he makes me feel.

Kiera: *Hi! I'm fine thank u*

Just as I send it through, I realize another text had come through. I had sent my response intended for Chandler to Josh.

I quickly glance up at the text Josh sent to see what it said.

Josh: *Hey.*

All he said was hey? He must be wondering why I answered with such a strange, "I'm fine thank you." But why do I care? I click back to Chandler's text and respond and say:

Kiera: *I'm doing ok*

Josh*: I'm glad you're alright. I was worried when I left. I hope I didn't come on too strong?!?*

Chandler: *I wish you were here…*

This is quite strange to try to carry on a conversation with both Chandler and Josh at the same time.

Josh: *Have you had time to think? Trying not to pressure but all I'm doing is thinking…*

Chandler: *or I was there*

Oh my God! This is a lot…Honestly, I must admit to myself, I kind of like this attention as odd as it is. Before I can respond to either of them, they each send another text.

Josh: *I feel like ass about everything.*

Chandler: *food?*

Holy cow! This is crazy. I respond to Chandler, who's actually made me laugh with the food comment. That man is always thinking food.

Kiera: *I'm not really hungry.*

Chandler: *Neither am I*

Josh: *Kier, say something*

I don't really know what to say to either of them. I text Chandler back first.

Kiera: *You're silly. I've gotta go to bed so I can wake up for work. We'll talk tomorrow*

Chandler: *got it. Nite <3*

Then I think about what to say to Josh.

Kiera: *sorry. I stepped away. I'm not ready to talk about it.*

Josh: *I understand.*

I feel sorry for him. Why I do not know, but I feel drawn to him like a lost puppy I need to save. I text him back.

Kiera: *calling dr tomorrow for appt. would u like to go?*

Josh: *YES*

Wow that was quick!

Danielle: *I'll let u know when.*

Josh: *I can't wait! Night Kier*

I analyze each of their texts for a few minutes. I note how much I enjoy Chandler's playful spirit, even the way he purposefully misspells goodnight. I suppose he does it to appear younger, which is cute.

I think about how Josh wouldn't dare do something like that. He's too caught up in being proper. I can't even believe Josh is in my thoughts as much as I hate him for everything he's put me through. Why did I even make room for him after everything?

Chapter 15

My alarm goes off and I quickly get out of bed. Like most mornings lately, I am extremely drowsy and nauseated. I reach for the saltine crackers I've been keeping next to my bed to help me with morning sickness, and I quickly eat two. I stretch over near my lamp and grab my water bottle I filled right before I went to bed. I read in my "Week-by-week" pregnancy app last week dehydration can cause morning sickness to be worse, so I've tried to stay hydrated. Once I get up, the nausea wave seems to have passed, but I feel hungry. I decide to grab a bagel from Absolute Bagel on the way in to the office. It's been a while since I've wanted breakfast, so I'm a bit excited.

Holy cow! Like most mornings the line is out the door, except it seems much worse today. I glance at my watch and then look back at the line. Judging from my place in line, I think it shouldn't take more than 30 min. I decide it'll be worth being late to work just to sink my teeth into one of their bagels. I calm myself by staring at my phone like everyone else in line.

The line is filled with mostly rude college kids sprinkled with occasional white collars. It's been a quiet morning so far, no texts from anyone. I feel a little tinge of resentment towards Josh, but I'm not sure why. Finally, I order my bagel.

"I'll have a plain bagel with walnut-raisin cream cheese."

The clerk looks annoyed by my order, and with her thick New York accent she sarcastically says, "Is that all?"

I wonder why she seems so miserable. I smile ridiculously big at her and tell her to have a nice day. Maybe that will brighten her mood. Nope, I'm almost positive she rolls her eyes back at me.

Once I get to the office, I turn my computer on and barely acknowledge Claire. I mean I see her and she sees me, but I don't really feel like dealing with her today. I'm still pissed about her coming over Saturday and making me feel awful about London. Actually, I'm quite happy Danielle and Sam have decided to get married the weekend I was supposed to be in London. After Claire left my apartment the other night, I was so pissed that I wanted to go to London just to spite her. Trust me, it's for the best Danielle is getting married and I can't go because I'd love nothing more than to get under hers, and Richard's skin about Josh. I smile at the thought of offending them, but then I feel relieved I already texted Claire I'm not going. I can't wait for her to ask me why. Better yet, I can't wait to hear what she has to say about Danielle getting married. I know it's childish, but sometimes I love to annoy her with Danielle's and my friendship, especially on days when she's pissed me off.

My calendar alert goes off reminding me to make an appointment with the doctor for the baby. I'm so mad at Claire, I decide not to use her gynecologist. Yet again, I know I sound a bit immature, but I don't really care. Instead, I text Danielle and get the number to her doctor. Of course, she texts me back immediately and asks what day I am looking at, but I don't answer her just yet.

I manage to wait until closer to 9:30 a.m. to call. Once I dial the number, the phone rings three times and then a kind voice answers and says, "Thank you for calling Dr. Saint's office. How may I help you?"

I say, "Hi. Good morning! I need to make an appointment."

"Are you a new patient?"

"Yes."

"Okay, what do you need to be seen for?"

I walk back near the break area and vending machine lounge in case anyone is eavesdropping. Still keeping my voice merely above a whisper just in case, I say, "I'm pregnant."

The nice voice says, "Has it been confirmed?"

"What do you mean? I took a test?"

"Okay. How far along are you, or do you think you are?"

"Probably about 8-9 weeks maybe more."

"Perfect. I'll need to get your insurance info, and then we can see what we have."

I give her all of my information, and we schedule an appointment for this Friday at 9:30 a.m. which is a lot sooner than what I'd expected. Surprisingly enough, I'm actually relieved by it being so soon. I hang up the phone and glance over to see Claire heading towards me. I sort of feel a knot forming in my stomach. *What is she going to say to me now?!?*

She nonchalantly says, “What’s up, Kier?”

I cautiously say, “Umm…not much.”

She puts some papers in the shredder and proceeds to her desk. She seems to be acting unusually odd, even for her, and I’m not quite sure what her deal is. I decide not to pay her too much attention and head back over to my cubical to get to work on a stack of files that I’ve been putting off for way too long. Feeling pretty accomplished, I’m able to get through the pile before lunch. Since the phones hardly ever ring on Mondays, it’s the day of the week Claire and I usually break away a few times. Today, I’m not feeling much like escaping with her, and she must not be interested either since she hasn’t asked. I glance up and see Claire putting her coat on. She grabs her bag, and heads out the door.

This seems awkward; but honestly, I don’t feel like putting up with her anyway. My cell alert chimes. It’s Chandler!

Chandler: *I’m downstairs. I brought lunch.*

I feel butterflies flittering around in my belly as I read his text. He’s truly a dream.

Kiera: *On my way down*

As I'm walking down, I send a quick text to Josh to clue him in on the doctor appointment in case he wants to go.

Kiera*: I got a doctor appointment for this Friday at 9:30 a.m. we can meet at my place if u like and head over together or I can send you the address…*

Immediately he texts me back.

Josh*: Oh crap! I can go any day but Friday. It won't work for me. I've a big meeting I can't miss. Sorry Kier*

Honestly, I'm super shocked after the way he seemed so interested yesterday, but I guess I have to be understanding of his job. He just texted back to ask me to move the appointment, but I really need to keep this appointment. I can't keep putting it off. I guess I'll go without him. I could always ask Danielle, but then I'll have to hear how she knew Josh would be un-invested, and I really don't need her shit right now either. I'll probably just go alone. Really, I'm fine with that anyways.

Once I get downstairs, I see Claire hasn't actually left the building and is just checking the mailboxes. I pretend not to notice and instead give Chandler a hug and thank him for bringing lunch. I say, "Let's walk outside and see if we can find a place to eat and chat."

He winks at me and follows me out. It's so cliché to say, but he makes me feel like a teenager again. I haven't felt this way in a long time. For a minute I feel guilty, and I'm not really sure why, but it quickly fades. We enjoy many laughs and little kisses over lunch. I feel like I'm on a lover's high. As we wrap things up Chandler says, "Have you made a doctor's appoint yet?"

I laugh and say, "Actually yes. I just made it this morning."

He says, "That's awesome! I've been wondering if you were ever going to get around to it. Question… Can I pick you up for dinner around 6:45 p.m. tonight?"

I smile. Without hesitation I say, "Answer… Sounds perfect! I'll see you then!"

Back at my cubical, I can barely keep my head up. I think I could literally lay my head down and fall to sleep. Must be pregnancy hormones acting crazy again. I feel tired, sick, and like I have to pee constantly. Really it's quite exhausting. It's no wonder I'm so tired all the time.

The rest of the day seems to drag on as slow as ever. The clock reads 4:49 when I decide to make a run for it and leave. I see Claire and avoid her as best I can, but she sees me leaving and says, "Heading out?"

I say. "Yeah, I need to get home. I'm not feeling too well."

I keep it short as I hate making small talk with people who I am usually close with, but who have completely pissed me off. I don't want to talk with her because she is acting so awkward.

Finally when I get home, I take a short nap before time for Chandler to pick me up. I set my kitchen timer to make sure I don't over sleep. I wake up and see the timer has a few minutes left before the alarm will go off. I go ahead and get up as I actually despise the sound my timer makes when it goes off.

Back in my bedroom, I pull out my old trusty Rag & Bone Dre's boyfriend jeans, except today I don't really feel like dressing them up, and opt for a white t-shirt look. I notice that the jeans are starting to feel a bit more snug, and decide they don't seem quite as comfy either. Oh well, I may be borrowing clothes from Danielle sooner than I thought. I suppose maybe I'll eventually break and buy a few maternity pieces, but…ugh…the thought of that is atrocious to me. It seems way too soon for that nonsense. Maybe I'll just buy some bigger clothes to avoid wearing maternity clothes all together.

I hear a knock at the door, and walk out glancing at the kitchen clock with a smile thinking about how early Chandler is. I look out the peep hole. I'm surprised to see it isn't Chandler!

My stomach flips and flops as I slowly open the door. I say, "Hi ,Josh. Umm come in."

He walks in and sits down on the couch. I'm curious if he'll notice I put the pictures of us away. I'm almost certain he'll notice the one missing from the coffee table for sure.

I walk over and sit down in the chair next him. Remembering that Chandler should be here in a few minutes, I start to sweat and get nervous. Josh is sort of just sitting here not saying anything, and that is making me even more uneasy. Finally, I break the silence and say, "I'm sorry I didn't text you back earlier about rescheduling the doctor, but I think I really should keep the appointment."

"Oh, it's no big deal really," he says. "I think you should keep it, too. I just can't miss my meeting so maybe you can fill me in on everything."

On some level, it makes me very sad he can't go with me. Part of me thinks this baby appointment is more important than anything else on either of our plates, and he should cancel whatever meeting he has scheduled. The way he's talking to me isn't very remorseful either, and I'm beginning to question his motives and sudden interest in me again. He seems so different from yesterday. It's almost like I'm talking to someone else, a different personality perhaps. I realize this is a lot for him to take in, but what about me? I'm the one who deals with this pregnancy on a daily basis. My mood is really slipping, and I just want him to leave. I say, "Josh why are you here?"

He says, "Excuse me?"

"I didn't stutter. You just show up, sit here, and you're not even saying much. What's going on?"

"I don't know, I just wanted to see you."

I'm having a hard time reading him, but I'm really not buying his story at all. He says, "Kier, I'm here because I thought I'd take you to dinner. I mean…I just assumed we'd pick up where we left off. We're having a baby. We need to make things right. Don't you think?"

And like always my mouth gets four steps ahead of my brain. I quickly say, "Yes, I do think we need to make it work. Of course I do, we're having a baby. I'm sorry I asked, I just wasn't sure what was going on. I guess I need to get used to the way things used to be again."

Immediately everything feels so wrong, and I'm not sure why I said this.

Shit, I feel guilty for saying that. Why did I say that when I'm not so sure inside. After all, Chandler will be here any minute, and things could really get awkward. I start to speak and say, "Josh, I'm expecting someone any minute, and tonight is probably not the best night for dinner."

Josh takes on a solemn face and says, "It's Chandler isn't it? He's coming to take you out? Am I right?"

I take in a deep breath. I say, "Yes, but it's just when everything went wrong with us, Chandler showed up. Things took off quick, I didn't mean for it to happen. I felt vulnerable and rejected, and he sort of swept me off my feet. I know it sounds incredibly cheesy… I know it does… but it's true. He makes me feel special and happy. I don't know if these are feelings that I should chase or not. Especially now. I mean you show up again, and we're having a baby together. It makes me think I have to give us a try for the baby. I feel so guilty. I feel guilty for getting on so quickly with Chandler, and I feel guilty for even considering a second go with you after all you've put me through. Does any of this make sense?"

Josh stands up and says, "Look, I'm leaving. When you decide what it is you want, let me know. Maybe I'll still be around, maybe not. I've told you my thoughts, and I don't have time for games. Fill me in on the doctor appointment Friday. I'm not going to be jerked around by you, Kier. I have done all I can do for you. This is on you."

I feel like he's being a jerk, and I'm not really sure what to say. Part of me feels sorry for him. As he turns to close the door, a part of me crumbles and I desperately say, "Josh wait! Come back."

He turns towards me. "Stop, Kier, just stop. There is nothing to say."

Feeling overwhelmed by his familiarity and longing for the way I used to feel in his arms, I grab hold of him and pull him in close to me. He doesn't resist, and we fall into a long passionate kiss. I tell him to please stay. He says, "Kier, are you sure? Do you really mean it?"

Although, I'm not one hundred percent certain why I'm falling into this, I say, "Without a doubt. I'm going to text Chandler not to come."

I pick up my phone to see Chandler has already texted me.

Chandler: *I can't wait to see you…*

Shit! He makes this so hard. I have to let him know. I can't be selfish. I'm having a baby with Josh, and we've got to give this a go for the baby. It's the right thing to do. I do my best and try to put my selfish desires away. It's so hard, but I text Chandler right away. I feel terribly sad as I hit send. *I hope I know what I'm doing. Josh can't let me down again. He just can't. I really think he's ready to be a family. He seems so serious about what he wants.*

Kiera: *I'm so sorry. I can't make it. I'll explain later. Please don't come by to check on me. I'm fine. Night.*

I grab Josh a beer and wait for a text back from Chandler. Five, maybe ten minutes have passed and nothing. *I hope he got the text and he doesn't just show up here.* Josh and I hardly speak for a few minutes. Finally I say, "What would you like to do?"

Josh says, "Awe, I don't know…let's just order in pizza."

"Pizza?"

He says, "Yeah, I don't really feel like going out. It was a long day."

We eat our pizza, and not too long after Josh passes out on my sofa. As I lay in my bed, I ponder what I've done and why I'm letting Josh back into my life so easily. Honestly, he seems half interested. I mean this is a guy who chickened out of a proposal and immediately started seeing someone else. I wrestle with my thoughts over-and-over in my brain all night long. What on earth am I doing? Why did I cancel with Chandler for this? This doesn't really feel right. Then I remember this has nothing to do with me or Josh; it's for the baby. I'm trying to help us make things right and be a family for this baby. I tell myself everything will be okay and I fall to sleep.

When my alarm goes off I stand up, have my crackers, go to the bathroom, and walk into the kitchen. When I see Josh, I physically feel sick. The funny thing is I don't think it's the pregnancy. He stretches and lifts his head and says, "Hiya! I fell asleep so quick after pizza. I better get home and get dressed for work."

He gathers up his wallet and comes in for the most awkward hug I've ever experienced. Things just seem so odd. I hope we can get past the weirdness and be a family for the baby. I tell him to call me tonight, and maybe we can have dinner. He seems mildly irritable and leaves barely saying good bye. What the hell is up with him?

Chapter 16

The last few days have been difficult. Today is Friday, and I've managed to not see Chandler all week. I miss him so much. Every night I try to suppress any thought of him. It gets harder every day I don't see him. I haven't explained anything to him, but I assume he's figured it out. It really has been hard not seeing him. I know I owe him an explanation, but I just can't face him right now. At times I think I may love him, but I try to stop myself for sake of my baby's future. I desperately want to give him, or her, a so called "normal family" with a mommy and a daddy. My mom called and she is coming in tomorrow, and I truthfully couldn't be more excited about her visit.

I can't believe I'm only an hour away from my doctor's appointment. I'm a little nervous and excited too. I wish so much Josh could have figured out a way to meet me there, even if only for a few minutes. I'm holding on to hope he'll come through at the last minute and surprise me. We've seen each other every day this week, and although we're trying to pick up the pieces of where we were before the proposal incident, we don't seem to be managing too well. There has been no intimacy between us, and no desire, at least on my part, quite yet. I feel like we both just need time to heal. Hopefully everything will work itself out and be alright. It has to work for the baby. We've got to be a family. We'll figure it out. We have no choice.

As I'm about to open my door to leave and lock up, I quickly glance across the hall to make sure Chandler isn't leaving too. The hallway looks clear. I open my door and immediately he opens his. He says, "Hi."

My heart melts into a million pieces just at the sound of his voice. *I really do love this man. I know I do, but I shouldn't, and I can't. I have to do what's right for the baby.*

I say, "Hi. How are you? You startled me?"

I'm not quite sure what I'm expecting him to say back, but I wait for his words. He says, "What's going on? I haven't heard from you since Monday. I wanted to give you some space and all, but I don't know what is adequately enough time."

I feel like such a bitch. I have to tell him about Josh. I know I need to tell him, but I really don't want to. All I want at this very moment is to fall into his arms and let him tell me everything is going to be okay. I know I can't. Instead, I avoid his comments and say, "Can we talk later? I'm heading to my first doctor's appointment, and I can't be late."

I notice a slight smile and he says, "Oh, that's wonderful! It's today? I suppose Josh is going with you right?"

Shit! He knows. Of course he knows. I'm sure he sees Josh coming and going. I want to crawl under something and hide but there isn't anything to crawl under.

Embarrassed that Josh isn't going I say, "No. I'm going alone."

"What? Alone? You can't go to your first prenatal appointment alone."

I say, "I don't really have a choice. Josh has a very important meeting he says he can't cancel."

"Can you stay right here for two seconds? I'll be really quick."

Feeling really sad and embarrassed by the fact he knows Josh isn't going, I manage to get past it pretty quickly. I'm not too sure why he wants me to stand in the hallway and wait, but I do anyway. A few seconds pass and Chandler pops back out of the door wearing his jacket and tennis shoes. He says, "I'm going with you."

I'm shocked. I don't really know what to say, but at the same time I feel happy that I don't have to go alone. I say, "What? Are you serious? You want to go?" *Something is very wrong here.*

He smiles and says, "I'm not letting you go alone. So the answer to the question is yes."

As we walk down the stairs I see Louie lurking. I know he's been watching me this week. He probably thinks I'm a slut with the back-and-forth between Josh and Chandler. Oh well, I guess I can't worry about him.

Chandler says, "I need to make a few calls and move some appointments. I'll be on my phone a few minutes, but don't mind me. I'll follow you."

I don't say anything back as he's already on the phone with someone whom I presume is his assistant.

Really? This is crazy. He's going with me to a prenatal appointment and it's not even his baby. Who does this kind of thing for someone? I think I know the answer, and it makes me feel even more feelings towards him that I shouldn't have. I'm just so impressed. He's made about five different phone calls rearranging his schedule to be with me so I didn't have to be alone. This is truly crazy. Chandler's flexibility makes me question Josh's priorities even more, and I realize I'm not really a top priority for him. I never have been. Why would I expect it to change now? What am I really expecting with Josh? Do I really think he'll change for me or the baby? Josh really is about Josh, and I hate that about him. I wish I didn't feel so old fashioned about us being a family and doing the right thing.

Inside the waiting room, after I fill out my paperwork, I look at Chandler and say, "Thank you for being here. It means more than you'll ever know."

He says, "Kier, honestly there is no place I'd rather be than with you. Even if it's here."

My heart flutters so fast I don't think I can keep up with my breath. I feel like I have to yawn in order to get enough air in. Why do things have to be like this? Why's it so difficult? If it weren't for this baby, I know exactly who I'd be with. I love him. I love Chandler. There, I said it and I know it's true. Being here with him, it's getting harder to fight my feelings for him. I didn't want to see him until I was sure I was through these feelings. I think he knows I love him. After spending this week with Josh, it's hard to see we'll ever heal. I feel like being with Josh is the right thing to do, but I don't think I love him. I guess the truth is I know I don't love him.

A nurse wearing blue scrubs swings open the door and calls my name. Chandler naturally places his arm around my waist as we walk back to follow her. She shows us to the room after she gets my weight and urine test. I was a little embarrassed I couldn't remember my last period, but she said it happens all the time. The exam room had the stirrups set up and a sonogram machine. Attached to the sonogram machine is a probe covered by a latex glove. Next to it stood a bottle of KY Jelly. I can only imagine where the probe will be going.

The room is very clinical, but at least there is a chair for Chandler. The nurse hands me a gown and says, "Get undressed from the waist down."

Chandler looks at me and says, "Want me to step out?"

I say, "I'm pretty sure you've seen it all, so you're fine."

We both make jokes about the probe and laugh hysterically. I feel very calm having him here.

For a moment, I forget about Josh. The doctor does a little jingle kind of knock, one that I felt like needed an extra few knocks to finish it off, but I guess that was my OCD. He walks in and says, "So we're having a baby, huh?"

He shakes Chandler's hand and says, "Congratulations, Dad." I almost speak up to say oh we're just friends, but I don't. Besides, Chandler is already accepting the congratulations and saying, "Thank you. Thank you very much." He smiles so goofy at me as he says, "We're very excited!" I can't help but giggle. The doctor says, "We're going to need to do a vaginal ultrasound to see how far along we are by measurements." I assumed that was what the probe was for, and I was right. Yuck!

I'm sure Chandler is dying over what he's about to witness. I tell him he doesn't have to watch, and he says, "Are you kidding me? I can't wait to see this baby."

This calms my nerves and my heart so much. Yet again, I'm glad he's here. He's standing up by my head as the doctor inserts the probe. It's cold at first, but once I see the picture on the screen in front of me, I don't notice or care anymore. It's a baby. It's my baby. Chandler is standing up by the bed next to me, and as I glance at his face, I see he too is as engrossed with what is on the screen. It's a heartbeat, a person, a miracle. "Truly amazing," he says.

I agree and say, "Wow! What a tiny miracle."

We can see all the parts of the baby. For me it is such an awakening moment making this pregnancy feel extremely real. I wasn't expecting to see an actual baby. It seems so big. The doctor is clicking and measuring. He says, "Well, according to my measurements this may or may not surprise you too much, but it looks like you're quite a ways along."

I'm not sure what to say, so I wait and he says, "You're measuring right around 22-23 weeks. Does that sound about right?" *Holy shit!*

I remain in a shocked state a few seconds longer. Finally, I say, "Wow! No, that's not what I was thinking at all! I really didn't think I was that far."

"Well these things don't really lie," he says. "They can be off by a week or two, one way or the other, but according to everything I see, I'd say it's dead on. You definitely look to be around the 22-23 week mark."

"So that's just over half way?"

He replies, "Yes, it is. Would you like to know the sex of the baby?"

I hadn't really thought about that, but before I can think it through I say, "Yes!"

"Okay, here is what we should do," he says. "Let's call the sonogram tech in to go ahead and do the anomaly check that we normally would do at 20 weeks if you have time? Basically, it just checks to make sure the baby is developing normally, and also we want to make sure the placenta is lying in the uterus."

I say, "Okay that sounds fine. I have plenty of time."

He walks out, closes the door, and Chandler says, "Wow, Kier, the baby is really there. This is so incredible. I am so happy I got to be here for this. I can't believe how big it is already. You're barely showing. I've never seen anything so amazing in my life."

Why does he always have to say the right things all the time? My heart melts yet again by his kindness and meaningful words. Chandler is so different from most other guys. He doesn't say things just to woo you. Everything about him is meaningful, on purpose, and sincere. He's perfect for me. He makes me happy, but as much as all of that sounds like a fairytale, we just can't be together. I really have to give Josh a chance for our little family.

The technician walks in and seems a bit cold, or maybe shy. I can't get a good read on her. She begins the sonogram. Aside from the nervous small talk, not much is said. She just keeps huffing and puffing. Finally, after a long silence I say, "So do you know what it is yet?"

She says with a bit more personality, "Yes. It's a boy!"

I am ecstatic, I'm having a boy!!

Chandler audibly lets out a, "Yes!"

The technician rudely says, "Daddies always say that when it's a boy."

Not quite sure what she means by that comment. The longer she stays in here, the more I dislike her. Terrible bedside manners, and she's so rude.

I hear my phone ringing. Chandler has it in his pocket as he took it from me when I had to lie down. He takes it out of his pocket and says, "It's your mom."

I smile at him and say, "It's a boy. A baby boy. I'm so happy."

Chandler hands me my phone and I send a quick text to my Mom.

Kiera: *At my dr appt I'll call in a few…*

Mom: *Okay. Hurry up and call!*

The technician says from the scan everything looks great, and she shakes our hands saying congratulations. *What a strange girl she was. She seemed so cold at first and through the scan, and now she's congratulating us?!?*

Once she closes the door I notice Chandler can't seem to stop beaming. You'd think he was the one having a baby boy. I get dressed and we leave the office. I'm hungry so we decide to grab a bite to eat. After finishing up my croissant, I decide I don't really feel like going in to work, and I really need to get my place clean for my mom's arrival. I call in and take the rest of the day off. I email Claire a brief message letting her know I'll sort of be working from home if she needs me. Chandler says, "Well, if you're taking the day off, I am too."

I'm relieved he's with me but also worried because being around him is making this too hard. I hate knowing this can't go on, and I'm not sure what I'm doing with him, but I just can't face it yet.

Back at my place I tell Chandler to have a seat on the sofa while I call my Mom. She answers right away. She says, "Oh my goodness! I thought you'd never call me back!"

I say, "Mom, it's only been a little over an hour."

I motion to Chandler that I'm going to step back to my bedroom. He doesn't seem to mind since he's emailing something to someone. I say, "Well, I'm actually 5 months along."

Mom says, "What? You're kidding me? How did you not know that, Kiera?"

"I don't know. I guess I just don't know my body that well."

"Well, does everything look good?"

"Yes! Actually everything looks great! And I know the sex. Would you like to know what your grandchild is going to be?"
"Of course I do, silly! What are we having?"

"It's a boy!"

"Awe, honey, that's wonderful news!" I can hear tears of joy in her response.

I'm so glad she's taking this so well and is so excited. Thank God, this must have all soaked in. I think she's actually eager to become a grandma. We finish up our conversation and she tells me her travel plans. She says she'll cab it over from the airport to my place and should be in around 11:30 a.m. I briefly mention Danielle is getting married and hopes she'll stay through next weekend. She's surprised by Danielle getting married since she didn't know there was even anyone serious. I tell her I'll explain when she's here. She doesn't seem to care too much. I can tell she's excited about the baby finally. She tells me she plans to stay at least two weeks. For once in my life it actually sounds nice to have her for that long.

I can hear Chandler is on a call, so I decide to go ahead and call Danielle. She also answers quickly. I'm sure she too was anticipating my call. She says, "Well?? How did everything go?"

"Great! Everything went awesome! He looks healthy and perfect!"

"He? It's a boy?"
Oh shit… "Yes, sorry it's a boy. I didn't mean to let that slip like that."

"Oh, Kier! This is so exciting! But wait, how could they already tell it's a boy?"
"Well, because I'm already between 22 and 23 weeks."

"You're kidding? Oh my! How did you not know that?"
"You sound like my mom."

"Sorry, but seriously?"

"Anyway, I need to get off and get my place ready. Mom's coming tomorrow."

Danielle starts to hang up and says, "Oh wait. I need you to come by and try on the dress for the wedding. When can you come?"

I say, "How about Sunday, and I'll bring mom?"
"Perfect! See ya both then!"

We hang up and I go back to the living room where Chandler is on his phone. I sit down beside him, but not too close and he starts laughing. I say, "What? What's so funny?"

He turns his phone around to show me the display. And he's on a website of boy baby names. He's laughing at the name Barnaby. He says, "Who names their kid Barnaby?"

We spend the next hour or so looking up crazy boy names to see who can find the best one. I love he is taking such an interest and doing this! We're having so much fun! I love being around him. Finally, after all the goofing around, I tell him that actually I've always wanted to name my son Noah. Not just because of the biblical content and what a strong man and symbol he was to the world, but also because I just like the name. He says, "I love it! Noah sounds like the perfect name for him. Noah it is!"

We spend the rest of the afternoon together, and I'm having the most fun I've had all week long. Time always seems to slip away so fast with Chandler. I look at the clock. It's a quarter until six, and for the first time I question why Josh hasn't bothered checking in. He must still be in meetings. I think Chandler knows what I'm thinking by the way he looks at me. He says, "Kier, we've pretty much avoided this all day, but what's going on between you and Josh? I've seen him over a lot. Not that I'm snooping or anything, but I know he's been in and out a lot this week. What's up?"

At first thought, I just want to lie to him. I want to tell him it's nothing, that Josh and I are just going to try to be friends for the baby, but I know I can't do that. I have to face this head on and tell him the truth. I clear the huge lump in my throat and say, "Chandler, I appreciate all you've done for me, and I appreciate how you're always here for me. I hate this, I really do. This is so hard for me, but I have to tell you something. Josh and I have been spending a lot of time together trying to figure things out. We feel like we have to try to work things out between us. You know like try to make things right with our relationship for this baby. Don't you agree?"

Chandler looks unfazed. He takes a hold of my hands and I am breathless as he says, "Kier, I know you love me, and I want you to know something…I love you too."

I feel as though I could collapse into his arms and give into the strong desire I have for him, but I manage to fight it. Instead, I say, "Chandler, it's not about me. There is a much bigger picture. Josh and I created this baby. We're going to do the right thing and be a family. I can't be selfish. I need you to understand."

Chandler stands up and walks towards the door. I know that what I just said to him needs to resonate a bit, but I really don't like the way it came out. I truly don't want him to leave. I know it's the right thing for him to go, but I don't like it. As he turns to the door, he looks back and says, "No pressure. I'll be here for you. I believe you'll get through this and figure it out. It may take a bit, but you'll get it, and I'll be here when you do." And he turns and walks away for what feels like a forever goodbye.

Chapter 17

I'm heaving between tears as I sit in my living room alone. A text comes through from Josh, and it says he'll not be coming by tonight. I guess it's just as good. I'm not sure how I could explain to a person whose baby I'm carrying that I'm in love with my neighbor anyways. I just need time, but the more time I have sitting here alone thinking, the more I realize how messed up things really are.

In the texts from Josh, not once has he asked me about the doctor appointment. I feel hurt and angry, like he doesn't really even care. Come to think of it, when I was making my phone calls to tell people about the baby, it never even occurred to me to reach out to Josh. He doesn't even know I'm half way through my term, or that we're having a boy. This should all make me run like hell as fast as I can in the other direction, but I just can't. I know I can't. I know I have to make things work out with him. We have to be a family. I know it doesn't feel right, but it's the right thing to do. Things will work themselves out. Besides I loved him once, and I know I can love him again. I'm sure when we have the baby it'll help me love him, too. Love can start circumstantial to an extent, and I know it'll progress to unconditional if I'm patient.

Slipping into my favorite pajamas, I notice how snug they've become. I glance at my profile in my full body mirror, and admire my beautiful baby bump for the first time. I smile at the thought of my son, rub my belly, and look down to speak to him. I say, "Everything is going to be all right. I know it may not seem that way right now, but we'll figure everything out. Just hold tight, my little man. I already love you so much, and I hope to be a great Mommy for you."

My bed looks inviting as I walk over feeling exhausted from my day. As I crawl into the layers of white heavy-threaded sheets, quilted down duvet, and pillows to try to forget my worries, I feel a little spirited thinking about tomorrow. I'm excited about my mom's visit. Tomorrow can't get here fast enough. I lay down and my thoughts race. I can't get Chandler off my mind. No matter how hard I try, I can't stop thinking about what he said just before he left. "No pressure. I'll be here for you. I believe in you, and I know you'll get through this and figure it all out. It may take a bit, but you'll get it, and I'll be here when you do." I'm not exactly sure what he meant, but I assume he thinks I'll come back for him. If only it were that easy….

Truly, if it were that easy I'd be across the hallway right now curled up next to him; or better yet, I'd have never let him leave. But it's not that easy, and my life must go on. That means it must go on without Chandler. I know we can't be together. I just wish he'd take the hint and understand. His response to me was too much to bear. How can he be so confident I'll decide I need him? Quite frankly, it makes me sad for him. It's hard to not think about him sitting around thinking I'll come back to him. I wish he'd just throw in the towel and let things be. Josh and I are having a baby and we need to be able to make a run at our relationship. If Chandler really cares, he'd make it easy and walk away.

I'm startled to hear my alarm clock buzzing loudly as I jump up out of my bed. I head straight to the bathroom to wash my face. As I'm washing, I realize for the first time in weeks something has changed, and I don't feel nauseated. *Ahh! Maybe that part has passed.* I slip into a pair of skinny legged jeans Danielle brought over since my jeans are all too snug. Danielle gave me all of her "fat girl" clothes, basically just the clothes she wears on her period.

Danielle has always had separate clothes for her period. She swears she gains an extra five to ten pounds during that time of the month. I have a little room still in them, but they seem to work wonderfully. I'm nowhere near ready, nor will I ever be, for maternity pants or clothes. I literally hate the thought of them. I just refuse to do it. I've found that as long as I wear loose fitting pants or leggings and flowy tops, I hopefully, will be able to evade the whole maternity clothes situation. Luckily, I just received one of the new flowy tunics I ordered from Anthropologie last week, and it looks perfect with Danielle's "fat girl" jeans. If I have to spend the next 3 to 4 months in tunics and leggings, I'll do it just to avoid my personal perception of the "moo moo" look of maternity clothing.

I pace around cleaning odds and ends around my apartment with anticipation of my mother's arrival. I simply cannot wait for her knock at the door. After glancing at the clock a million times, I decide I'll wait for her downstairs. Once I'm in the lobby, I feel Louie's eyes directly on me. I look at him and say, "Hi Louie! How are you?"

I swear he's staring straight down at my belly. *Am I showing that much? I guess it's enough that strangers can now see I'm expecting?* I choose to ignore his glare, and Louie and I continue on with pleasantries. As I reach down in my purse to pull out my Nars Peachy Pink Lip Gloss, I hear the most soothing noise in the distance saying, "Kiera, Kiera honey!"

"Mom!" I manage to screech as loudly and as enthusiastically as I could. We run to each other and embrace as if we haven't seen each other in a year. It feels so good to be hugging her. Feeling relived by her mere presence, I cry and cry as she hugs me tightly. She says, "There, there honey, everything's okay. It's all going to be alright."

There standing in my building lobby, just as simple as a finger snap, I finally feel like everything really is going to be okay. It's amazing how a Mom can make you feel that way. *I hope I can make little man instantly feel like everything is going to be okay if he ever faces adversity in this life.*

Louie asks to help my Mom with her bags, and we both say thank you as we head up to my apartment. I notice Louie again staring daggers at my belly. I shoot him a look. He doesn't seem to be bothered by it, but the cat is out of the bag when my Mom says, "Oh honey, look at that sweet little bump on your belly! You look simply beautiful pregnant! Your skin is glowing and radiant."

I'm not sure why, but I feel ashamed as Louie says, "You're expecting?"

I nod my head. Louie, hesitates and says, "Wow! Well, congratulations Kiera! What spectacular news!"

I show Louie out and say, "Thank you, Louie. I appreciate your help."

Just as I'm about to close up the door, I hear Chandler's door opening. For some reason, I just can't bear the thought of not seeing him. I wait until he's out locking up before I say "Hi." Immediately, he turns to me and says, "Hi. Back at you."

His smile melts my heart the same as it always has, and I feel light and dizzy. My mom comes to the door and says, "Well, hello there. Kier who's this?"

I introduce my mom and Chandler and notice right away how impressed my mom is with him. She asks him to come in for a drink. I feel like I'm going to die as he accepts.

Once we're in my apartment, Chandler makes himself right at home as he always has on my sofa and keeps shooting flirty smiles over at me. I can feel my cheeks flush every time he looks at me. He's enjoying this way too much. There is a knock at the door, and I'm certain it's Josh. I walk over to let him in trying to conjure up an explanation as to why Chandler is here. Nothing comes to mind. I open the door and I'm surprised to see it's only Danielle. Part of me is a bit disappointed I guess. In some sick way, I was secretly hoping for Josh. It does him good to see Chandler is so interested in me. I guess it's the whole idea of "you don't know what you have until someone else wants it." Danielle seems extremely happy to see both mom and Chandler here. She says, "Chandler, I hope you're coming to the wedding next weekend with Kier?"

How dare she!

Mom looks confused. She says, "Are you friends with Danielle as well?"

Chandler stands up to leave and says, "Yes, we're all very good friends."

He flashes his beautiful white pearly smile at my mom, takes her hand, and lightly kisses it. *Why does he have to be such a charmer?!?* He says, "It was so very lovely meeting you, and wonderful to see where Kier gets her poise and beauty. I hope you ladies have a terrific evening. Stay out of trouble."

As he leaves and my door closes, I try to mask myself as I catch my breath. It must be obvious to my Mom how enticed I become around Chandler, because she says, "Kier, you've got some explaining to do. I've never seen you look at a man the way you were just looking at him, and I must say, I can't blame you for it. The magnetic force between the two of you was beyond obvious. It was electrifying. Electrifying, wouldn't you agree Danielle?"

Danielle looks over at me, and in her best Grease impersonation she begins singing, "I got chills, they're multiplying, and I'm losing control. 'Cause the power, you're supplying, it's electrifying! You're the one that I want! You're the one I want! Ooh! Ooh! Ooh!"

I roll my eyes and ask, "Are you done? Seriously?"

I swear she's crazy! She played the beauty school dropout part in the high school production of Grease at our school a bazillion years ago, and still bursts into songs from the play when she deems appropriate. It's really annoying. She hasn't done it very often lately, but I guess she couldn't pass it up. Especially after Mom used the word "electrifying."

My mom says, "Honestly, Danielle, that was hilarious! But seriously, Kier, what's going on with you and Chandler? I wasn't born yesterday."

Danielle pipes back in and says, "Boy does she have some explaining to do. I can't wait for you to hear every…single…detail of it so you can hopefully help slap her back into her senses."

My mom's ears perk up. She says, "Do tell. I want every detail, and none of that G rated business either. Danielle, I'd love to slap her into her senses nonetheless."

My eyes are going to roll out of my head. I look at Danielle and say, "Go ahead. You started it. Spill the beans."

Danielle laughs and says, "Don't cop an attitude with me, Juliet! You and Romeo are the ones who can't hide your mutual attraction."

I smile uncontrollably, like a teenager, and then immediately regain my composure as I catch myself letting out a giggle. "Danielle, are you sure you want to refer to us as Romeo and Juliet and not Sandy and Danny? That would work better with your Grease theme today?"

She says, "Good idea, Smart ass!"

Quickly my smile fades, and my mind races to reality. I have to stay strong and show my mom and Danielle how important it is for Josh and me to make our family work.

They need to see that I can't chase school-girl fantasies with Chandler. I have to help Danielle understand it isn't about me and my feelings. We have to do what is right for this baby. For Josh and my son.

My Mom says, "Will someone tell me please… what in the world is going on? Go ahead Kier, I'm listening. What is going on with you two?"

"Mom," I say. "Seriously, nothing. Okay? Just stop it! Ugh!"

I can tell right away she's not going to stop until she thinks she knows every detail there is to know. I can't say I blame her; she's my mom. Finally, I say, "I guess I won't totally lie to you. He's definitely special to me, and he's been here a lot for me lately, but what Danielle doesn't seem to understand or chooses to forget is that he's not the father of this baby, and being with him is not the right thing to do."

I pause with a deep sigh before proceeding, "Now that Josh has come back into the picture and we've decided to make things work, I can't be chasing my hot next-door neighbor around to see where things might go. It's time to be grounded and grow up, something that's hard for Danielle to understand. No time for hypothetical what-could-be relationships. I know who I am with, Josh. I know where I belong, and this baby just solidifies the security that's so important for us to be a family. The rest is just details."

My mom and Danielle are being very quiet, intently listening to my every word. Actually they make me quite nervous with their silence. My Mom looks at me with a sincere face. She places her hand on my shoulder and simply says, "Ok dear, thank you for explaining. I guess there is really nothing more to tell me. Just know one thing, Kier, sometimes what is noble isn't always what is right… So then where's Josh?"

Shit! I'm not quite sure. Playing it safe and without letting on that I haven't spoken to him, I quickly say, "I was just about to text him and let him know you're here."

Danielle shoots a stare my way as if to say she knows I haven't seen or heard from him at all since Thursday. I choose to ignore her "best friend super abilities." *Damn it! I hate how well she knows my life sometimes.* I grab my phone and type away.

Kiera: *My Mom is over and would like to see you… When will you be here?*

Josh: *Just woke up. Last night was rough. I'll text you when I get out of bed. I'll catch you all later… or maybe tomorrow*

WHAT??? I don't know what to say… tomorrow?!? I'm so pissed at his response and the way he's behaving. I could scream. I can literally feel the blood boiling under my skin. *How could he be so inconsiderate?* From the kitchen I hear Danielle suggest to mom we should take a walk out and grab lunch together. I hear her say she wants to fill my Mom in on Sam. I hear Mom say, "Yes, Danielle. I can't wait to hear all about Sam and you. I'm so excited about your wedding, although it's rather quick! You don't have a bun in the oven there, too, do you?"

I try to keep my composure and not let on that I heard her question. Too funny. Danielle laughs and says, "Oh no! Not a chance. We're just in love, and when you know it's right, why wait? We're just so happy and in love! You'll love him! I can't wait for you to meet him."

As I walk towards the living room I send Josh a text back.

Kiera: *R U seriously thinking about not coming to see my mom until tomorrow?*

Chapter 18

Sitting in Joe's Pizza, I keep glancing down at my phone in hopes that a text has come through from Josh. I'm disappointed with each look as he still hasn't responded. I'm beginning to bore listening to Danielle go on-and-on about her and Sam to my mom. Things are just so perfect between the two of them. I know I sound jealous, but it's probably because I am. If only Josh would text me back, maybe I could enjoy Danielle's wonderful stories about Sam with a bit more enthusiasm. I order a slice of pizza and a glass of water. Mom orders a calzone and a beer. Oh how I'd love to have a beer with my mom. Danielle is sweet to order a water with me though.

The rest of lunch I try to seem interested in Danielle's discussion of her wedding plans. If she questions the dress fitting me one more time, I may slap her. Finally, I look at her and say, "Seriously, have I gotten that big? It's only been a little over three weeks since I tried it on."

Danielle tilts her head in a sympathetic manner and says, "Kiera, you look beautiful and I'm sorry. I don't really care if the dress still fits anyway. I don't know why I keep making a big deal about it. I'm sorry I'm worrying you with such bullshit with everything you're going through. I never thought I'd be such a "bridezilla." Please forgive me. I'm seriously ready for this wedding to be done. I love Sam, but sometimes I wish we could skip the ceremony and be married already!"

Mom butts in and says, "Speaking of Sam, I truly can't wait to meet him! The way you and Kiera both speak of him, he sounds like a wonderful man."

I don't know why, but hearing my mom say how wonderful Sam seems to Danielle makes me feel like a failure with my current relationship. I wish I could make her happy, or at least comfortable with Josh and me trying to work it out, but it seemed obvious back at my apartment she's not buying the story. Before I can change the subject and get off of relationships, Mom says, "Kiera, honey, did Josh ever respond? What time is he coming over?"

Knowing my mom, she's not trying to make me upset by asking. She's smart enough to say things to prove a point. No matter what I say to her or Danielle, they both can see right through me. They know Josh isn't coming. They know what I'm thinking and how I feel about Chandler. There is no hiding it. Clearly my Mom knows Josh hasn't responded, and she wants to prove her point. Mom and Danielle have never been too keen on Josh, but for some reason that's made me more determined to make things work out between us. It sounds silly admitting it, but as much as I doubt things too, at times I can't imagine failing in anything, especially a relationship. Since the recent events with Josh, my determination to go full force with our relationship and come out on the other end has strengthened. I want us to be the couple everyone always says will never make it, but we do and defy all logic.

Mom says, "Kier? Did you hear me? Did Josh respond yet?"

I love how she has put me on the spot again. Quickly I say, "Not yet. He had meetings late last night and said he'd call sometime tonight. Maybe we can have dinner with him."

Mom and Danielle say nothing. Instead Danielle asks if we'd like to go to her place so Mom can meet Sam. We agree. I say, "I'll try on that stupid dress again for you, too!" She laughs and we head over to her apartment.

Danielle must have texted Sam to let him know we were coming because when we arrived he had snacks laid out on the table and drinks poured. I walk in and give Sam a hug. He truly is growing on me. He treats Danielle so wonderfully there's not much to not like. Danielle introduces mom to Sam. She says, "Sam, this is Kiera's mom, and my second mom, Gretchen." Sam takes Mom's hand and kisses it with the same chivalry that Chandler did. The thought of Chandler makes me miss him. I miss everything about him. After he gently places her hand down, Sam says, "Gretchen, I've heard so much about you. All positive things. Danielle adores you, and she and I are so happy you'll be at our wedding."

Mom seems to hang on Sam's every word as they have a beer. Danielle and I go back to try my dress on again. I slip into it, and this time I'm a bit worried as the zipper seems caught. Danielle looks over and says, "Oh shit! Kier!"

We burst into laughter. My belly looks huge in this get up! We're laughing so hard tears start running down my cheeks. Finally, Danielle is able to get the dress zipped up and we giggle some more. I say, "I literally can't gain another inch before next Saturday. Little man has just blossomed in the last two weeks." I look at my belly. "You better stop growing little man!"

Danielle takes my hands and says, "Kier, you look beautiful, incredibly beautiful! I need you to listen to me please and I mean it. Please, whatever you do, don't just settle with Josh because of the baby. Make sure a life with him is what you really want. You know things aren't right with the two of you. Kier, I know you love Chandler, and I want you to be happy. Chandler loves you and he wants to be with you, baby and all. He loves you unconditionally, and I feel Josh is the opposite. Josh would still be out of the picture if it weren't for the baby. Don't you agree?"

She doesn't really give me a chance to respond and she says, "Please don't make this mistake. Please don't let Chandler walk away and spend the rest of your life wondering what might have been. Look, I'll stand by you know matter what, but please make sure you know what you're doing first. Just take some time to clear your mind and look at the big picture. Josh has betrayed you once, and I'm just so scared he'll do it again."

I don't respond to Danielle, but I can feel my eyes swelling up with tears. If I'm honest with myself, I truly appreciate what Danielle is trying to say, but at the same time I can't let her know what I'm thinking. It's true, I do love Chandler, but I also know I need to give Josh a chance. I can't compromise my child's chance of normalcy with a traditional family life for my selfish desires. I have to make sure, without a doubt, Josh and I can't work out. If it means taking a chance on losing my opportunity with Chandler, then it wasn't meant to be. *"Que Sera, Sera" Whatever will be, will be.*

Back in the living room, Sam and Mom seem to still be hitting it off pretty well. When I walk in Mom says, "Well, how does the dress fit?"

Danielle and I laugh. I say, "It fits nice and snug."

Danielle says, "Umm let's just say little man may need to not eat too much this week. He's getting BIG!"

We all giggle, and I throw in a joke about maybe wearing a girdle just for the ceremony. Luckily, it's going to be a quick ceremony, and only dinner afterwards, so I won't have to be in the dress too long.

Mom and I leave Danielle's and decide to go shopping for a while. At some point, maybe I'll tell her I don't think Josh is coming today, but I'm hoping maybe she'll forget. Then I won't have to mention it at all. It's highly unlikely she'll forget something like that, but a girl can hope. While walking around Upper Manhattan mostly window shopping, Mom spots a baby boutique and begins dragging me towards the entrance. I must admit, now that I know it's a boy, I am pretty excited at the idea of going into a baby store. I've been in these kinds of stores before, but never for myself. I've only had to buy a baby shower gift for someone else. Ironically enough, the thought of buying anything for the baby hadn't yet occurred to me during my pregnancy. I suppose I've been so busy just getting used to the idea that I never considered how much fun I could have shopping for the baby.

As we walk in, I'm immediately drawn to the sweet baby blue hues. I hear my mom take on a silly baby talking tone as she picks up different items. She screeches and says, "Kier, look at these sweet little booties (except it comes out boooooottttttiiiieeeesss)."

They are very precious, only they look like something my Great Grandma Mae would have made. I think they would probably work better on a girl baby. Looking around, I am getting some good ideas of what I like and don't like for my baby. Apparently, I don't like crocheted items for my boy.

We're having so much fun in this boutique. It must be obvious to the sales clerk this is a first time pregnancy, and even more obvious my Mom is a first time grandma, because she is standing in the corner with a smile and shaking her head. Mom seems so happy. She looks so cute as she picks up each item. Her excitement about the baby couldn't make me happier.

I walk around for a few seconds looking at different outfits on various racks, and when my eyes catch this certain outfit, I know immediately my little man must have it. I place my bag down below on the floor in front of me, and pick it up. The almost white-blue hue makes me smile. The organic cotton is so soft and gentle against my hands. The outfit has little footies and mittens for the hands. It's lined in a darker, light blue with a small appliquéd train on the left side matching the darker, light blue trim. I hold it up next to my belly as Mom walks over to see what I have found. In her newly formed baby voice she says, "Oh, Kier, that's so sweet! It will make a perfect "going home outfit."

I say, "What?"

Mom laughs at me. She says, "You're so silly! A 'going home outfit' is a nice outfit for the baby to wear to go home from the hospital. It's kind of a big deal. Let's get it!"

"Are you sure?" I ask.

She of course says, "Yes. I'm having a blast picking out little outfits for my first grandbaby!" We go to the cashier and I see Mom has quite a few additional items waiting on the counter. She has at least seven adorable outfits and footies, but thank God she hasn't chosen any crocheted booties! Whoever would have thought I minded crocheted items for my son, but boy do I despise those booties. The sales associate asks if we need any of the items monogrammed and I'm not sure what to say. Mom looks at me and says, "Well, it would be precious to do that. Kier, do we have a name?"

I've never been surer of anything as I am at this very moment. I say emphatically, "Noah."

The sales associate looks at me oddly and says, "Generally, we need all three names to monogram unless you'd just like to use an 'N' or spell out the name 'Noah'?"

I say, "Oh I see. I haven't thought it all out that far, I just know his name will be Noah so can we just go with an 'N'?"

The sales associate seems even more confused and says, "Umm sure. Whatever you like."

Mom and I start laughing after she whispers to me about how priceless the face on the lady was when I said I wasn't sure about the other names yet. I'm not sure why it was so funny, but it was. Not knowing what the baby's last name will be is definitely not ideal, but in this situation picking something as silly as a monogram, we're able to find some humor.

We pay and as we walk out I say, "Wow! That was a lot of fun! What shall we do now?"

Mom wastes no time answering and says, "Have you thought about decorating your spare room for the nursery?"

Of course the answer is "no." I'm not real sure what I was expecting my little man to wear, or where I was anticipating his room to be. I am glad Mom sure seems to have everything under control. Thank goodness she's here. We both look at each other and with a high five our next move is underway!

"I hadn't thought of a nursery at all," I say. "But, I've always loved Pottery Barn Kids. How about we go there… I can get furniture, bedding and all!"

Mom looks overjoyed as we hop into a cab. I give the cab driver the address, "We're headed to 1311 2nd Ave please."

As soon as we walk in the doors of PBK, it feels as if tiny little butterflies are swarming my tummy, or better yet, maybe I feel Noah. *Awe! I love the sound of his sweet little name.* Either way, I'm sure this is the most excitement I've experienced since seeing Noah for the first time on Friday. I can feel my phone vibrating with a text through my bag. I start fishing around for it. Finally, when I pull it out, I look at the screen to see it's from Chandler. I hate how excited I get when I see his name. It really makes things hard for me. I open the text while Mom is occupied looking at cribs.

Chandler: *Hello, beautiful! I hope you're enjoying your day.*

Why does he have to be so, so, ugh… just him? Why does he have to be so perfect?

I try carefully to not be teasing or flirty, and I text him back.

Kiera: *Hello. Shopping with my mom.*

He wastes no time and texts back immediately.

Chandler: *I know… I just saw the two of you walk into PBK!*

What? How did he see us?

Kiera: *where are you?*

Chandler: *I was at Barnes & Noble… don't worry I wasn't following you!*

Like I'd worry about that. The problem is, I'd be flattered if he were.

As I'm about to text him back, I hear Mom say, "Oh, what a lovely surprise! What are you doing here?"

I already know who it is before I turn around. I say, "Hello, Chandler."

He flashes that million dollar smile I can't resist, and I can't help but smile back. Again, I feel myself becoming giddy, and I try to hold back. The only problem is I feel like I'm in a different world around him, and I can't control how silly I feel. I'm certain it's obvious to everyone around how much I love this man. Suppressing my feelings keeps getting harder and harder.

Mom says, "I hope you'll join us. We're looking for everything baby boy! Everything Noah! Ooh, I love the way that sounds!"

Chandler says, "Oh, so you decided for sure? I'm so glad. I love the name Noah!"

I don't really answer but keep looking at cribs. Surly he isn't staying to shop for things for Noah with us, but I must admit I sort of hope he does.

Chapter 19

Chandler has been so helpful. He has stayed with us the whole shopping trip. At one point, he said he'd scoot out of our way, but Mom insisted he stay. Surprisingly, I was actually relieved she did. Together we've picked out Noah's crib, changing table, night stand, chest of drawers, bedding, and even some precious teddy bears to place on his shelf. The bedding is adorable and like my taste, classic in theme. I didn't really care for any sort of print, like alligators, trains, or animals. I chose basic white from the Harper collection.

The white bed quilt has a navy band trimming the outside, and inside framing a place to again add monogramming. This time I chose to have 'Noah' put on it, also in navy. The sheets are navy and white polka dot to add a mild pop of character but everything else is basic white and navy.

I chose charcoal gray for his furniture, and I love the way the navy and white look against the charcoal color. At the register, I set up delivery. As I'm about to pay, the lady says, "Actually your husband already took care of everything."

I say, "My what?"

"Your husband," she replies.

I'm not sure where Chandler has wondered off, but I imagine it's a bone I'll need to pick with him. I can't believe he paid for everything.

Mom is beaming from ear-to-ear about Chandler's shenanigans, and I'm not sure how I feel quite yet. I'm not a charity case. I make plenty of money and can certainly afford to furnish my baby's room. Mom says, "What a sweet thing to do. Kier, I think you may want to think things through a bit more before you go writing him off. It's not about him purchasing your baby room for you, but there is more and you know it. He is here for you."
She's right. I hate her for it, but she's right again. I don't know why this man loves me, and I don't know why things have happened the way they have, but I have a lot of thinking to do. I can't keep hiding these strong feelings for Chandler, and where the hell is Josh anyways?!? Mom and I

grab the bags that we'll be taking with us today, and head out of the store.

As soon as we get to the door, Chandler is standing holding water bottles for my mom and me. We both take our water and say thank you. Chandler says, "I'd love to take you two out for dinner if you'll allow me to?"

Before I can say anything, Mom emphatically says, "Absolutely!"

Mom walks ahead of us for a minute to allow us space to talk. I ask, "Why did you pay for the baby furniture? You know I'm not a charity case right? I make great money… well for a single person anyway. Besides, I can't let you do that. I'm writing you a check as soon as I get home."

Chandler stops walking and grabs my arms to stop with him. He says, "Let me love you. Don't stop what we have. Don't be so stubborn about us. I know I'm not Noah's dad, but I can love you better than he can and you know it. I already love you more than he does. No matter what, I'll not accept any repayment from you for Noah's room. It was a gift and I intend to keep it that way."

I say nothing, mainly because I'm breathless. God! He's not giving up and it's making it really hard. I don't even know why I think I want him to give up. I guess it would make things easier on me to at least try with Josh, but damn it, where in the hell is he anyway! Josh still has no idea how far along I am, or that we're having a boy. He literally knows nothing, and he doesn't seem to care at all. He hasn't even asked how my appointment went. Why I'm even having trouble deciding between the two is beyond me.

We catch up with Mom and decide to grab a Chinese take-out once we get closer to my place since I'm feeling exhausted from the day on my feet. Chandler says, "Kier, why don't you and your mom go ahead and head back to your place. I'll pick up the Chinese. Okay?"

"That sounds perfect!" I say. "Thanks Chandler!!"

In the cab on the way back to my place, Mom starts in on me. She says, "Kier, seriously what is so hard for you to figure out? Chandler is present. Josh is… well… not!"

I roll my eyes like when I was a teenager and say, "Mom, I know. Chandler is utterly perfect, and I know it's hard for everyone to understand, but I feel like I have to give Josh a chance for us to make things right for Noah."

Mom says, "No Kier, no you don't. I disagree with you. You owe him nothing except a chance to be a dad if he is willing. You deserve happiness, and I don't think you'll find happiness unless Chandler is a part of your life. He loves you. That man absolutely loves everything there is to love about you, and you're just so damn stubborn. I'm just hoping you make the right decision before it's too late."

I keep quiet the rest of the ride home. My thoughts are racing, and yet again I can't stop thinking about Chandler. I think about what life would be like together and how visitation would work with Josh. On the flip side, I think about life with Josh and try to imagine forgetting Chandler for good. The thought of never seeing Chandler again frightens me. Mom looks over at me. I can feel her staring me down. Finally, she breaks the silence and says, "I'm sorry if I hurt you, or if I said something you didn't want to hear. I love you, Kier, and I just want what's best for you."

"I know, Mom."

Back at my apartment, we are having so much fun going through the bags of loot we purchased for Noah. I can't help squealing with each outfit! Things are really beginning to seem real. Chandler sent me a text saying he was about 15 minutes behind us. From the bathroom, I hear someone knock on the front door, and I hear Mom say she's got it. *It's probably Danielle.* I flush the toilet and head out to the living room. I can hear my mom say, "I haven't seen you for a while."

I know immediately by her tone it's Josh. He embraces me with an awkward hug and peck on the cheek. I flinch and he looks cross at me. He smells like a bottle of Jack, and I can tell by the way he's acting he's been drinking. I am disgusted to see him. Surely, that cannot be a good sign. Feeling anxious Chandler will be here any minute, I say, "Josh, Mom and I were about to eat dinner. Maybe we can hook back up tomorrow?"

I can tell right away he's not falling for it. He says, "Oh well, we can all eat together then. Right? I mean you've practically begged me to come all day. I'm here now, so let's make it work."

What the hell does he mean by that? I try to remain calm as my mom looks like she might blow off at him at any minute. I say, "Josh, seriously I think you should go. Have you been drinking?" "What the hell?" Josh says. "So I have a drink and it's a problem?"

"Don't be silly," I say. "I just thought maybe you had more than one drink."

He ignores me and says, "So what I really came for, and what I want to know is, how the doctor appointment was?" *Oh, now he asks…*

I hesitate and decide now is as good of a time as any. I say, "Everything looks great! I'm a little further along than I thought. I'm five months pregnant. Far enough along they were able to tell me the sex. Would you like to know?"

Josh pokes his chest out and says, "I'm sure it's a boy. All first born babies in my family are boys. Am I right?"

I simply shake my head implying "yes." Josh reaches in his pocket and pulls out a tiny wrapped up wad of gift tissue. Handing it to me he says, "I told my Mom last week about the pregnancy. She mailed me these to give you, and for what it's worth, she said she sends her love."

I reach for the package and cringe once I un-ravel the paper and see a tiny white pair of crocheted booties. *My worst nightmare has come true. I hate them just like the ones in the store! Holy cow these are the ugliest socks ever… maybe for a girl, but not my boy.*

I say, "Tell her thank you for me."

Josh says, "Wow! Five months along already… that's a surprise. Well, at least it's a boy." He sounds like a total asshole; and quite frankly, I can't stand the sight of him right now.

Mom stands up and walks over to the dining area where we're talking. She says, "Josh, if you don't mind, Kiera and I were talking and could we all just meet for lunch tomorrow?"

Josh looks taken aback at the fact that my mom is pretty much asking him to leave. He says, "I can take a hint. I'm not too sure why you both want me to leave, but I'll go. I'm sorry I had a few drinks before I came, but I think I'm acting pretty normal. My apologies if I've offended either of you."

Josh walks over to the door and just like a scene straight off of a Lifetime movie, Chandler walks in with the Chinese to-go bags.

Josh sarcastically says, "Oh well, lookie who we have here… Hello there. Look what the cat drug in...And Chinese food and all. You shouldn't have gone to all of that trouble just for me." Chandler nonchalantly ignores Josh's remarks and walks the food over to the kitchen. He places it on the counter. He washes his hands, and walks over to shake Josh's hand. Mom and I are in disbelief at his manners. Josh of course shakes his hand back and makes an asinine comment about hoping he's worthy enough to shake such a high profile lawyer's hand.

Chandler again ignores Josh, and goes on about his business. He walks over to the door and lets himself out. As he steps into the hall he says, "I hope you all have a lovely evening."

Quickly, I say, "No Chandler, wait, don't go."

He puts his hand up and says, "We'll talk later." He closes the door behind him. I feel knots forming in my gut. I hate the way I feel, and I hate seeing Chandler so disappointed when he saw Josh was here.

Anger comes over me. I look at Josh and say, "Get out! Get out right now! We'll talk later. Just go."

Josh says, "Fine. I'll go so you can call your little boy toy back over. This is bullshit, Kiera, and you know it. You can't make things work out with me and our little family as long as you're still messing around with your little boy toy."

My Mom stands back up from the bar stool and says, "Josh, get the hell out now!"

Josh turns towards the door and leaves. I immediately feel relieved. Not even 30 seconds pass by and Mom opens my front door, walks across the hall, and knocks on Chandler's door. She left my door cracked, and I can see Chandler open the door. Mom says, "Are you coming back over or not?"

I bust out laughing at her, and when Chandler hears me, he starts laughing, too. He says, "Is the coast clear?"

I laugh even harder and say, "Who even says that anymore?"

Chandler walks across the hall back into my apartment. We all sit in the living room and eat our Chinese food. No one brings up anything about what just happened with Josh.

After dinner, Mom and I continue looking through the things we got for Noah today. I say, "I can't wait to pick up his going home outfit they are monogramming. It's so sweet looking." Mom says, "It was precious."

Chandler appears to be very content just hanging out watching us ooh and ahh over baby items. Finally, he speaks up in a very concerned manner. He says, "What are these?"

I glance over at what he is holding. Mom and I both burst into uncontrollable laughter. Chandler is holding the pair of crocheted booties Josh's mom sent. Mom says, "Oh, those are Kiera's favorites!"

I throw my yellow and white chevron pillow at her. "Stop it!" I say. "You've lost it."

We're laughing so hard we can't even speak. I have tears rolling down my cheeks, and Mom is literally on the floor laughing hysterically. Chandler says, "I hope you're not going to let Noah wear these. They look like girl socks."

I'm so relieved to hear him say that! Eventually, we gain our composure and I'm able to tell Chandler the story. I say, "While Mom and I were shopping today, I saw a pair of these booties in a baby boutique. Until today, I never realized I actually hate crocheted booties. Maybe if I were having a girl, I might not feel so strongly about this, but I definitely know I don't like them. It's so funny because, ironically Josh's mom mailed these booties to me and he just gave them to me tonight. I thought I was going to die when I saw them. Mom and I haven't really had a chance to laugh about them yet. It doesn't sound as funny now that I'm telling you, but trust me it's just exactly what I'd expect from Josh's mom."

Chandler lets out a laugh and says, "Well, thank God you didn't buy them for the little guy. I'd be embarrassed for him if you made him wear these."

Again I think… *Finally someone who understands!*

Mom went to bed about thirty minutes ago with a headache. As she was turning in she winked at me and smiled. I know she really likes Chandler, and it makes things that much harder for me because I really like him, too. The rest of the night Chandler helps me look at paint samples, and we decide on a color to paint Noah's room. I'm a sucker for Benjamin Moore paints, and we choose a color called "Silver Chain" which is a light silver-gray for the top of the wall, and for the bead board on the bottom, we choose a color called "Temptation" which is a deep, dark gray.

Chandler had a great idea to use letters to spell Noah's name over the crib, so I order some from Etsy. I get the kind that hang onto hooks with white ribbon, and they match everything perfectly. I love how into this baby Chandler seems to be. He's literally interested in every single aspect, even proposing ideas of his own.

It's getting late and Chandler is a complete gentleman as he says, "I guess I better get to bed. Kier, I want you to know this has been one of the best nights of my life. Everything I've said to you over the last few days holds truer than ever. I'm not trying to make things hard for you. I know Josh and you have a past. I'm trying to respect your wishes and give you space, but I'm so in love with you I can't see straight. I want to be with you. I want to spend forever with you and Noah. I mean it Kiera… Look, tonight was fun, and I hope I can see you tomorrow, and the next day, and the next day, and the next day. I'm trying to be patient with you and I understand…"

I hold my hand up to make him stop talking.

I try to catch my breath. Everything in me is screaming don't go. I melt into his words and give over to my feelings. I say, "I'd like that a lot."

He kisses my cheek and says, "Goodnight," and then he leans down to my belly and says, "You have such a wonderful Mommy. Night Noah!"

Closing the door behind Chandler, still feeling breathless, I hear Mom obnoxiously make her presence known. She clears her throat loudly. I turn towards her and she says, "If you don't marry him, I will."

I smile and say, "Goodnight, Mom."

Chapter 20

It's Monday morning, and my alarm clock is blasting loudly. Yesterday, much to my expectation, Chandler ended up coming over again. To our surprise, he brought Mom and me over breakfast and stayed most of the day. Danielle and Sam came by with last minute plans regarding their wedding reception. Basically, the last minute plans involved Danielle giving me a piece of paper where she'd written exactly, word-for-word the speech she wants me to give at her reception. I wasn't surprised she'd written the speech, nor was I offended by her giving it to me to read. It's typical behavior for her and very much Danielle's personality.

As Danielle and Sam were leaving, she turned to Chandler and said, "I meant what I said the other day. Sam and I hope you'll be accompanying Kier to the wedding!"

Chandler looked at me and said, "I will if she'll allow me to."

I smiled after being put on the spot, and said, "Yes. Of course."

Then Danielle winked at me, walked out the door, and Sam closed the door as they walked away. I wanted to crawl under the table. How very nice of her to make things awkward for me and Chandler. I knew she meant well and just wants Chandler and me to be together, but that was cold in front of him. I felt pissed at her, but strangely excited by her insistence all at the same time. Especially since he clearly wants to come along.

I never heard from Josh yesterday, and I certainly didn't intend on calling him after his escapades Saturday evening in my apartment. He'll eventually call, and when he does I'm not sure how I'll react. Things just aren't right between us. Just like Mom and Tanya Tucker have always said, "If it don't come easy, you gotta let it go."

I find this statement to be completely true, especially in the beginning when things should be easy. Many times I've thought failed relationships meant you were a failure. After all of the relationships Mom has been in and out of, I just thought it was an easy excuse. I'm beginning to see the truth in the saying now. I feel like I'm the one who's doing all the trying, especially with Josh showing up unannounced after avoiding me and being two sheets to the wind. It sure makes him seem useless and uninterested in trying to work on our relationship for Noah.

The truth is I don't love Josh, and I know in my heart I don't. I know where my heart is, and I just have to see if I can let go of the guilt I feel not trying to make it work with Josh. I hope I can reach a place of solitude knowing that I'm not giving up my chance at happiness. Noah will be loved no matter if Josh and I are together or not. It's better for us to be friends for Noah, than for him to think his Mom and Dad hate each other.

I get out of the shower and get dressed into my work clothes. I choose a Jimmy Choo cotton, black flowy A-line dress, and pair it with my favorite solid black Tory Burch flats. I do minimal make-up - mascara, powder, and light eye shadow - but I do top my lips with Nars Jungle Red Lipstick, followed by honey lip-gloss. I love red lipstick with a black outfit. I'm looking forward to being at work today. I hope Mom can find something to keep her occupied while I'm gone.

I walk into the kitchen and Mom is sitting at the table. She whistles and says, "Kier, you don't even look pregnant in that dress. I've never seen anyone as stunning at five months pregnant as you."

I say, "Oh Mom, you're just saying that because I'm yours and you have to."

We smile at each other. I say, "Sure wish I could talk Danielle into letting me wear this to the wedding instead of the number she's picked out. I seriously hate pink, and she knows it too! So what cha got on the docket today without me?"

"Not much," she says. "I may go for a massage and facial. Where should I go?"

I give her the address to my favorite spot, Premier 57, and tell her to plan for all day. Also, I tell her she better call early.

The ride over to the office is surprisingly quiet and nice. You never know exactly what to expect on the subway, especially on Monday mornings. Sometimes it's full of tourists and people heading to the airport, but today it's quiet and even a tad enjoyable. I walk into the office and immediately see Claire heading straight towards me. She acts as if nothing has happened between us. Very strangely she says, “So, have you been to the doctor yet?”

It’s pretty clear she has no idea about Josh and me because she would have mentioned that first. I think it’s probably for the best Josh hasn’t mentioned anything to Richard about us since I’m pretty sure there isn’t even going to be an “us” after all. At least that’s where I’m leaning. Trying to keep things short and sweet I say, “Yes. I’m five months now, and it’s a boy.”

“Five months?” she says. “A boy? I had no idea you were that far along! How exciting!”

I say, “Thank you.”

I pick up a few folders and move them around on my desk thinking maybe she’ll get the hint. Without saying anything back to me, she walks away. My work phone rings and I answer it right away. “Whitaker and Bluff. This is Kiera!”

It’s Susan my boss. She says, “Kier, can you come see me at your earliest convenience? Like right away.”

“Absolutely, I’ll come straight there.”

We hang up the phone. Susan is three floors up from my cubical on the 9th floor. I head up right away. As I walk into her office, Susan is staring down at her desk, but I feel like she should know I'm standing there. She keeps her head down and seems rather starchy. She seems a bit cold and stand offish. I can tell something is off. Assuming she's not having a good morning, I hesitate a moment before I say, "Hi Susan! How are things?"

As soon as the words are out of my mouth, I can feel it wasn't the appropriate word choice. Susan says, "Kiera, we've gotta talk. I really hate this, truly I do."

I say, "Okay, what do we need to talk about?"

She looks at me and says, "Listen, I'm really sorry, but things aren't working out too well in your department. I'm afraid corporate sent in the consultants and they found your position to be redundant. They've decided to eliminate the role altogether. I'm assuming the redundancy would be between you and Claire, but it wasn't noted."

My heart sinks. *I love my job…this can't be happening. Eliminate?* Trying to maintain composure I say, "Oh, I see. What does this mean for me? Eliminate my position, but you'll find me something else right? Another fit for me?"

I can read the look in Susan's eyes well enough to know the answer is "no." She says, "Kiera, I'm so sorry. I tried everything in my power to keep you on. There just isn't anything open currently that would be a good fit, and honestly the budget won't allow it anyhow."

I feel like I could faint. I place my hand on the wall just in case. Susan hands me an envelope. She says, "I know with the baby and all, this is quite a surprise". *How does she know about the baby?*

She continues on, "I was able to get you a nice severance package though, and I think you'll be pleased with it. It's enough to carry you through twelve weeks post-partum. That's more than anyone else around here gets. I hope this will help ease your worries."

I take the envelope and say, "So this is it? I'm leaving today?"

Susan nods her head in the affirmative and hands me a small box to pack my personal belongings. *I can't believe this is happening… I love this job, and this place. I can't believe this is really it. I feel like I'm going to cry.* Back at my desk I start placing things into the box. I can see people staring at me. Everyone knows what the brown box means. Claire glances up at me, and throws her hands up as if to say "what's going on?"

As if it isn't obvious, I ignore her gesture and continue packing. There isn't really much to pack. I open my drawer and see Chap-Stick, lip-glosses, nail polish, and little notes I'd collected between Claire and me, mostly making fun of other co-workers. Through the corner of my eye, I see Claire coming over. She says, "Kier, what happened?"

I can't speak or I'll cry. I keep on moving around my cubical checking for items to place in the box. Claire takes my hand and says, "What are you going to do?"

I shake my head and say, "I'm not sure, but I really don't feel like talking."

She turns away, and quietly goes back to her desk. I finish clearing things out of my cubicle and packing them into the box, and then I head downstairs.

The subway is a little busier this time of day as I head back to my apartment. When I walk into my apartment, Mom is still there. I guess I've only been gone around an hour and a half. She looks surprised to see me, but once she sees the brown box I think she catches on. She says, "Why are you back so early?" as she eyes the box questionably.

I nod my head "yes" answering the question she never asked. She says, "Oh, honey! I'm so sorry. Did they say why? You were such a hard, passionate worker for them. You loved that job. It was your dream job."

"I know," I say. "I did. They said my job was redundant and that I'm not needed anymore. I guess Claire does my job better than I do. It sucks badly, but on the bright side, they paid me a severance covering me until twelve weeks post-partum. At least I won't have to look for work at five months pregnant."

Mom says, "I'm pretty sure they were just covering their asses doing that so you won't sue them."

I say, "Probably so. Look, I think I'm going back to bed for a while if you don't mind?"

She says, "I think you should. I don't mind at all. I'm going to head on to the spa you told me about unless you need me here? I made an 11 o'clock with them. Will you be fine?"

"Oh yes! Please enjoy your time in New York. I need rest anyway. Don't worry about me."

She smiles and says, "Ok. Well I'll be back later. Rest well my love!"

Within moments of my head hitting the pillow, I fall asleep. I keep waking up by my phone. It keeps making noises alerting me of texts, and finally I get up to see who it is. I have three texts- one from Danielle, one from Josh, and one from Chandler. I open Danielle's first.

Danielle: *not sure if u thought about this, but if u r interested… I got a number to a highly qualified nanny agency for the baby from a very reliable source from work… I'm sure you'll interview several so let me know if u want info... LY*

Shit! I hadn't actually thought about a nanny. I suppose that's something I'll have to consider. Especially once I find a job after the baby. All of the sudden, a sad feeling comes over me. I haven't even met Noah yet, but the thought of leaving him makes me feel terrible. And the thought of not returning to my job makes me sad too. *Ugh!* I try to not think about it for now. I look at the text from Chandler.

Chandler: *Thinking about you. I hope your day is going good.*

He always makes me smile, and I wish he were here. I feel so safe when he's near. Much to my dismay, I decide to look at Josh's text.

Josh: *Look, I'm sorry.*

Seriously! Now I'm pissed. Is that all he can say? I should've gone with my gut and not even looked at his text. I delete it, and try to get it out of my mind.

I decide to text Chandler back.

Kiera: *Awe… Today's interesting to say the least. I'm already home… Hope you're good!*

I smile and tap send.

Sitting on my couch listening to Spotify, I quickly glance through a job search site. It's hard to separate out legitimate jobs from bogus ones. I'm pretty sure if it sounds too good to be true, then it's too good to be true. After about fifteen minutes of my job search going nowhere, I Google Nanny businesses in the area. I decide to look mainly so I won't seem completely oblivious to the idea when Danielle brings it back up again. After all, I'm sure whoever she suggests is the best. I see a couple of places that look alright, but still the idea of a stranger raising my baby through the day seems off-putting and uncomfortable. I shut the computer and curl up on the sofa to watch TV.

I turn on the Food Network and relax. *The Pioneer Woman* is on, and it's actually one of my favorite shows. I'm not sure why I love it so much. I can't really relate to her, but I love to watch her cook. The only thing I really know about *The Pioneer Woman*, other than her show, is that she grew up fairly well off and now she lives on a cattle ranch. That's enough to fascinate me beyond end. I also love her recipes. I watch the show and feel myself drifting off right before the door buzzer goes off. I roll my eyes at the sound of the door as I make my way over and peep through the hole.

I'm happy to see Chandler standing outside my door. As usual, millions of butterflies flitter in my tummy as I open the door to let him in. Immediately, he hands me a bouquet of Juliet roses with a tag that reads Banchet Flowers. This is a well renowned top florist in New York, and a box of Chocopologie chocolates.

"Yummy, Chocopologie chocolates! And these flowers are just beautiful!" I say.

He has such amazing taste, and is so thoughtful! He walks in and places his arms around me. He asks, "So, what's so interesting about today?"

I laugh and say, "Well not much, except I got laid off."

Chandler looks surprised and says, "Oh no! You loved that job… I'm so sorry, Kier. Well it looks like I made the right choice with the chocolates. That'll make everything feel better! Are you all right?"

I shrug my shoulders and say, "I think so. I'll find something. They were very generous and gave me a severance package to get me through twelve weeks post-partum, so I really can't complain."

"Wow," Chandler says. "They must have really liked you. I've never heard of that kind of a severance."

Smelling my beautiful bouquet of Juliette roses I say, "Do you mind if we talk about something else? I don't really want to think about it anymore."

He says, "Sure" and then changes the subject asking me where my Mom is. I say, "She's having a day at the spa. I guess I've worn her out."

We both smile. I open the box of Chocopologie chocolates and we share them while sitting on the couch watching *The Pioneer Woman.* Not once has he asked me to change the channel from the Cooking Network. I love that about him.

During a commercial, Chandler says he needs to ask me a question. I say, "Sure what is it?"

He says, "Well, I want to make sure I'm not overstepping my boundaries… you know, since the other night when you told me to give you space, and then I sort of told you I wanted to be with you forever? I don't know, but sometimes I feel like you want me to not bother you so you can figure it out with Josh. Then other times, I feel like you want me around. Can you just kindly let me know if I'm too much, because I don't want to mess things up with you? I'll respect whatever you decide?"

Bless this wonderful man's heart. God! I'm so in love with how awesome he is. I smile and place my hand on his knee. Looking in his beautiful eyes I say, "Chandler, I'm so sorry for the way I've been acting. I'll let you know if I need space, but right now it feels good. It's true I've been so confused with Josh and the baby, trying to do the right thing. I have been pulling you around, and that's so unfair. The only problem is, I don't love Josh. I love you. I just have to figure out logistics, and I don't want to feel guilty with my choice. I think I'm finally at a place where I don't think I'll feel guilty. I'm working through it all now, but I think everything will be fine."

Chandler says, "Rewind. That's a problem that you love me?"

I quickly say, "No! No, it's not a problem at all. I just have to figure out what all of this means. Somehow I have to work through everything, including Josh. I'm so sorry for all I've put you through. Please forgive me."

It's relieving to tell him how I really feel. I hope he can find peace with what I'm saying, and we can move from there.

Chapter 21

Mom comes in all cheery from her spa day. She's pleasantly surprised to see Chandler next to me on the sofa. She says, "What a lovely surprise! How are you today, Chandler?"

He stands to greet Mom with a kiss on the cheek and a quick neck hug. He says, "I'm well. How about you Gretchen?"

She says, "I couldn't be better! I'm so glad you've come to cheer Kier up!"

I smile because the truth is, he really has cheered me up. I have a flashback to my teen years and recall how all the boys my mom liked, I hated. It's so ironic now to finally make a pleasing choice for Mom. I suppose its normal for teenagers to not like boys their parents like. Funny how things change. I love how much Mom adores Chandler, it makes things easier to have her approval, especially after how much she didn't care for Josh.

My phone beeps and I see it's Josh again. I never responded to his last text. I'm still so pissed at him. Regardless of if I have no intention of making things work with him or not, now I know he'll still have to be a part of my life with Noah. I open the text in my bedroom to avoid Mom and Chandler's remarks.

Josh: Kier, I suck! I'm so, so, so sorry for the way I acted. I shouldn't have come over unannounced and drunk. Please talk to me. Can you break away from work and meet me at Magnolia's bakery in an hour? There is something I need to say in person…

What the hell does he need to tell me? I don't know why I feel I owe him the opportunity, but I text him back.

Kiera: Sure.

Luckily, when I come out of the bedroom, Chandler is standing up putting on his lightweight Burberry breaker. He says, "Listen, I have a few more meetings this afternoon I have to be at, so I need to go prepare for them, but can I see you tonight?"

Mom says "Yes!" before I can even manage to speak. I laugh and say, "I'd like that a lot!"

Chandler softly kisses me on the lips, and I feel warm sensations everywhere as he says, "I hope you have a beautiful afternoon, and I'll take care of dinner tonight. I'll bring something over. See you in a bit!"

As I close the door behind him, Mom says, "Kier, you're making the right choice."

How she knows I've made any choice is beyond me, but having her approval feels good for once. I say, "Mom, I gotta run a quick errand. Do you mind?"

"Not at all. I think I need a nap after the spa anyway. I'll see you later on."

I walk into Magnolia's for the first time since Josh and I were here last. I'm completely and utterly shocked at how I do not want a cupcake. Must be the pregnancy. It's so funny how some of the foods I loved before are a turn off to me now, and foods I hated before the pregnancy sometimes sound good now. Hormones are a crazy thing. I see Josh at a table and walk over. I'm actually about fifteen minutes early. I say, "So you wanted to talk. Here I am."

He says, "I deserve that tone."

Josh's demeanor changes, and for the first time in a while he seems sincere. He says, "Kier, I brought you here because I wanted to work backwards from where it all went wrong."

I'm sure the look on my face is dazed and confused, maybe even unfazed. I say nothing and just listen. Josh takes my hand, and at first I flinch, but then I give into his familiarity and let him hold it while he speaks. *I hate him for being so smooth and able to turn it on so easily. I'm not going to fall for his games again. I'll stay strong.* He says, "I'll take forever if I have to. I'll show you that we can make this work. I hate what happened between us last time we were here, but you know what I hate the most?... Myself for letting you down. Look, Kier, I love you. I always have. It scares the shit out of me how much I love you. Now we're having a baby. Don't you see? It's what was supposed to happen. Us? We were supposed to be engaged and I screwed up. I'm going to take care of you and make everything right. Can we go for a walk?"

I stand up behind him and follow him out of Magnolia's. The bakery people probably appreciate us leaving since neither of us ordered anything. We walk towards the park, and I'm beginning to see where we're headed, but I'm not quite sure why. I follow Josh anyways. He stops in the exact spot where we stood not that long ago when our lives changed forever. He looks into my eyes and I look into his. My heart begins to thump so hard I feel like it's going to pop out of my chest. Again, I find myself in a vulnerable state. I want marriage so badly, and I'm scared I might say yes. He says, "Kiera, I love you. I love our son. I want to make everything right between us."

He ever so comfortably gets down on one knee and opens up a tiny box with the most beautiful emerald shaped diamond ring inside. He says, "Kiera, will you, and my son, marry me?"

I feel like I can't breathe. I can feel beads of sweat forming under my arms and face as I look down at the beautiful ring. I allow Josh to place it on my finger. I'm so grateful for this moment. I'm so grateful for what happened the last time we found ourselves in this very same spot in Central Park. I'm thankful that Josh crumbled the way he did and the initial engagement went wrong, because as I stand here in the moment I'm overwhelmed by the most wonderful feeling. For once in my life, I know exactly what I want and I'm not afraid of it at all! I'm surer than I've ever been as I look deeply into Josh's eyes. I say, "No! Hell, No! I won't marry you. I don't love you that way, and I never will. What happened to us in this park the first time was a blessing. Don't you see? If you'd have gone through with the proposal I'd have said yes, and we'd have gotten married. I can't marry you, and I'm so grateful for the circumstances that brought us back here. Noah will have a better chance with us remaining friends instead of being enemies from a broken marriage, and that's a wonderful thing!"

Josh says, "What in the hell are you talking about? Who's Noah?"

Oops! I say, "I want to name the baby Noah. You never asked, and I like the name."

"It's a fine name I guess, but you're confusing the hell out of me… I thought we talked and wanted to try to make things work out for our family, and now you're telling me you don't love me. Which is it, Kier? What the hell do you want from me?"

"I'm sorry, Josh. I don't love you. Maybe I had to experience all of the shit you've put me through lately to realize it. Maybe I needed a true proposal from you to see my true feelings, but I don't want to marry you. It's really over now. We can still parent Noah, and I believe we'll do it well. We just won't do it together. I'm sorry, it's just the way it is."

As I say, "Look, I've gotta go," Josh pulls me back by my arm and he says, "You're in love with Chandler aren't you?"

I look him in the eye, and I actually feel sorry for him for a second. Then remembering all we've been through, the feeling fades. I nod my head "yes" and emphatically say, "I am."

Feeling so confident and empowered, I turn and walk away without any urge to glance back.

I feel incredible! I've never been so sure of anything in my entire life. It feels great! Finally, I'm certain Chandler is the one, and I can't wait to tell him. I send him a text.

Kiera: *what time will you come over later?*

Immediately he responds.

Chandler: *what time do you want me?*

I smile at his flirt. As I think this through more, I decide I want to be with him alone. I say:

Kiera: *can I just come over to your place?*

Chandler: *Mom too?*

Kiera: *just me. 6?*

Chandler: *what, you don't want to share me with your Mom? Sounds perfect… I can't wait*

Once I get back to my apartment, Mom is still napping. I clean up the kitchen and bathroom quietly. When she wakes up, she asks me what time Chandler is coming over tonight. I say, "Mom, actually I'm going to go over to his place so we can talk alone. I can order you a pizza if you would like? You don't mind do you?"

"Of course not, sweetheart, as long as what you have to tell him is good?" She looks at me questionably, and I smile consoling her thoughts. She smiles back and says, "I'm so proud of you!"

How does she know everything I'm thinking? One day, maybe I'll understand how she does it. Maybe when Noah's older I will have motherly powers too. It's crazy really how little I have to say, and she already knows what I'm going to tell Chandler. I suppose she knew I'd come around and follow my heart. She and Danielle probably have already planned Chandler's and my wedding. Mom says, "Don't worry about pizza. I might go try the new restaurant that just opened one block up. Is that a safe area?"

I laugh and say, "Mom, its New York City! Just go and be back before dark."

She says, "Okay I will. Don't you worry about me. Just have a nice night with Chandler."

I heard Chandler come home a few minutes ago. I wanted to wait a couple minutes past six in case he needs a few extra minutes. It's 6:15, and I walk over. I knock on his door two times as usual. Chandler opens and greets me with a kiss on the forehead and a chocolate covered strawberry. I say, "Yummy! You know just how to get to a pregnant woman's heart! What smells so delicious?"

"I'm making baked spaghetti and garlic knots. I hope it sounds good? I decided against take out."

"Oh my goodness, it sounds and smells wonderful! You didn't have to cook, you know?"

"I wanted to! Now, let's sit. Dinners got about another forty-five minutes. What was it you wanted to talk to me about?"

"How do you know I want to talk to you about something?"

"Because you wanted to be away from your mom, so I just assumed you needed to talk."

I smile. He knows me so well. I am so happy, I must be beaming. He says, "What? What's so funny?"

"Nothing really... It's just that I actually did want to talk to you about something, but it seems so silly because I think you probably already know. I just feel so…so juvenile."

Chandler reaches his hand over onto my lap and says, "You are sort of juvenile."

I slap at him in a flirtatious manner. He says, "Seriously, stop. Don't be silly. What is it, I'm starting to get scared?"

"Well, as you know I've spent a lot of time thinking and torturing myself and you. I don't know or fully understand how things transpired between us so quickly, but they definitely did. Words can't describe how thankful I am for you being a part of everything like you have been. I actually could get a little emotional over it if I don't stop. Look Chandler, I just want you to know that not only do I finally get it, but also I'm finally ready to admit it and face up to it. I'm ready to accept it and give into it!"

He looks at me and says, "You get and accept what?"

I say, "Don't you remember silly? You told me that you believed in me, and that you knew I loved you and you loved me. You said you would wait as long as it took, because you believed I'd eventually get it? Well I do… I get it, and I love you Chandler. I want us to be together too, and I'm so happy that you waited for me to come around. I'm so happy you came into my life. I want us to be together if you'll still have me?"

Chapter 22

At first Chandler says nothing and seems a little bothered, but then he reaches for me and embraces me with a warm passionate kiss. I suppose he was caught off guard. He holds my cheeks close to his face and finally says, "You've just made me the happiest man alive."

We continue kissing, and he hugs me up against him. I laugh as I feel Noah kicking. Chandler says, "Was that a kick?"

I smile and say, "Yes! I think he must be giving his approval."

Chandler says, "Well, I'm glad to have it."

We lean back on the sofa, and I place my head on his shoulder. He puts his hand on my belly to feel Noah moving. He says, "I can't imagine how amazing it must be to feel a human life moving around like that in your tummy. What a miracle!"

I smile and say, "It really is. For the longest, I didn't even know it was him kicking. I'm not sure what I thought it was, but now there is no mistaking."

As we sit down to dinner, there is a knock at the door. Chandler walks over and peeps out. He says, "It's your Mom." He opens the door and says, "Hi, Gretchen! It's so lovely to see you. Please come in."

Seeming to be frazzled, Mom walks in and emotionally says, "I'm so, so sorry to bother you two, but Kier do you think you can step over to your place real quick?"

I can see my Mom must really need something because she wouldn't normally intrude like this. I stand up and say, "Certainly."

In the hallway I ask, "What's going on? Is everything ok?"

Not answering me she continues to walk over to my place. As I open the door, I can immediately see what the problem is. Josh is sitting on the sofa. Not knowing what else to do, I say, "Hi, Josh… Ummm…What are you doing here?"

Yet again, he looks drunk and disheveled, which is not exactly out of his character lately. I'm growing impatient as I wait for his response. Finally, after a few awkward moments he says, "I came by to let you know I'm about to go on vacation. Gina and I are taking a cruise."

He's slurring with each sentence, and I'm having to focus intently on his words. I don't comment and let him finish, mostly because I'm not sure why he's telling me his life details. He continues on, "I planned this getaway, and I was going to take you, but when you ditched me at Central Park, after I just proposed, I figured you wouldn't want to go."

As awkward as I feel not saying anything, I still remain quiet. He then says, "Look, I think things are clear to me now, and I'm going to propose to Gina on the trip. I just wanted you to hear it from me first."

What in the hell is going through this man's mind? Again, I remain quiet. He says, "Look, the only reason I'm here is because I want to make sure you're positive about not wanting to marry me? I'm giving you one last opportunity before it's too late…"

Yet again, I find myself speechless by his arrogance and bravado. I take in a deep breath as not to be emotional, and

I decisively say, "I've never been more positive about not wanting something in my whole life than I am right now. Josh, I wish you and Gina the best of luck! I hope you two have so much fun on the cruise. Are we done here?"

He stands to leave my apartment, and looks back at me. "You don't know what a relief this is to me. Kiera, the only reason I proposed again was to make certain you didn't want to get back together, or come after me for this baby. I wanted to do what was right, but in reality I didn't really want to be with you either. I've not been completely honest. Gina and I have been together for several months now. Your being pregnant complicated things, but I'm just happy to have closure with you and to see you've moved on as well."

Just when I thought he'd ran out of asinine comments, he turns back around and says, "So, you're not really going to be keeping the baby now, right? Like, I mean, you'll put him up for adoption or something? So we won't have to actually worry about anything like that, right?"

Mom jumps up off of the sofa and slaps him across his cheek. Josh says, "What the hell was that for?" Then Mom slaps his other cheek. I can't help but laugh as she says, "You get the hell out of here. You're just a loser, and Kiera is worth so much more than you'd ever have to offer her. Kiera and Noah will be just fine without you. Just leave!"

When Mom is done, I somehow maintain my dignity and say, "Josh, to answer your question, yes, as a matter of fact I'm keeping Noah. With you or without you. If you decide not to be a part of his life, that's your choice…it's on you. I'll not force you one way or another, but Mom is right, you really should leave for now."

Josh looks perplexed as I walk towards the door and open it. It's kind of humorous how he's staring at me so confused. I motion my hand towards the hallway, and he walks out. We close the door behind him, and Mom pulls me in for a hug. She says, "Kiera, I'm so sorry you have to go through all of this alone. He's such a sorry person. I mean, what a jerk! I guess I never realized he was that bad. He has some audacity to act the way he does. I think he seriously thought he was doing you a favor by double checking to see if you'd changed your mind. Does he not realize his leaving is the best favor he's done for you?"

Some way, somehow I feel completely numb and unmoved by Josh's behavior. I suppose it's because I have no feelings for him. I've come to grips with my feelings for Chandler, and I know that he's exactly who I want. I look at Mom and say, “Honestly, Mom, I don’t care. I really don’t, and for once in my life, that feels good! He can’t hurt me anymore. You and I both know who really matters to me, and he’s right across the hallway waiting for me to have dinner with him. Would you like to join us?”

Mom smiles. She says, “You don’t know how happy I am to hear you say that, and no, I’ll not intrude on your dinner with Chandler tonight. Go be with your man, I’ll be here when you get back waiting for all the details! I love you, Kiera, and I’m so proud for you!”

Hearing my mom say she’s proud of me feels so good. I open Chandler’s door and see he’s setting the table. I walk in and he says, “Everything okay?”

I say, “Everything is simply perfect!” I don’t mention anything about what just happened and we sit down to enjoy our dinner.

Chapter 23

Chandler pours me a glass of fresh squeezed lemonade and a glass of water. He's such a wonderful cook. I tell him how delicious everything tastes. The baked spaghetti is the best I've ever had. As we eat our dinner, we make small talk about Noah and the nursery. I love how interested he is in all things Noah.

All of a sudden, his demeanor changes and he solemnly says, "So Kier, there is something I need to talk to you about, but before I say anything, I don't want you to get scared by what it is. I have figured everything out in my head, and now all I need to do is convince you I'm right on with my plan. Everything will be perfect!"

I must admit, when anyone tells me not to be scared, it scares me. This is no exception to that rule. I'm not sure what he's about to say, but I try to brace myself for the worst, just in case. He says, "Kier, I don't talk too much about work because I don't really want to bore you."

I nervously laugh and say, "You couldn't bore me, trust me."

He continues on, "Alright, well here goes… I had a pretty big day today. Our law firm's biggest client is under investigation for some serious accusations, and I'm like 95% certain the company is being set up and our client is innocent. They're based out of Zurich, Switzerland, and I've been offered the opportunity to go and investigate it, and personally represent this client. The two head partners of my firm said if I could turn this around in a reasonable time frame and essentially win, they'll give me ownership interest as a senior partner. It's truly a dream come true. The only thing is, I just don't think I can leave you… So."

I say, "Stop it right there! Okay, first of all, Yay for you! I'm so happy for you and this opportunity. This is awesome Chandler!"

He puts his hand on mine and says, "Kiera, I need you to listen. I could be gone anywhere from six months to a year, or even over a year. So I've decided I'm not going to leave you. I simply won't leave you and Noah. Not after everything we've been through to get where we are."

I stand up and say, "Chandler, look, you have no choice. This is a once in a lifetime opportunity, you said it yourself. Sure I'm sad, and I'll miss you like crazy! Maybe I can visit. We can talk on the phone and text, besides no matter what, I'll be here when you get back."

Chandler, too, is standing now. He takes a hold of my hands, and says, "Kier, don't you get it? I'm not leaving you here. I love you, and I love Noah. I want to be with you both. I don't want to risk losing you again. That's why I'm asking you if you'll consider going with me to Switzerland? I know it may sound crazy to some, but I make plenty of money to support you and Noah. You can stay home with him, which if that is something you want, I want you to have that opportunity more than anything. I know it's a lot to think about, that's why I'm telling you now. Will you think about it? Chances are I'll have to leave in two weeks."

Wow two weeks! I say, "Wow! Okay. Well this is kind of a lot for me to think about. I've never even been to Switzerland before. You've really thought this through?"

"Yes! The only thing I had to think through was that I want you and Noah to go with me."

"That means I'd have to possibly deliver Noah there?"

"Yes," Chandler says. "He'd be born there. We will find the best doctors, and it will be great!"

I take a few moments to myself, and while everything inside me is screaming yes, I don't quite know how to convey my enthusiasm. I say, "I'm definitely going to need a bit to gather my thoughts. I mean it's obvious I love you, and I don't want to be away from you, but this is a lot. I mean leaving the country while I'm pregnant, and all of the uncertainty… I just really need a few days to process."

Chandler says, "I assumed you would, but I wanted to give you the facts and explain to you how perfect things will be with my plan. All I need is a yes from you, and we'll be on our merry little way… But I'll give you time. I truly do understand and respect your thoughts."

He quickly changes the subject and asks about Danielle's wedding. I can't seem to get this Switzerland thing, or the whole situation with Chandler, off of my mind. A gazillion thoughts are racing through my mind. *What if I go? We're not even married. I feel like this is crazy. None of this is how I planned it to be. Are we even boyfriend and girlfriend, or is that just logistics?* I must have dazed too long because Chandler says, "Kier? Kier? Are you okay?"

I quickly try to snap out of it. I apologize and say, "I'm so sorry. I think I was day dreaming or something. Umm, what were you asking? Oh, the wedding. Yes, I think we'll need to be there around 5 o'clock. It's really going to be small, but I think it's for the best, especially for Danielle."

Chandler says, "What about you? What kind of wedding do you want?"

I'm not sure why he's asking me, but I suppose he's letting me know how serious he is with me. I say, "I want a small wedding with only people I'm closest to. How about you?"

Chandler says, exactly what I expected him to say since he doesn't really have much family. His parents both passed away after a tragic car accident ten years ago. He says, "Me too. I want small and quaint. I want my bride to look just like you."

It wasn't a proposal, but at least I know where his thoughts are. He leans in for a kiss and yet again we find ourselves lost into each other with passion, giving in to one another as we make our way to his bedroom.

It's crazy really how fast things have progressed between us. My thoughts go back to our earlier conversation, and as I lay in his arms I feel sad. *If only there were no Switzerland.* I know in my heart I can't go to Switzerland, but I just don't want to face the truth yet. In theory, Switzerland sounds lovely, but I can't leave the country 6 months, or 6 ½ months, pregnant by then with a man who's not the father, and rely on him solely for living expenses. I'm not a charity case and I have to maintain some sort of a reputation. Switzerland just can't happen.

I get up and get dressed. I say, "If my mom weren't here I'd stay, but I really need to go over and keep her company."

Chandler says, "I understand… I suppose Gretchen would miss you if you stayed."

He stands and walks me over to the door. He leans down to kiss me and says, "I mean all of what I said to you tonight. I want you to think seriously about every detail. I love you and Noah, and I want us to be together. Goodnight, Kier." He kisses my forehead, and I am breathless.

I walk in and Mom is sprawled out, covered up with my navy chenille throw on the sofa watching HGTV. She says, "Hi honey! Did you and Chandler have a nice time?"

I suck at hiding my feelings from my mom. Patting a place for me to come and join her she says, "Oh no. Do you want to talk about it?"

I shake my head no, and she says, "Kiera, it'll be fine whatever it is. I know Chandler is a good man. If you don't want to talk about it now, we don't have to, but I think you'd feel better to get it out."

She's good. She always knows the right words to say to get my lips to moving. I smile at her word choice, and sort of let out a giggle as I say, "You're so funny, Mom!"

She looks at me so innocently as if she doesn't realize she is using tactics to get me to spill, and says, "I don't know what you're talking about?"

Ignoring her playing dumb, I say, "You're good, and you know it! You can always get me to talk. I suppose it's your motherly gift. Anyways, tonight was interesting. Chandler had something to tell me and well, let's just say I've got some big decisions to make. I'm a bit scared of my choices."

Mom says, "Okay, well first things first, you need to stop talking cryptic and tell me what in the hell is going on. What are the big decisions?"

I say, "Well… Chandler has been offered a remarkable opportunity to go to Zurich, Switzerland, to represent his firm's biggest client. If he wins the case, or does a good job, then the law firm says they'll make him a senior partner. It's just a really huge opportunity for him, and he can't pass it up. The only problem is he could be gone anywhere from 6 months to a year or more."

Mom says, "That's wonderful news for him. So what's the problem?"

"Well, he, wants me to go, too."

"Well, I figured that much! And what's wrong with that? You're going right?"

"I told him I need time to think, but he's leaving in two weeks."

"What on earth do you need to think about? Of course you'll go with him. You love him don't you? I don't understand what there is to think about. Kiera, everything you want is right here in front of you. Don't let him slip away. I know you'll make the right choice. What are you so afraid of anyways?"

"Seriously," I say, "When he told me this, he said he couldn't go unless I went too, and everything inside of me was screaming "Yes," but then I started to think. The more he said, the more I questioned the decision. He said that he wanted me to go, and that he made plenty of money to support me and Noah. He said I could have Noah there, and stay home with him. I love that part. Of course I'd love to stay home with Noah, but not at Chandler's expense. I mean we aren't even married. How crazy would I look to traipse around the country with him un-married while carrying Josh's baby. I mean, I have to maintain a bit of dignity somehow."

"Kier, I trust you. I know you'll make the best choice. I also know how independent you are and I admire that about you. So, I understand why you wouldn't want to just follow him out of the country. I really do… I just really love the way you two get on with each other, but you know what? There is no amount of miles that can stop love if it's meant to be. So you go ahead and think your little heart out. I'll support whatever you decide."

I hug my Mom and say, "That's why you're the most wonderful Mom ever! Thanks for supporting me. You're the best! Truly I really appreciate your not pressuring me about this. I mean it. Truly, thanks Mom."

She smiles and says, “Tomorrow may be a different story, and especially if we tell Danielle.”

“Ha ha,” I say. “I suppose I’ll tell her when the time comes, but she’s so busy right now I don’t want to bother her.”

Mom says, “I think tomorrow morning I may go out and buy a dress for the wedding.” You can come if you like?”

I say, “That depends on what time you’re going because I definitely need to sleep. I feel so worn out, and with the wedding festivities to come, I know I need to rest up. So we’ll see how long I sleep and if you’re still here when I wake up.”

Mom says, “Fair enough! I’m heading to bed. Goodnight!”

“Goodnight, Mom! I love you.”

Chapter 24

Just as I'm about to fall asleep, I hear my cell alert going off. Feeling sleepy headed, I reach for my phone. I see Chandler's name and rub my eyes as the text looks blurry.

Chandler: *Hi love… I miss you being here next to me. I hope you have sweet dreams.*

My heart feels sad as I imagine this text is the kind of texts he'll send when he's in Switzerland and I'm here in New York. I feel pain thinking about our future living arrangements. I can't imagine him not being right across the hall. I really hate the idea of a long distance relationship, especially considering our circumstances. I consider why I'm so stubborn. I want to be happy; after all, that's why I chose to be with Chandler and not Josh in the first place. I'm seriously making things harder than they have to be. Why am I doing this to myself? Why am I torturing myself for the sake of how things look? For goodness sake I'm already pregnant, why do I care?

And then a light bulb goes off! Feeling empowered, I sit straight up in my bed and out loud I say, "Of course I'll go with Chandler to Switzerland, why did I feel the need to make that decision so hard?!?" I hit reply on the text:

Kiera: *Hi! I miss u too. I'm sorry about earlier, it just took me by surprise. I've thought about it all night and I've decided to go!!!*

After I hit send, I can see three dots moving indicating Chandler is typing. It takes a few minutes before a text comes through. I have an exciting feeling as I read his text:

Chandler: *Oh thank God! I seriously would not have gone had you said no. I mean it! I was going to quit my job and start my own law firm… I'm so happy! Tomorrow we can search for doctors for you and Noah and look at hospitals. God I wish I could hug you right now! I'm so happy!*

I love this man so much. He's so sincere, I can't believe how much he wants me, and even Noah. He's truly a gift from God. I decide to get out of bed and run across the hallway. I leave Mom a note on the counter that says "At Chandler's". At this moment, I don't think she'd disapprove of anything I wanted to do with Chandler.

I knock on his door, and he opens fairly quickly! He picks me up, kisses me, and says, "Oh Kier, I'm so happy! We're going to be so happy together. This is the best thing ever. I mean it! I love you so much!"

I kiss Chandler and say, "I love you too! I can't imagine not being with you that long. I'm crazy excited too." Not feeling like I want to leave, I say, "Can I sleep here?"

Chandler says, "Of course, I'd love that!" On the way back to his bedroom he says, "This night couldn't get any better!"

My smile is so big, I feel like Chandler can hear it. As we lay in the dark all curled up next to each other tightly, we fall to sleep.

I wake up before Chandler and mess around on my phone a while. I decide to text Danielle to see how things are going with the wedding plans. Also, I conclude, if I don't fill her in soon about everything that's happened lately she'll be mad. I know she's preoccupied with the wedding, but she'll still make time for all of my drama too! I have to tell her about Josh's visit, and the latest with Chandler. Let's see, how do I summarize all of this? Hmmm… I start typing.

Kiera: *ok so lots going on try stay with me… can't remember what all I may have already told u… here goes: 1. Josh proposed again in Central Park 2. I said no. 3. Told Chandler I want to be with him and I love him! 4. Josh came by apartment when Mom was there - said he and Gina are going on a trip and he's going to ask her to marry him. Also, they've been together a few months but he wanted to give me one last shot. (haha) oh yeah, he asked if I was giving Noah up and Mom slapped him across both cheeks! Lol… 5. Chandler has been offered an opportunity to go to Zurich, Switzerland for 3 months to a year… if he wins the case or does a good job then the law firm says they'll make him senior partner. 6. He wants Noah and me to go. 7. I'm going! 8. We leave in 2 weeks (Noah would be born there)!!!! WHEW that was a lot… thoughts?*

I can see she's read it. I suppose it's all sinking in. It seems to be taking her forever to respond. Finally, I can see she's typing back…

Danielle: *WHAT?!?! This is a lot. I just saw you… you've been busy! Ok, we need to squeeze in time to chat before the wedding? What do you have today? I'm free from now until lunch. I have a run through for my wedding hair at noon… want to go?*

Kiera: *Okay. I'm at Chandler's and he's sleeping. I can meet u at Magnolia's in like 40 min…*

Danielle: *Done! Add me to your crazy list! See ya then!!!!*

From the sound of it, I think she's pretty excited for me. I am too. I try to slide out of bed without waking Chandler, but he pulls me back in bed and begins kissing me. He says, "Where you sneaking off to?"

I say, "Danielle and I are meeting up for a quick coffee. I'll be back in a couple hours. You're going to work right?"

"Yes," he says. "There are a few things I need to tie up at the office before tomorrow. I decided I'd take tomorrow off since it's the rehearsal dinner and all. I mean, you do want me at the wedding right?"

"Umm… YES! Of course I want you at the wedding! Okay, well I'm sure I'll see you in a bit!"

I open the door to my apartment and pick out my clothes for the day. I hop in the shower. After I am done in the shower, I towel dry my hair, put on my Skin Waffle-Knit white robe, and walk out to the kitchen. Mom is already awake and eating breakfast. She smiles great big at me and says, "You decided to go to Switzerland didn't you?"

I laugh and say, "You amaze me! Yes, I did."

She stands and gives me the biggest hug ever. "Oh Kier, I'm so happy for the life you're about to start living!"

I say, "Thank you Mom!"

I tell her I have to get ready quickly so I can meet Danielle. I joke and say, "She needs to be filled in on everything."

Mom agrees.

I say, "You're welcome to join us."

"No, remember I'm going dress shopping for the wedding, but I'll be here when you get back! Besides, I'm sure you and Danielle will have lots to talk about without me!"

Walking into Magnolia's doesn't seem as strange as I thought it might. I suppose it's possible to put the bad memories of Josh aside and enjoy my favorite spot again. It was complete habit having Danielle meet me here, and I'm sure she didn't think about it too much either. I take in a deep breath as I look around. I see Danielle sitting, so I walk over. She looks beautiful as always. She greets me with a hug and a quick kiss on the cheek. We sit down and Danielle says, "Holy shit, Kier! What in the world? I can't believe all I've missed! I feel like you've lived a whole year in only a couple days!"

I laugh and say, "I feel the same way. It's crazy really. I mean things have been wild! Everything happened so fast, and without time to really think through. I mean the stuff with Chandler has been a no brainer, but then Josh showing up out of the blue with his news had me taken back. I was quickly able to decide things weren't right, and thank God!"

After I catch Danielle up to speed, we talk about all things wedding. Danielle seems so happy and vibrant. Her beautiful hair is super shiny from her recent smoothing treatment from Fringe, one of our favorite hair salons in the City. Her tanned skin is extra "bride perfect," and her nails are freshly done. I tell her how great she looks and she accepts the compliment. We finish up and head over to Fringe for her hair run through. Danielle tells me she's having bridal and boudoir pictures taken this afternoon and says I can join her. Honestly, this does not sound like something I want to be a part of, so I lie and say I made plans with Mom. She says, "I understand and I'm so glad we met up for this coffee and talk. I can't believe I'm going to be married in two days!!! Oh my gosh! Or, that you're moving out of the country with Chandler. This all seems so much like a dream."

I laugh and say, "I know. Everything has happened so fast!"

Danielle says, "I guess we'll be planning your wedding soon too, huh?"

"Ha! I certainly hope so, but not until I have my waist back!"

We both laugh. As we walk out of the bakery, I'm overwhelmed and a bit nostalgic. I mentally take note of how I feel. How leaving this time feels different than ever before. I try to hide my feelings from Danielle. I don't want to be too sappy. I know it may seem strange to feel this way, but Danielle and I are changing. Our lives are moving on. This may be the last time she and I meet like this. The last time we're two single women meeting at Magnolia's. We're growing up. I don't mean we won't still be a part of each other's lives, but things will definitely be different. Things will especially be different for at least 6 months to a year or more with me being out of the country. Who knows what Danielle will be up to when I get back? I stop walking, and she stops too. I think she may be having the same thoughts. She leans in and whispers, "Nothing is going to change! I promise."

I smile back and so want to believe her. I throw my arms around her and say, "I'll see you at the rehearsal dinner tomorrow night! I can't wait. Oh, and by the way, Chandler is super excited too!"

"Yay! I'm so glad you're bringing him! I love you, Kier!"

"I love you too, Danielle!"

For the last time, standing in front of Magnolia's as single ladies, we say goodbye.

Chapter 25

An older lady with golden shoulder length hair welcomes Chandler, Mom, and me as we walk into the ballroom door of The Sanctuary Hotel. She greets each of us and thanks us for coming. I introduce myself, Mom, and Chandler. She says, "Oh, of course…I've heard so much about you! Your Danielle's best friend. I'm Shelly, Sam's Mom."

Standing next to her is a very handsome older man with salt and pepper hair wearing a black suit. Sally says, "And this is Sam's father, Gary."

We all say hello and shake hands, exchanging pleasantries. I look around and become a little confused as to why we're in this oversized ballroom for such a small wedding. *This is so Danielle*! *Of course her small is gigantic!* Finally, after walking around looking at all of the decorations on the tables and baby pictures of Danielle and Sam, I walk Chandler and Mom over to our table and get them settled in. Mom places her bag down in her chair and asks Chandler if he'd like to walk over to the bar and grab a cocktail. They excuse themselves and I sit down.

I hear a loud screeching voice coming my way, and immediately know its Danielle. Every time she gets excited or nervous she adopts this voice, and it's quite irritating actually. One time a few years back we were at a party and she spotted who she thought was Adam Sandler. Her voice and laughter got so loud, we were asked to leave the party. On the way out the man who she thought was Adam Sandler had taken his sunglasses off and Danielle was mortified she'd been wrong. She blamed him, and actually got in his face and said, "I can't believe you'd walk into a party trying to pose as an actor like that… I hope you got the rouse you were looking for. You JERK!"

Her behavior can be quite embarrassing, but after being friends with her for so long I'm used to this screech. Besides, it's her rehearsal dinner, I don't think she'll get kicked out of here.

I slowly turn around and say, "Danielle, everything looks beautiful! I knew it would, but really it's just lovely!"

She says, "Oh Kier! I'm just so excited and happy you're here with Chandler and your mom, everything is simply wonderful! Have you met Sam's parents Sally and Gary?"

"Yes, and they seem lovely. So, show me everything…"

Danielle walks me around the ballroom to show me the details. In addition to the rehearsal dinner being held in this ballroom, the ceremony will take place here, too. Truly, it's beautiful. Every detail is astounding. From the orchids to the chocolate waterfall, the ambiance is breath- taking. She walks me over to the area where the ceremony will be held. There is a white runner for the aisle with chairs on either side. I'm surprised to see only about fifty chairs. *This really will be a small wedding after all.* Danielle will not have a flower girl or ring bearer, so there are already flower petals leading to the canopied arbor where Sam and Danielle will say their vows. The whole scene is simply elegant. It looks like something out of a movie.

Danielle introduces me to the priest and to a few familiar faces I'd seen through the years. Mostly just her two aunts and uncles and a few cousins. I'd met most of them before at her college graduation gala, but I never mentioned a prior meeting. Most of her extended family was from out of town so, although she and I'd been friends forever, most of them did not know me too well.

Finally, I see Danielle's Mom, and run to embrace her in a long hug. I haven't seen her in at least a year or more. She says, "Kiera, you look so beautiful! Danielle tried to fill me in on all of your news, and boy was that some scoop." She winks at me and then begins rubbing on my belly, which I'm not too sure how I feel about it. It sort of feels awkward. I'm happy when she stops. She says, "It's a boy, right?"

"Yes, his name is going to be Noah."

"I love the name Noah!"

I'm not too sure why, but I'm beginning to feel uncomfortable, and I want to sit down with Mom and Chandler. I excuse myself from the conversation and walk over to the table. Dinner is beginning to be served, and we make small talk around the table with a few of Danielle's co-workers. I know most of them and do wonder how much they know about me, because two of the ladies are staring daggers at Chandler, and I've caught a few whispers.

Dinner seems to go on forever. It seems as though Danielle invited the whole guest list to this event. I joke with

Chandler, and say, "If she invited the whole guest list to the rehearsal, couldn't she have just done the real wedding tonight."

He smiles and says, "I'm sure she knew they were all in town and just wanted to include them for food purposes."

Feeling embarrassed I say, "Do you always find the good in people?"

"I try to," he says.

I smile and lay my head on his shoulder. I see Mom stand up in the corner of my eye where she and Danielle's mom are talking. They always liked each other pretty well and definitely kept open communication between themselves to keep us out of trouble growing up.

Danielle raises her voice, "Okay, wedding party!" (Which consists of Danielle, Sam, me, Seth (the blind date), the priest, and Danielle's dad)… Danielle continues, "It's time to do a run through, and if everyone not in the wedding party wouldn't mind stepping out into the vestibule, there will be cocktails and dessert for you."

No one seems to mind, and they all scatter rather quickly. I think about if I weren't pregnant I, too may have snuck out for the cocktails, because at this point I could really use one.

Once I see Seth (the blind date), better known as Sam's best friend, I'm reminded of how awkward that night was. It was the night my life changed forever. Seth is being really cool and friendly. He hasn't even mentioned the blind date night. Thank God! He has a date with him and she looks pretty cute and cheerful. I'm sure he's moved past the awkwardness of that dreadful night a few weeks back. It's crazy to think of everything that's transpired since the events unfolded with the pregnancy. I'm just content with how things are turning out.

The rehearsal literally takes ten minutes, and that was two times through. Not feeling too well, I tell Danielle I'm going to grab Mom and Chandler so I can go back home for an early night. I say, "I need to get some rest for tomorrow!"

She's understanding and in her lightened, excited, squeaky voice she says, "I'll see you tomorrow!" And she seals it with an, "EEK!"

Back at my apartment Mom says she's going to bed. Chandler says he'll stay a while if I'd like. I say, "Of course I want you to stay. Make yourself comfortable, I'm going to step back to the bathroom real quick. My back is kind of hurting. I must have lifted something wrong, or something. I'm going to take a couple Tylenol and get my heating pad. I'll be right back."

Chandler rubs my feet as I lay on the heating pad, and we talk about the rehearsal dinner. He says only positive things as usual, which I love about him. "It was a nice time" he whispers.

Finally, the Tylenol and heating pad have relieved the pain, and we say goodnight. As I'm closing the door behind him he says, "I'll bring over breakfast in the morning."

I smile back and say, "That'd be wonderful!"

I go back to my bed and quickly jump onto Instagram. I look at pictures from the evening. Danielle has posted several collages and various other photos. She's so photogenic. I scroll down and see a picture of Josh and Gina. My mouth drops wide open. *Why am I still following her I wonder?* It's a picture of the two of them on an island with crystal clear water behind them and she's flashing a ring. I literally laugh out loud…he used the same ring. *How original.* A strange feeling overwhelms me, and I realize if Josh decides to have anything to do with Noah, Gina will be his step-mom. This makes me feel very odd. I decide to unfollow Gina. I've seen enough. I'm not sad or hurt. I just honestly don't want to think about either of them right now.

I let out another chuckle as I think about how funny it is she's wearing the ring he proposed to me with. I have to tell Danielle because I know she'll see the picture on Instagram. I send her a text:

Kiera: *Ha! Did you see they're engaged?*

Danielle: *Yes… what a Jerk!*

Kiera: *same ring!!! Lol*

Danielle: *you're kidding right?*

Kiera: *nope… I'll sleep with a big smile tonight!!*

Danielle: *I bet… night…see ya tomorrow!*

As I try to lay down, I notice the pain in my back again. I don't really want to take anymore Tylenol, so I decide to ignore it and eventually fall asleep.

I hear a knock at the door and throw on my Skin Waffle-Knit robe and go to the door. It's my love. He walks in with the yummiest smelling breakfast. Mom comes out of the guest room and says, "Yummy! This looks divine!"

Chandler sets the table and asks us to have a seat. He's just amazing. We eat breakfast and relax on the couch. Feeling a little lightheaded, I say, "I'm still having a dull aching pain in my back, but I'll just take another Tylenol. I can't imagine what I must have done to it."

Chandler says, "Are you sure you're okay? We could go to a quick clinic and have it checked."

I say, "No. I'm fine. Besides, I need to start getting ready for the wedding soon. I have to shower and do my hair."

"Ok. Well let me know if you change your mind. I don't mind taking you by one on the way to the wedding. I guess I'll go back to my place so you and your Mom can get ready. Tell your Mom since you're going over early, she and I can grab a cab together."

I say, "Okay. She'll like that."

Looking in my mirror after my shower, I can already see the girdle is going to be a necessity, so I throw it in my bag. I'm not getting dressed until I get to Danielle's hotel room. She has a photographer coming to take pictures of us getting dressed. I'm sure it sounds wonderful to her and her flat tummy, but being six months pregnant, I'm not looking forward to that part. Oh well, just part of the sacrificing I have to do in order to make this her perfect day!

Before I leave, I tell Mom what Chandler said about them cabbing it over to the hotel. She says, "I'd love to cab over with him." I kiss her goodbye, and she notices me holding my back and says, "Kier, are you sure you didn't hurt yourself?"

I say, "No, I'm not sure, but it'll have to wait until after this wedding."

She rolls her eyes at me, and my stubbornness I suppose, and I head off for the hotel. I see Louie in the lobby of my building. He says, "You look simply gorgeous, love."

I smile and say, "Thank you, Louie!" I hail a cab on the first try. *How awesome!*

As I walk into the hotel room, I hear Danielle and her Mom talking about something. I say, "Oops, should I give you two a minute?"

Sally says, "Don't be silly, Kier, come on in."

Feeling awkwardly out of place and a tad like I'm interrupting a moment, I continue in anyways. Danielle looks amazing! Her hair and make-up are all done, and the photographer is on the way. I say, "Wow! You're the most beautiful bride I've ever seen. Honestly!"

She smiles and gives me a long hug.

I walk over to my bag and pull out my good friend "the girdle," and we both laugh. I say, "Yep, today won't happen without her! I sure hope I can still zip up this dress."

We both laugh. There is truly no way to hide my pregnancy, and I'm becoming okay with that problem. A sharp pain tinges through my back so strong I have to sit down. Danielle says, "Holy cow! You okay?"

I say, "Yeah, I think I must have hurt myself somehow, or something yesterday. I'm not too sure. Don't worry about me, let's focus on this wedding! I'm fine."

We continue to get ready. The time flies by so fast, we can hardly believe we're less than an hour away from show time. I say, "How does it feel, Danielle? I mean, we've dreamed of this our whole lives and talked about it often, but I just can't imagine how you actually are feeling to be this close to being married?"

Danielle holds both of my hands in hers and says, "Wonderful! Wonderfully happy! That's how it feels! I'm utterly past excited and nervous, but it feels amazing!

Something tells me you'll be feeling the exact same way real soon!"

I smile at the thought of marrying Chandler.

Chapter 26

Standing in front of even this small group of people up here waiting on the doors to open, seems to take an eternity. Sam, surprisingly for a groom, seems very calm. He and Seth are teasing each other about something, but I'm not too sure what. I imagine it's something like what happened at the royal wedding when Prince Harry supposedly teased Prince William about it not being too late to back out of the marriage commitment.

As I'm looking around listening to the dreadful wedding music, I see Danielle's family and friends on one side and Sam's family and friends on the other. Sally looks a little emotional, and I can see she's holding a wadded up handkerchief. I suppose she plans on crying. *Oh hell! What if my crazy preggo emotions take me over, and I cry too? I'll surely look like a mess if so…* I look at Mom and Chandler. They each flash a smile at me, and smiling back, I feel at peace.

Finally, without inescapability, Danielle and Gary are walking down the aisle. She looks exquisitely elegant. She went a tad overboard on her dress since she opted for a small wedding. She's wearing an Allure, off-white gown, Mermaid style. It fits her body like a glove. She opted for no veil, and instead has a beaded halo head-piece draped around her forehead. Tears are streaming down Sally's face, and as I look at Sam he seems awestruck by Danielle's beauty.

Everyone is standing when Gary and Danielle reach the front of the room. Gary squeezes her hand and whispers something into her ear. I see he, too, is wiping away a tear. Danielle hugs him tightly, and the priest says, "Who gives this woman to this man?"

Gary not being able to keep things seriously (probably for sake of his own sanity), looks at Sally and says, "Do we?" Everyone laughs, and eventually he agrees by saying, "Her Mom and I."

The ceremony is over rather quickly, and I'm quite relieved. Not because it wasn't lovely, but my back feels so painfully dreadful. I don't think I could have stood much longer. I sit down at the table next to Chandler. Mom is mingling around the room with guests. She appears to be having a wonderful time. Chandler is worried about my back pain. I pop a couple of Tylenols, and agree that as soon as the wedding reception is over, I'll go to the hospital to see what's going on. We're pretty sure I've pulled something.

The D.J. calls for the "Best Man" and "Maid of Honor." Seth and I make our way to the front. I have my written speech from Danielle in one pocket, and my own ideas in the other. Since the other pocket with my own idea is actually empty, I decide I'll pull out her speech, and opt to add a few words of my own. I don't think she'll mind. I begin…

"Okay… Everyone listen up! Seriously, umm, I have three pages to get through here, and it could take some time." Everyone laughs. I wonder if I should tell them Danielle wrote the speech. Probably not… I continue on "Sam and Danielle, I'm so honored to be here today. To be a part of your special day..."

I'm boring myself as I read. Surely she doesn't expect me to read this. I feel like it was copied from a wedding speech site. I take a bold move, hoping not to cause Danielle to hyperventilate. I rip up her hand written speech and toss it up in the air. She doesn't seem surprised, so I decide to go ahead and wing it.

I say, "Well that was boring… let's try again. Alright guys, Sam you're getting a great girl, and Danielle, even though I feel like I just met Sam, probably because it's somewhat true, I think you're getting a great guy! Really, I do. Danielle and I go waaaay back. I'm talking waaaay back. Like so far back, I can't remember life without her. I remember when she fell in love with Leonardo Dicaprio. Do you remember that? You were like gonna marry him and stuff. You had a plan to meet him by the time you turned 15… like a mapped out, time lined plan! I mean he was totally hot, right? Especially, in *Titanic* with Rose and all. Anyways, enough about Leo! Danielle, I've always adored our friendship, our love, and life growing up together…Getting into trouble together; we've had some crazy times! Sam, this girl adores you as if you were Leo. Take that for what it's worth and run with it! I wish you two the most happiness you could ever dream of! Oh, and by the way Sam, if you hurt her I'll come after you!" At this, I hold up my glass of water and say, "Cheers to the two of you!"

Everyone claps and I sit down. Seth's speech literally consists of "Good luck you two! I love you man." And Sam stands up and chest bumps Seth making some disgruntled noise. It's quite awkward. I think I definitely win the award for the best speech!

After all of the customary dances, Chandler and I slow dance to Ed Sheeran's "Thinking Out Loud." When I lean over in obvious pain after the dance, Chandler says, "Okay, when are we going to the ER? This is ridiculous. You need to be examined to see what in the world is wrong with you."

I say, "I can't leave before it's over. How tacky would that be? She's my best friend…"

Chandler says, "Fair enough, I think it's almost over anyways because people are congregating by the back door."

He's right. Sam and Danielle are getting ready to leave in the limo. Everyone heads outside to send them off.

Sally is hot on Danielle's tail, not sure what she's doing but she seems to be on a mission. Once outside, I peek over the man's shoulder in front of me to try to see what Sally is doing. She appears to be whispering something to Danielle and handing her a check. They probably gave her some money for the honeymoon. It's so funny, Danielle does not need handouts. She makes a lot of money, but her parents are always giving her money. She hates when they do that, but this time she takes it. I guess it makes them feel like they are helping. I've always thought it was sweet.

I hug Danielle and say, "I'll miss you while you're gone."

"You'll be too busy with Chandler to miss me."

We blow bubbles as the limo drives off.

Chandler looks at me and says, "Well, that was a beautiful wedding, and now it's time to see what you've done to your back."

The Tylenol must have kicked in because I barely feel any pain, but I agree to go. We tell Mom we're going to get me checked out at the hospital. Mom says if it's okay she's going to go back to the apartment but to let her know if we need anything.

Chapter 27

We've been at NYU Langone Medical Center for two hours. They are pretty certain nothing is broken, and instead they think the pain is due to pre-term labor. Apparently the pain I've been feeling was contractions. I feel so stupid. We had no idea this could be the cause of the pain I'd been experiencing. I just thought I'd pulled something, but according to the doctor, my cervix has started dilating. I can't believe the back pain was actually labor pain.

Chandler is calling Mom on his cell to fill her in. We're waiting on someone to come back and give me a shot with Terbutaline in it to stop the labor. Apparently, I'm having way too many contractions for the doctor's comfort. I guess really, any contractions causing me to dilate this early is a concern, so I understand. I'm a little scared.

Chandler is being completely wonderful through this whole experience. We're both just relieved I came in and that Noah looks good on the ultrasound. Thank God I didn't keep putting this off. Chandler hangs up the phone with Mom and says, "Your Mom is on the way. I told her she didn't have to come, but she insisted."

I smile and say, "I'm sure she did."

The nurse comes in and administers the shot of Terbutaline. After she leaves the OBGYN comes back in. He says, "Well, after reviewing everything, we're going to keep you overnight for observation to make sure the contractions have stopped. Also, I spoke with your routine OB doctor, and he and I agree we should probably go ahead and do a small procedure to ensure you sustain the pregnancy."

I look at him intently, not sure what he means. He must see the confusion on my face because he says, "It's called a Cervical Cerclage. Basically, we put some stitches in to close the cervix up until it's time for delivery. It's an outpatient procedure, and we do it fairly often."

He stands staring at me, I suppose wanting my approval. Finally, after looking at Chandler for support, I say, "Okay. When can we do it?"

He says, "While you're here, works for me. The sooner the better really. So if that's good with you, then just relax and I'll have someone come up and take you down soon."

I say, "Okay, I got nothing else planned, so we might as well."

The doctor walks out of the room.

"Well, this is a bit more to digest than a pulled back muscle," I say to Chandler.

He says, "It sure is sweetie but everything will be alright. I promise…" He leans over the bed and gives me a kiss.

Mom walks in, and I ask Chandler if he can fill her in on the latest. I'm a bit overwhelmed. Luckily, as Chandler begins telling Mom the news, a nurse wearing blue scrubs comes in to take me down for the procedure. I say, "I've eaten a lot today, is that a problem?"

The nurse says, "Oh, not at all. You'll probably be awake. Usually they just give local anesthesia. It's a quick procedure."

As everyone said, the procedure seems to go by pretty quickly. I'm already on the way back up to my room. The nurse wheels me in, and Mom and Chandler both smile.

Chandler says, "Wow! Surgery… and you still look every bit as amazing!"

I reply, "That was hardly surgery."

Mom says, "So, it wasn't that bad?"

I say, "Not at all."

It's getting late, and I know Mom and Chandler must be tired from the wedding festivities and now the hospital. I say, "Why don't you two grab a cab and go home to sleep. I'll be fine until morning. If I need anything, I'll text you."

Chandler immediately says, "I'm not leaving. I'll stay here all night. Gretchen, why don't you go get rest. Honestly, I don't mind at all."

Mom looks so tired. She looks over at me while standing up grabbing her bag, and says, "This is a good man, Kier! A really good man. If you two really don't mind, then I think I'll go ahead and head back. I'm not as spry as the two of you, and apparently my new grandson, too."

Mom kisses my cheek and says, "Get some rest. Have Chandler text me if you need anything. I love you."

"I love you too, Mom."

Chandler gently closes the door behind Mom, and he lies down on the stretch out chair. He looks miserably uncomfortable, but doesn't complain one time. The nurse gives him a blanket and says, "Here is a daddy blanket for you."

Neither of us correct her, mostly because it seems natural I suppose. I mean he may not biologically be Noah's dad, but he's the only dad present. We try to close our eyes, but every time we fall asleep either beeping noises of machines or nurses come in and interrupt.

At around 4 a.m., a nurse puts monitors on my belly to listen to Noah's heartbeat. Any other time, I'd love to listen to his little heartbeat, but at four in the morning, and after not getting much sleep, it sounds like a stampede of horses. Not so sweet.

By the time 9:30 a.m. rolls around, I'm dying to leave this room and place. I've asked every person who's come in when I'll be able to leave. There is a knock at the door before whoever it is barges in. I've learned privacy doesn't exist in hospitals. It's the doctor. He says, "I got great news! Everything looks wonderful! Baby is fine, and the procedure went well. I think you can go home now. I do want you to follow up with your regular OB next week, but I think you're good to go."

As he turns to walk out, he spins back around and says, "Oh, I forgot a couple things. No intercourse until your OB says, and for a while you should stay in bed as much as possible. Lastly, no travel for probably the rest of your term."

He leaves the room. I feel like my heart has just been ripped from my chest. No travel for the rest of my term. I can see Chandler is letting that soak in, too. He says, "I'm not going. I won't leave without you."

Quickly I say, "Stop that nonsense, now. I mean it, Chandler. Seriously, stop it. I only have about 3 months left until delivery. That's not long. Really we can do this. You have to go. I can come after the baby is born."

Chandler says, "I don't even want to think about this right now. I just want to get you home and get you all snuggled in your bed. I will take care of you for the rest of the weekend and not worry about anything else.

I pat him on the shoulder as he's leaned over the hospital bed. I say, "That sounds nice… I can't complain about that. I've never wanted to be home as bad as I do this minute."

I never knew it can take up to a million years to finally be discharged from a hospital, but apparently it's true. We were told we could go around 9:30 a.m. and we're just now being released at 12:45 p.m. I'm starving. The hospital food is nasty, so I haven't eaten too much since yesterday. Chandler knows how hungry I am. He said as soon as we get home, he'll get us some food.

I can't help but think about the possibility of him leaving for Switzerland without me. I feel so sad and lonely imagining life without him, even for a short time. I thought everything was set to go, and now here we are again pending this brutal, unwanted separation. I can see it in his eyes. I know he's thinking about it, too. I must admit, I thought it was sweet he didn't want to leave me, but I won't let that happen. He has to do this. Things will work out, I just know it. It's such a huge career opportunity, and besides it's only like three or four months.

Downstairs, I wait inside the lobby while Chandler grabs a cab for us. A text comes through from Mom. Since she's been staying here, she's been texting me more and calling less. It's really nice actually. I open the text:

Mom: *I sent Danielle a text just now letting her know everything that's going on. I figured she'd want to know. Not sure if they've* *boarded their flight yet, but she'll get it and when she does I just want you to not know it was me who filled her in.*

I guess the next thing I need to work on with her are shorter texts. This is like a novel!

Kiera: *Got it! Thanks Mom!*

Chandler comes in and says, "Got a cab. Let's go."

Back at my apartment, Chandler does exactly what he says he'd do. He pulls my covers back like a turn-down service, and tucks me in ever so gently. He says, "I'll go to get you some yummy food. What sounds good to you?"

Without hesitation I say, "Steak!"

He says, "Then steak it is!"

After Chandler leaves, Mom comes in my room and says, "Why the sad face?"

I tell her what the doctor said about travel. She says, "Oh dear. I'm so sorry, but three months isn't that long, right? It'll go by fast. You'll see, it will. I can come visit more frequently, too. I know it's not ideal, but you two can make it work."

I say, "I know, it just seems so sad. I love him so much, I can't imagine not seeing him every day. When the doctor said no travel, his face looked so disappointed. As soon as the doctor left the room he looked at me and said he wasn't going without me. I know he meant it, but I told him that was nonsense, and that three months would go by so fast. He has to go. I can't let him know how sad I am about it. He really wants this career move. I'll support him, even if it's painful and I'm screaming 'PLEASE STAY' on the inside. I'll never let him know."

Mom says, "You're doing the right thing, and that's true love. You can't hold him back. He'd always wonder what might have been. Let him go. Encourage him to go. Three months really isn't that long. The two of you'll have plenty of time, probably the rest of your lives to be together anyways."

She tells me to get some rest, and I fall to sleep. When I wake up and look at the clock I'm shocked at how long I slept. It's after 4 p.m. I suppose when Chandler got back with my food, he didn't want to wake me, and I'm grateful for that. I can hear Mom and Chandler talking in the living room. I try to listen in on what they're saying, but I can't make it out, so finally I say, "Hello! I'm hungry! Got food or what?"

Chandler walks back towards my room and says, "Well look who decided to wake up? I'll heat up your food and bring it to you."

I blow a kiss at him and wait for my food. I inhale every bite until my plate is clean. Chandler cleans up my dishes and says, "Move over, I want to lay here with you."

I scoot over in the bed making room for Chandler as he crawls in beside me. The TV is on, and as we lay here with our heads together, I turn the channel to our go-to station, The Food Network. We snuggle up as close as we can, and spend the rest of the evening like this. It's approaching 10:30 p.m., and Mom comes in to say goodnight. Chandler says, "Yeah, I guess I should turn in, too."

Not wanting him to leave I say, "Just stay here. Do you mind?"

He says, "Of course not. I'd like that."

In my mind, I'm thinking what I just said is exactly what my selfish-self wants to say about Switzerland, 'Just stay here', but I know better.

Chapter 28

The last three and a half weeks have flown by so fast. Chandler was able to leave a week and a half later than originally planned for Switzerland. This is good because now we only have about two months and 3 weeks before we can be together, or at least until I can travel. Saying two months sounds so much better than three months.

Chandler and I have spent every single moment together, soaking in as much of each other as we possibly can. There have been numerous conversations over the last few weeks about him not going. All of those conversations were initiated by him. I've remained strong and encouraging. I think we're both finally at as much peace about the situation as we can be. When we went for my OB follow-up, the doctor pretty much agreed with everything the hospital had suggested. I guess I was holding out hope, at least for the travel part, but he said it really wasn't a good idea. I think having two doctors say the exact same thing solidified that part for us.

He's leaving tomorrow, and I don't think it'll actually hit me until he boards the plane. I'm trying to stay strong and talk positively, but in reality, I'm scared as shit to be alone. Especially without him. It's so weird because this isn't my personality at all. I'm generally very independent, but he's done such a great job taking care of me that I think I may go insane alone. This bed-rest thing is for the birds! Mom left three weeks ago, on the Wednesday after Danielle's wedding, but she calls or sends texts daily. Her texts have gotten shorter, thank God!

Danielle got back last week from her honeymoon in Belize, and she promises to come by at least three times a week to hang out once Chandler is gone. Sam works late a lot, so I'm sure her frequent visits won't be a problem with him. Chandler is so awesome, he's been spending his evenings cooking up dinners and freezing them in my freezer. He says this was so I'll always have food available in case no one is around.

We've decided for the long run, to break my lease and live together at his place since he has a lot more room once Noah is born. I can't believe how fast this is all happening.

Of course, if he isn't done with his job over in Switzerland, we'll be there for a while and rent something to get us through however long the assignment takes. Until we see how long the Switzerland job lasts, we really won't know exact plans.

While Chandler is gone, he's given me a couple names of handy men to get some estimates for creating Noah's room the way I'd like. I chose one after calling all of them the day before yesterday. The one I selected came over right away.

We're using one of his spare bedrooms as the nursery. I'm happy to at least have that to work on while he's gone. It'll be something fun to keep me entertained. The room is so much bigger than my guest bedroom. We'll even have room for a twin bed in the room. The window has a window seat, and the room is airy and calm. It's truly the perfect nursery.

We finally got all of the furniture in, and I'm storing it in my guest room until everything is ready at his place. Once we get the nursery painted and bead-boarded, Chandler said I can pay Bob, the handyman, to set everything up in the way I want it. Also, I won't need to hire movers since it's just across the hall. Between Bob, Mom (when she visits),

Danielle, and Sam we should be able to manage the whole move. Really, that'll all work out perfectly!

I get out of the shower, and slip into my new silky, cream Araks robe Chandler got me last week. As much as I love my favorite white Waffle Knit Skin robe, it was beginning to get old after a while. Chandler was probably getting sick of seeing me in the same robe. Going from choosing Jimmy Choo or Prada outfits for work, to which robe is best for the day is a way different experience for me, but I'm adapting. The best part is no maternity clothes! My belly is definitely poking out in a major way. I look in the mirror at my profile, and long for my flat tummy to soon return.

As I walk out of the bathroom all wrapped up in my robe, Chandler whistles. *The man is truly crazy, or blind.* He says, "You look sexier than ever."

Over the last few weeks, we've talked about getting married a lot. I know we will, but I continue to tell him I don't want to rush anything. I definitely won't be getting married in my current condition at 28 and a ½ weeks pregnant, and with a belly the size of a basketball.

I've been really good about the bed-rest situation, but every once and a while a girl has to get out. Today Chandler and I are going to take lunch for a picnic in the park. I can't wait to get out of my apartment. The last time I left this place was almost a week ago for a doctor's appointment. I'm considered a "high-risk pregnancy"; therefore, I now go weekly to the doctor. So far, everything has been good. The best thing about the weekly appointment is getting out of the house.

I see Chandler standing in the kitchen looking into the picnic basket. I say, "Did you get everything?"

"As a matter of fact I did," he says. "I have two beef brisket croissants with my special BBQ sauce, two Fuji apples, two balsamic salads with cucumbers and craisens, two bottles of orange soda, and key lime pie for dessert. Can you think of anything else?"

I say, "Wow! Nope, I sure can't…I never should have questioned you! It sounds delicious! You're remarkable!" and then it slips, and I say, "I'm going to miss you."

He embraces me as tightly as my belly allows. He says, "Not as much as I'm going to miss you. Kier, I'm going to work non-stop to wrap things up over there as fast as I can. You're my motivation, and I can't wait to get to be with you and Noah. I hate it that you can't go. It's true in the beginning, I thought there was no way I could go without you. I'm so glad you're making me go. This will be a major life change for our future. This success will take us very far. I love you for your selflessness. It's going to be really hard to get on that plane tomorrow, and I couldn't have done it without your support. I love you, Kier, and I can't wait to spend the rest of our lives together. The time will go by fast. It will."

I lean in to kiss him. One, because a speech like that deserves a kiss, but two, because I can't speak. I feel a major lump in my throat as I hold back my tears. If I speak the tears will fall, and I have to remain strong. *'Que Sera, Sera', whatever will be, will be.* Everything will be fine. Chandler grabs the picnic basket, and we walk down to grab a cab.

The chances of him being here for Noah's birth are zero, and I've come to grips with that. I mean, it'll probably happen spontaneously, and he'll not have enough notice. He keeps telling me he's going to make every effort to come, but I'm not going to hold him to it. I've wondered if Josh will want to know when the baby will be born. I haven't heard from him since the night at my apartment when he came to give me "one last chance," and then said he was asking Gina to marry him. Who knows what to expect. One thing I know for sure is that Danielle says she'll be there, day or night with bells on, and I know she will, that I can count on.

Mom actually called yesterday to tell me she and Gage had broken up. I wasn't too surprised. When she was here visiting, they hardly spoke to each other. When they did, it never seemed too meaningful. She said she may try to plan on coming and staying from my 34th week on, and honestly I hope she does. That would be next month, so it gives me something to look forward to.

The cab stops on Central Park West (8th avenue), and we hop out. We walk for a few minutes until we see a nice spot for a blanket and picnic. It just so happens it's in view of Heckscher Playground, and a million little kids running wild. I smile at the sight and Chandler seems to be smiling too. We're both watching a little blonde headed three year old running freely, and finally I say, "One day that'll be Noah."

Chandler nods his head and says, "I can't wait to watch him grow."

We open our picnic basket and begin eating our food. Everything is perfect. Everything except that each passing moment is bringing us closer to his departure. He's leaving first thing in the morning, and I can't get it off of my mind.

It's the elephant in the room, or in this case the park. We finish eating our food in silence.

Once we pack up, Chandler lays back on the blanket and pats his chest for me to lay my head down too. We lay there in silence for a while before Chandler says, "I love you so much." I say nothing, and can feel the tears begin to flow freely down my cheeks. I already miss him and he's still here. I dread tomorrow immensely.

Back at my apartment, we sit on the couch all cuddled up. We're enjoying each second wrapped up together in each other's bodies. I don't want this night to end because I know if we close our eyes morning will come too fast, and he'll be leaving.

Chapter 29

Finally around 2:00 a.m. last night, we made our way back to my bedroom to go to sleep. It took me forever to fall asleep, and I'm really not sure if I ever fully did. I'd equate the overall night to hotel sleep. Basically, I was in and out. Mostly in.

The alarm clock buzzes, and I look over at it, 6:00 a.m. Chandler shoots out of bed as I hit the off button. Chandler has been staying at my place since Bob the handy man started working on the nursery, and the paint fumes are quite strong. I get up, too. I'm so sleepy I can't focus too much on my feelings about today. I'm not going with him to the airport for many reasons. The biggest reason is the bed rest thing, and also I think it'll be easier to say goodbye from here as opposed to dragging it out at the airport before he walks through security.

It's for the best that I not go to the airport. While Chandler is in the shower, I make him a cup of coffee to go. As I hear the water in the shower shut off, I feel so sad because I know he'll be gone in a few short minutes. Danielle said she'll be by this morning to hang out, and I hope she comes soon. I know I'm about to be a mess when he walks out the door. I shoot Danielle a quick text:

Kiera: *Hey! When can u come? He's about to leave and I'm already sad and dreading it…*

Immediately, she texts me back:

Danielle: *20 min…*

Okay! 20 minutes, that's not so bad. I can make it that long. Besides, I need to brush my teeth and clean up a bit myself. Chandler comes out of the bathroom and he's rolling his luggage towards the living area. It took us forever to pack for this trip. With a half-smile on his face he says, "Yum, the coffee smells so good."

I look at him and feel as if I could crumble. I seriously want to cry. Secretly, I still want him to change his mind, but I know it's an important career move and two and a half months isn't that long when you have a lifetime to spend together. *I can do this!* I swallow the gulp of emotions rising up in my throat with a large glass of water. Chandler picks up his coffee and rolls his luggage over closer to the door. It's obvious he doesn't really want to leave.

I walk over next to him. He wraps his arms around me and says, "I'm going to miss you. I love you, I love Noah, and I pray to God that this time soars by so we can begin the rest of our lives together."

Standing by the door, he gets down on his knee, reaches in his pocket and says, "Kiera, I had plans to do this some place special, but the more I think about it the more it makes sense. Listen, I love you more than I've ever loved anyone. I want to spend the rest of my life with you and Noah."

He opens the tiny little box, pulls out a beautiful round cut diamond ring, and says, "Kiera, before I go, I want to know one thing… Will you marry me?"

This is the most incredible moment of my life! It's exactly what I've always dreamed of. I've never felt surer of anything as I say, "YES! YES! I'll marry you! I love you so much Chandler!" We kiss and hug in a swaying motion, back-and-forth for a few moments.

As we say goodbye, I no longer feel as sad, but I actually feel my spirit's been lifted. We're ENGAGED! I'm

ENGAGED! I suppose Chandler did this on purpose… he probably knew being engaged would help me through our separate time. I'm not sure if it will, but it sure does help with our goodbyes. I feel elated about the future. It's hard for me to focus on him leaving, as good as I feel in this moment. I can't wait to tell Danielle! I have to call Mom! This is so wonderful. I mean we've talked about it, and I knew it was coming, but what perfect timing. This really softens the blow of him leaving. Not only do I have Noah to look forward to, but now I get to plan a wedding! In some crazy way, even with Chandler's leaving, this feels like the best day of my life.

As I close the door behind Chandler, I look down at my ring. I'm excited beyond compare. My ring is gorgeous! It appears to be about a carrot and a half, or more. The perfect size really. I can't stop staring at it. Surprisingly, I'm not crying at all. Chandler was so smart to do this today. I mean, he knows me so well. I think about him saying he wanted to propose in a special place, and my thoughts go to Josh's proposal, and how the place he chose seemed perfect at the time. I'm reminded of how our lives weren't right for each other. I laugh at the irony. For once I can see it isn't about the scene being perfect for an engagement, it's about love. I'm so in love, and I feel so happy it's with Chandler.

The door buzzes. Quickly I hide my ring behind my back as I run over to let Danielle in. I open the door and can barely contain myself as I screech, "HI!!!"

She says, "Hi! I wasn't expecting you to be so chipper. How long has he been gone?"

Ignoring her question, I smile, and can't keep it a secret any longer! I say, "LOOK!"

I hold out my ring finger, and Danielle and I both start jumping up and down in circles holding onto each other's arms, squealing like little girls in a candy store. Immediately, I realize women on bed rest probably shouldn't jump, so I sit down on the sofa. She says, "OH MY! This is so wonderful, Kier! I'm so happy for you! He's completely brilliant to do this before leaving the country! I think he's truly amazing, and I couldn't have hand-picked one better for you! Gosh Kier, I'm just so flipping excited for you and Noah! So when's the wedding?"

Laughing I say, "I've literally been engaged for 15 minutes. We didn't discuss the date, but I can for sure say when I have my flat tummy back, so at least a while after Noah is born."

Danielle says, "I agree. No rush anyways! Have you told your Mom? She's going to be so thrilled. She knew you two were right for each other from the first time she saw you both together!"

"That's true. She totally called it. I'm going to call her in a little bit! She's probably not up yet."

Danielle says, "You should totally Facetime her! Then she could see the ring and all!"

Again, laughing hysterically at Danielle, I say, "She's just learned to text. Do you really think she could Facetime? Besides, she doesn't even own an iPhone."

Danielle says, "Oh well, that won't work then. Anyways, just call her!"

"I will in a little bit."

We walk over to Chandler's place, and I show Danielle the plans we've come up with for the nursery. Of course she loves everything, and like me, gets really giddy over every detail. Danielle asks me if I called the nanny agency, and I say, "No."

She says, "They can have a really long waiting list. You really should call them soon."

"I don't think I'll be needing a nanny after all," I say. "I'm going to stay home with Noah. Chandler wants me to, and I really can't imagine leaving him. With Chandler being away, and us not really knowing when he'll be done, it really makes since for me to stay home since we might have to travel back-and-forth from here to Switzerland."

Danielle seems super excited about this plan. She says, "Oh my gosh! This is perfect! I think it's wonderful you'll stay home with Noah! Truly, I'm super happy. I wonder what I'll do if I get pregnant… it has to be really hard to watch someone else raise your baby. I guess I haven't given too much thought to it. Hmm. Definitely something to think about. It would be hard not to work though."

I say, "Well, I'm sure whatever you choose will be right for you. If this all would have happened to me this time last year, I'm not sure I'd be staying home. It seems like the right thing to me now."

Around 9 a.m. I call Mom. She answers on the first ring. She knew Chandler was leaving today, and I suppose she expected me to call. Immediately upon answering the phone she says, "How are you?"

I giggle and say, "I'm okay."

Then before we can make any small talk or pleasantries, I excitedly say, "Mom, Chandler and I got engaged this morning before he left!"

She says, "Oh Kier! You have no idea how happy I am to hear this wonderful news! This is fantastic! I mean I thought it would happen, but what an appropriate moment. He's just marvelous, dear! I love it!"

We continue on with our conversation a few more minutes. She, too, asks if we've set a date, and I say the same thing I said to Danielle. Basically we didn't discuss the date, but it for sure would be when I have my flat tummy back, so sometime after Noah is born. It seems to suffice her because she tells me about her travel plans, and when she'll be back. She says, "I know I said I'd come and stay from your 34th week on, but I've been thinking. Since Gage and I broke up, there is really no reason I need to wait five more weeks, so if you don't mind I was thinking I might come sooner? I figure you could probably use my help around your place anyways. So is that a problem?"

Feeling overly excited my Mom is coming sooner, I say, "Not a problem at all! I'd love you to come earlier! Sounds like a perfect idea to me!"

She says, "Fantastic! That settles that! I'll start looking a tickets, and maybe be there by the end of the week or sometime next week. I'll text you in a bit and let you know what I get." I say, "Perfect!"

I hang up my phone and tell Danielle Mom is coming either this week or next week instead of my 34th week. She says, "That'll be really good. I think you'll feel so much better having someone here with you."

I agree with her. I walk into the kitchen to heat up some of the homemade food Chandler left, and Danielle is extremely impressed with my fully stocked refrigerator. She says, "Holy cow! Chandler did this, didn't he?"

I smile really big and say, "Yep!"

She looks through the endless supply of casseroles, sandwiches, pastas, and pizzas and says, "He's incredible, Kier…"

"I think so too, but if you think this is a lot, you should see his refrigerator. It's full, too!" Danielle says, "Get out? You're joking…"

Laughing I say, "Seriously! He's that incredible!"

Danielle stays with me until around noon, and then she says she needs to go into the office, only if I think I will be okay. I tell her I'm fine, and thank her for staying with me. I really am so happy I got engaged today. I know we didn't really get to celebrate, but it really was an awesome distraction to my sadness, and I'm so thankful he chose today.

Chandler called to tell me he'd boarded this morning around 10. I think the flight is about 8 to 8 and 1/2 hours, so he should land sometime around six or so tonight. The six hour time difference should make things interesting… Switzerland is six hours ahead of me.

Surprisingly, I wasn't sad when he called. I'm still so happy about us being engaged, I'm in a lackadaisical state of mind. I'm also feeling upbeat over my Mom's arrival soon, and everything seems to be falling into perfect timing.

Chapter 30

Even with the crazy time difference, Chandler has called every day at least three to four times, just like he said he would. We also text a lot throughout the day, which is nice. A couple of times we've Facetimed so he could see my belly. Still he says I'm the most beautiful woman he's ever seen… *God I love that man.* He also makes me put the phone next to my belly while he talks to Noah. It's really sweet. He may not be Noah's biological dad, but he's as wonderful as it gets, and Noah and I are super lucky for a future with him!

I can't believe it's already been two weeks. I miss him a lot, but the plans with the nursery and the move are keeping me busy while helping the time to go by very quickly. At 32 and a half weeks pregnant, time moving quickly is a good thing. I can't sleep at night. I toss and turn constantly, and I feel uncomfortable no matter what position. I'm so ready for this pregnancy to be over. I mean, it's sweet at times, like when I feel Noah moving around in my stomach, but for the most part I'm over it! Sometimes, it's hard to believe I'm this close, but I guess that's what happens when you're halfway through your pregnancy before you even know you're pregnant.

I haven't moved any of my furniture over just yet because I'm waiting to have the nursery done first, and then I'll move on to that part. My lease is up in twenty days so there is still some time.

To my benefit, Bob the handy man has been pleasantly quick, and extremely thorough. Noah's nursery has already been painted the color we chose a while back, Silver Chain by Benjamin Moore, which was the light silver-ish gray for the top of the wall. We stayed consistent with our original plan, and put the bead board on the bottom. We painted it the Temptation color which was the deep, dark gray. The furniture has all been put together and placed methodically where I told Bob to place it. I watched everything from the rocking chair in the corner of the nursery.

Everything looks great. It's better than I ever imagined! Being in the nursery makes things seem surreal! When we hung the letters spelling Noah over the crib like Chandler suggested, I felt so warm and fuzzy. It literally made it look complete. I texted him a picture of it, and he immediately texted me back how awesome it looked. For the most part, the nursery is close to being finished. I have a few loose ends to tie up, like making sure we have everything a new baby needs and luckily I have a check list from one of the thousands of magazines about babies I'm using to help me know what to do. Every time Danielle comes by, she has a baby book or magazine with her in tow. It's a good thing, because I need all of the reading material I can get. It's been a long time since I've been around any babies. Sure, I babysat in junior high and high school, but that was a gazillion years ago. In a lot of ways, I'm depending on these books to get me through!

My Mom was able to catch an early flight like she planned and came in late last night. I'm so happy she's here. She came in and pretty much went straight to bed. She said she might sleep in, and of course I told her it would be fine. When she wakes up, we're going across the hall. I'm going to show her the nursery. I can't wait for her to see it. She did comment on my protruding belly, and how cute I looked before going to bed last night. I suppose it has poked out a bit more since she was here last. I feel like it doubles in size daily!

I really hope she wakes up soon because I need to get out, and a walk across the hall usually suffices. This bed rest stuff is getting old fast. At my last doctor visit, he said I still need to be taking it easy since I was having more contractions than he would like to see. Luckily for me, between my Mom and Danielle, they will make certain I barely have to lift a finger.

The doctor said our goal is to keep the baby inside for at least another 4 weeks at a minimum. He said I shouldn't worry because survival rate gets better with each day, and the baby looks healthy. The main thing is I need to stay off my feet as much as possible. I asked if the cerclage was doing its job, since I thought it would prevent preterm labor. The doctor said it would only help if I have an incompetent cervix. He is now suggesting with the amount of contractions I've had at the last two visits, he's not sure the cerclage will be enough for me to carry full-term. He says most likely I won't carry full-term and depending on how early Noah comes, they can do some sort of steroid to help mature the baby's lungs. It all sounds a little scary to me, but the doctor doesn't seem too worried. I've come to accept it, and I'm trying not to worry too much. I'm leaving it in God's hands.

Finally at 9:45 a.m., I decide Mom has slept long enough. I really want to show her the nursery, so I intentionally start making loud noises in the kitchen. I open up the bottom freezer drawer and fumble around looking for one of the breakfast burritos Chandler made. I would have starved had he not left me with all of this yummy food. He even labeled everything so I could see what it was. I decide on an egg and cheese burrito with bacon. He wrote on it to warm it in the microwave for one minute and a half.

I sort of close the freezer harder than normal, and abruptly grab a plate letting the door slam behind me. I place the breakfast burrito on the plate and slam the microwave door shut. When the minute and a half is up, I let the beeping go the whole time, instead of stopping it early. I'm pretty sure my noisy kitchen escapades have worked, because I can hear Mom in the bathroom as she just flushed the toilet. I kind of giggle under my breath at how juvenile I am for intentionally trying to wake her up, and also that my plan worked.

She comes out while I'm sitting at the table eating my breakfast burrito and comments on how wonderful breakfast smells. I tell her there are about thirty of them in the freezer. She too was just as impressed as Danielle by all of the food Chandler made, and left for me. I say, "You didn't think I actually cooked, did you?"

She laughs and says, "I was wondering…"

She heats up her burrito, and sits down next to me. I say, "I can't wait to show you the nursery. You're going to love it!"

She says, "I can't wait to see it! I loved everything we picked out the day we all went shopping. What time does the handy man come? Will we be in his way?"

I almost choke laughing because I'm always around when Bob's there. I probably drive him insane, but some days he is the only human interaction I have not through a phone. Finally I say, "He doesn't mind. Besides, I need to start having him move some things from here to there. I'm not putting stuff in boxes, because there really isn't any reason to since we're just moving them across the hall."

Mom says, "When's your lease up here?"

"We've actually changed it a couple of times. Now it's at the end of the month. We are breaking the lease, or else I would have to pay another six months. I'm really excited to get moved over to his place. Hopefully, I can have everything switched within the next couple of weeks.

Chandler's place is much bigger and nicer. It'll be great! Plus it reminds me of him."

Mom says, "Surely we can move quicker than two weeks since I'm here. I can take care of most everything, except the big furniture. I don't want it to take too long in case little Noah decides to come early. Plus, you need to feel settled and do some nesting. I'll start moving stuff over once you show me around. I'm so excited for you and Noah, Kier! Chandler is so good to you, and I think Noah will be so happy with him! Have you heard anything from Josh?"

I shake my head no and say, "Honestly, Mom, I don't really expect to anytime soon."

"What about the birth certificate?" she says. "Will you give Noah his last name?"

Thank goodness I had already done my research on this. I say, "Well actually, a few weeks ago before Chandler left, he and I did some research. He even spoke to an attorney friend from law school who practices family law here in New York. Interestingly enough, protocol in the state of New York says an unwed father's name cannot be listed on the birth certificate without his consent. So I suppose I will do what's right and ask Josh if he wants his name listed. I mean it's the noble thing to do, right?"

Mom nods her head "yes" although I know she's thinking exactly what I'm thinking. Neither of us want him to share his name with Noah, but I have to do what's right. She says, "Well, why don't you just send him a text? I would like to know what he's thinking about that. And just because you list him as the father, doesn't mean you have to give Noah his last name."

"I'm not so sure this is a text conversation, but the more I think about it, I don't really want to meet up with him or talk to him on the phone either. Ugh! I'm not sure what to do."

I hastily grab my phone and begin typing. "I'll just type it out and see what it looks like before I decide to send it." I read it to my Mom.

Kiera: *Hate to bother you… I need to know if you want your name on the birth certificate or not?*

I delete the text. It sounds too direct. *Hmmm.* I think for a few seconds before I start typing again.

Kiera: *Umm. Hi, I'm getting things in order for delivery and need to know if you'd like your name to be on the birth certificate. It's something I need to know.*

After reading it through aloud two times for Mom to hear, we both shake our heads and say, "No."

I attempt to come up with another text…

Kiera: *do you want your name on the birth certificate?*

My mom says she loves it, and I kind of do, too. Without hesitation I hit send.

Mom and I clean up our breakfast. She grabs a pile of my clothes that were sitting on my chair next to my sofa to take over to Chandler's apartment. She says, "Might as well go ahead and take some stuff now. No sense in going empty handed."

The smell of paint fumes becomes very prevalent, even in the hallway as I open the door to Chandler's apartment. I'm not sure at what point I will stop calling it Chandler's apartment, I guess once I move in things. As we walk in I say, "Bob? Are you here?"

I can hear him in the nursery. I show Mom to Chandler's closet and where to hang my clothes. Chandler cleared out his closet and made room for me before he left. It's a decent size closet for New York, but thank God he also has a wardrobe. I walk into the nursery and see Bob doing some last minute touch ups. I say, "Bob, this looks great!"

He's not a man of many words and simply says, "Glad you like it."

Bob steps out to get something to drink. I call for Mom. She walks in and says, "Oh my! Kier, this is the most handsome room I've ever seen for a baby boy! It looks like a designer did this. I love the furniture! The navy and gray hues complement the white, crisp linens so lovely. It's simply perfect! You two have an eye for this. Oh, and his sweet little name on the wall…It's just precious."

I'm so happy to hear how much she loves the room. I knew she would. Danielle says it makes her want to go ahead and have a baby so she can have me create her nursery. It truly is adorable. I can't wait to meet this little guy.

I hear my phone go off and wonder if it is Josh responding or Chandler sending me a text. I look at the clock to see what time it is in Switzerland, it's around 4 o'clock in the afternoon. I suppose it might be Chandler. I go pull my phone out of my purse and see it's a text from Danielle.

Danielle: *did your Mom make it? How are you?*

Kiera: *Yes she's here. We're over at Chandler's she's helping move a few things over today. She loves the nursery!*

Danielle: *glad she's there! I love the nursery too!!! I'll text you later.*

While I have my phone out, I send a text to Chandler since we haven't spoken yet today. Last night when he called before bed, I told him I might sleep in. I suppose that's why he hasn't sent me anything yet.

Kiera: *Good morning! Over at your place… Love you!*

I place my phone in my pocket and go back to the nursery where Mom is sitting in the rocking chair holding a teddy bear. She says, "What did he say?"

Confused I say, "Who?"

She says, "Was it Josh? Did he not respond to your text?"

I say, "Oh… No, that wasn't him. It was just Danielle, and then I sent Chandler a good morning text. Josh hasn't responded at all."

I pull my phone out, and look at the text I sent Josh. I can see it is marked as 'read', so I know he saw it. There is no response. I suppose he maybe is thinking about things. I'm not sure what I expect from him. I'm just trying to do the right thing.

We go back over to my place and I show my Mom some other things that we can move over. She says, "Okay, well, why don't you go rest on the couch over at Chandler's while I move this stuff?"

I smile and walk back over. Once inside, Bob says, "Chandler mentioned I'd be helping you move things over from your place. Want to tell me what to do?"

I say, "Today my Mom is going to try to move most of the small stuff. Why don't you wait until we're done with that, and then maybe we can get you to do the bigger stuff?"

He says, "Alright, maybe I'll come back later in the week with help."

"That would be perfect!" I say.

Bob closes the door behind him, and a few moments later my Mom is coming through with a pile of what looks like the rest of my clothes.

I laugh so hard at her and say, "Oh my goodness! Are you carrying all of my clothes?"

She says, "Not all of them, but as much as I could. No need to drag this out."

Feeling useless the rest of the afternoon, I sit on the couch with my feet propped up and watch as Mom goes back-and-forth between my place and Chandler's place with my belongings. It's now almost two o'clock, and I'm hungry. I ask my Mom if she wants some food. She says she'll run across the hall and grab one of the frozen meals Chandler left. I say, "No need to run across the hall, his refrigerator is just as full as mine. He stocked both!"

Mom is in disbelief as she says, "You're joking right?"

Shaking my head "no", I say, "What do you think?"

As she opens Chandler's freezer she says, "You're not joking?!? He is amazing, Kier… Truly, amazing."

We heat up some lasagna, and Mom makes us a salad. We have lunch. I keep checking my phone for a text from Chandler, but nothing has come through yet. He's usually called or texted by this time, and I'm a little unsure what's going on. I send another quick text.

Kiera: *Hi! Not sure if you got my last text? I hope you're having a great day! Love you*

I hit send. For some reason, I'm not feeling quite right. I don't want to alarm my mom, so I decide to tell her I'm going to take a short nap. I lay down on the sofa and cover up with a white, fuzzy throw. Mom doesn't ask any questions, and continues moving my things over from my apartment. As Mom shuts the door behind her walking in with another load of my belongings, I look down and see I have soaked myself. Feeling frantic, I scream for Mom. She comes running towards me and I say, "I peed myself."

My mom looks worried and she says, "Oh no! Honey, I think your water broke. We've got to get to a hospital quick. Are you in any pain?"

I say, "A little in my back, but nothing too bad."

My mom gets the first taxi she sees, and tells the guy to get us to NYU Langone Medical Center as quickly as possible. I look at Mom and say, "Mom, I'm so scared."

Chapter 31

Luckily when your water breaks, they seem to attend to you right away. Unfortunately though, my regular doctor isn't here, so the on-call doctor came in immediately. I'm a little bummed that my regular doctor isn't in, but I guess it's like playing the lottery for them to always be available for every patient. The on call doctor has already been back in to the room two times and spoken with me about all of the possible outcomes.

The main thing is, I won't be going home this time, and that is for certain. The nurses came in following the doctor, and we've started the round of steroids to strengthen Noah's lungs. At this point, we are preparing for an early delivery. My water has definitely broken and I'm still having contractions. Mom is on the phone with Danielle telling her everything.

Danielle is so loud I can hear her all the way across the room, and I know she is on her way. I say, "Mom, please text Chandler again. I haven't heard from him today, and I'm worried. Plus, I want him to know Noah is probably coming pretty soon. Also, tell him I won't be leaving the hospital until I have him." Surely he'll respond to that.

For some crazy reason, I'm having little to no pain. The doctor seems to think that's the craziest thing ever with the size of my contractions. Last time he checked my cervix, he took out the cerclage. It wasn't too bad having it removed, there was a little pinching and bleeding, but nothing severe.

I'm still sort of in shock that I'm here, and this is happening, but I feel surprisingly peaceful about it all. The only thing that could make me feel better would be if I could hear from Chandler. *Why in the world has he not responded? So unlike him…*

I keep checking my phone. It's been fifteen minutes since my Mom texted him for me, and nothing. Danielle walks in and looks so concerned. I say, "Why the weird face?"

She rolls her eyes at me and says, "Oh great, are you going to be one of those?"

I cock my head at her and say, "What do you mean, one of those?"

She says, "A pain in the butt patient… I bet you'll even be one of those loud, crazy screamer moms when you're pushing through delivery… You pain!"

"Come closer so I can slap you across the face." We both laugh. Mom rolls her eyes at us and says, "You two are something else. Danielle, we're glad you're here."

A nurse pops in without even a knock. I recall this is exactly how they ran things here last time we were in. I suppose when you're here to have a baby, there isn't much in the way of modesty anyhow. The nurse walks over to my bed and says the doctor wants me to check your cervix from the cerclage removal, as well as to see if there is any dilation.

Mom and Danielle step out to grab some coffee. The nurse does her thing and says, "You're about 4 and a half centimeters dilated. Let me tell the doctor. Usually, we would prefer the baby get a little more of the steroids before you go into active labor, but with your water broke, it's not looking like it will be too much longer."

Then, not saying anything, she pulls the mile and a half long strip of paper with the recorded contractions up from the floor and looks it over for a minute. She says, "These are very consistent and strong contractions. You should start dilating fast at this rate."

I must look worried because she softens a bit and says, "Your baby will be alright. You're at the best place. Trust me we've delivered much earlier than this. No worries."

I feel a little better. I'm still in shock this is happening so fast. I mean I know they told me I probably wouldn't make it full-term, but I didn't imagine it to be this early either. The nurse brushes my hair back off of my face and says, "Let us know if the pain gets bad and we can get you an epidural. If I were you, I'd go ahead and have one because once you're past 8 centimeters, there is no turning back. You're already at 4 and a ½, there is no telling how fast this could go. Once you start dilating more, the harder the contractions become. It's up to you?"

I say, "Okay. I guess let's do one. So you really think I'm having the baby soon? Like today? I mean, I just thought I was here having some contractions and that the baby would get some steroids, and I would hang out a few days to weeks."

The nurse sort of chuckles and says, "Oh no, honey, your water broke. You're dilating and having heavy contractions. This baby is coming soon!"

My mom and Danielle walk in as the nurse says, "This baby is coming soon."

Danielle says, "Woo hoo! It's time to boogie on out, Noah!"

She's literally insane. Feeling completely emotionally drained, I start crying. I'm not even sure why. I guess I'm so scared and feel so uncertain of everything. I don't know what to expect with getting a baby out, and I wish Chandler were here, or that I could at least talk to him.

Ignoring Danielle and my mom, I reach to the bed table for my cell phone. This time I call Chandler's phone. There is no answer. It goes to voicemail. I leave a message.

"Hi Chandler, I'm at the hospital. It looks like Noah will be making an early appearance after all. Please call me as soon as you can. I know you may be busy, but I just need to hear your voice. I love you…"

I'm not sure why, but that made me cry even more. I can't stand this. Of all days for him not to text, call, or answer, it had to be today. I feel awful, and now I have to worry about him.

The anesthesiologist comes in with the largest needle I've ever seen in my entire life. I feel as though I might faint as I look on his tray. I've heard stories, but really I thought people exaggerated the size of the needle. Danielle says, "Oh my goodness! Is that for real the shot?"

My mom hushes her, and I can hear them giggling over in the corner. Finally, I'm bent over the bed and my mom has walked over to hold my hand. I feel the needle go in, and all is well once it is over. I lie back in the bed and try to remain calm.

About thirty minutes have past, and I can't feel my legs or anything… it's quite annoying actually. According to Danielle, my contractions are regular. She keeps staring at the screen. I guess she's not really bothering me too much. The machine begins to beep loud and annoyingly. I ask Danielle if she touched something and she says, "No smart one… it's probably because of your contractions, they're really close together…"

All of a sudden the door bursts open without a knock which again is not unusual around here, and there are about three, maybe four people standing around in the room. I'm not sure what's happening, but there seems to be major concern in their eyes. They are looking at Noah's heartbeat and saying the monitor is picking up a drop in his rhythm. I'm feeling very nervous and I keep asking, "What's going on? What does this mean? Is he okay?"

No one is answering me, and I'm scared. Feeling more frantic, I fight to sit up and say, "What's happening?"

Eventually, the doctor puts a mask over my face, and finally he responds and says, "The oxygen will help the baby's heartbeat go up. I'm going to check you and see if you're about ready to start pushing."

I hear one of the nurses say, "Dropping. Dropping, it's dropping."

I'm so scared. Pulling the mask back so I can speak, I say, "What's going on? Is everything okay? Is my baby okay?"

Again no one answers. Mom is up by my face. She says, "Everything is going to be alright sweetie. I promise, Noah will be fine."

The doctor says, "Alright dear, I'm going to need some really big pushes. The baby is in distress and it's probably a cord situation. This happens often, and we're going to try pushing first. If it doesn't work, we'll rush over to the O.R. for a caesarian section."

Hearing exactly what the doctor said, I can recall many of the magazines and baby books I'd read about this very situation. Danielle says, "Don't worry, Kier, Noah's going to be alright. Everything is fine sweetie. Give them the biggest pushes you have…"

The doctor looks up at me and says, "Alright, three good, strong pushes. You can do it. You ready?"

I shake my head, and can feel sweat and tears pouring down my face. I push with all of my might. I push once, and the doctor says, "Okay good job…wait till I say go, and let's do it again." We wait for the next contraction and he says, "Okay, another push."

I push again with all of my might. The doctor looks at the nurse, and he says something I wasn't able to make out. He then looks back at me and says, "One last push…"

I push as hard as I can, with all of my might, but nothing happens.

All of the sudden, I feel the bed rolling and know exactly what this means. Walking along side my bed the doctor says, "We're going to the operating room for an emergency c-section. Don't worry we just need to get the baby out as fast as we can, and everything will be okay."

Everything is happening so fast, I see a white sheet go up and I try to close my eyes to say a quick prayer. They make me drink chalky stuff called Bicitra to calm my stomach acid. Mom comes in suited up in scrubs and a mask. I'm happy she's here, I did not want to do this alone. I still wish I could have spoken to Chandler. He better have a good reason when I finally talk to him. I suppose I'll send him a picture of me holding Noah, or I'll Facetime him while holding Noah.

Finally, I can feel them prepping the area and prodding around. I feel like they are acting urgently. I hear the doctor say, "You may feel some painless movement, I'm just moving the baby's head into position. I'm just going to reach my hand in to cradle his head so we can pull him out. Hang in there, Mom, you're doing great!"

Something about the way he called me Mom made me tear up again. I'm so emotional. The doctor says, "Not bad at all. The cord isn't wrapped around his neck or anything. He looks great. I'm pulling him out now. Alright, we have our baby boy!"

I immediately say, "Is he okay?"

I hear a familiar voice from behind me say, "He's absolutely perfect! Just perfect, Kier."

I look at Mom because I think I may be delusional, and she's looking up smiling at the voice. I turn my head and I see him. I say, "Chandler, oh my God! You're here. How are you here? I mean… I'm glad you're here but…but… how? I was so mad at you. I kept texting you and calling, and you were…I didn't know where you were… I guess you were on your way here? Back to New York?"

He leans over to kiss my forehead and says, "We'll talk about it later. You look so beautiful. You're amazing Kier. How's our little man?"

The doctor looks over the curtain. He says, "You must be dad?"

Chandler looks at me for what seems like approval, and I nod my head 'yes'. He says, "Yes, I'm dad. How's our little man?"

The doctor says, "He actually doesn't look too bad. The lungs of course will need a little more maturing." By this time, the doctor is talking to the both of us on my side of the curtain. He continues, "The Apgar results aren't bad really. The weight is pretty good. I'm thinking you're closer to 34 weeks gestation by the size of the baby and Apgar. Don't get me wrong, we will want to keep him here in NICU for a week, or even up to three weeks, so be prepared for this. Overall, he's breathing well on his own, we'll need to get him eating soon, and all of these things will tell us exactly how long. I'm not worried about him, though. Your baby will recover and develop just fine. He looks good." The doctor reaches his hand towards Chandler and says, "Congratulations."

I say, "When can we see him?"

The doctor says, "How about right now!"

A nurse rolls him over by the bed. He is hooked up to some tubes and seems so tiny and fragile. They let me hold him briefly before taking him to NICU. Chandler kisses him on the cheek and says, "Noah, you're so perfect. You look just like your beautiful Mommy."

I kiss Chandler on the lips and smile. I don't want to forget the way I feel right now forever. The nurse places Noah in the incubator crib, and they roll him to the NICU.

We're finally in a room, and Mom and Danielle go down to grab some dinner in the cafeteria. I look at Chandler who is right beside my bed holding my hand. I say, "What happened?"

He says, "I hated being away from you. My life sucks without you, Kier. I left. I told the guys at the firm I couldn't be there for the investigation, and that they could either agree or fire me. They told me I could keep my job. They said having me on their firm was far more beneficial than this client. Can you believe that?"

I say, "So what about your dream and making senior partner?"

Chandler smiles. He says, "That's the best part! I got to leave and come home to you and Noah, and I made senior partner!"

"You're kidding? That's awesome, Chandler! I'm so happy for you and for us!"

EPILOGUE

Today we get to take Noah home. The last three weeks have been kind of crazy and draining going back-and-forth to the hospital, visiting him. I can't wait to bring him home and be with him all the time. I think things will sink in and feel real once we have him home. He's just so perfect! I can't believe I love him so much. It sounds silly to say, but I almost can't remember life without him.

Mom went home the week I came home from the hospital, but now she's back helping us prepare to bring Noah home. She plans to stay a while and help me get on a schedule with Noah. I'm so happy for her to be here. I really love having her around. We've finally got all of my stuff moved out of my apartment and moved in here. Everything for the most part is in it's place, and I now am beginning to feel comfortable and at home here. I'm feeling so at home that when we left the hospital last night from visiting Noah, I said, "Let's go home for the last time without him."

Chandler said, "You called it home, finally."

I grab my bag, and head for the door. Chandler is carrying Noah's car-seat in one hand, and the diaper bag in the other. Mom is just as excited as we are. She is beaming from ear-to-ear as we lock the door behind us.

At the hospital, the nurses seem to be as excited as the three of us are. Everyone is all smiles as we say our goodbyes. I know it may sound weird, but I've kind of grown attached to the nurses around here. It was a bittersweet goodbye, but mostly sweet, as I look down into Noah's precious face. On the way home, I can't take my eyes off of Chandler. He is staring at Noah and talking to him as though he had always been his dad.

Josh never responded to my text about the birth certificate, so I didn't list him as the father. I'm happy with the way things have turned out. It's funny really to think back to that day in the park when I thought everything was perfect. I was about to get engaged to Josh. I was feeling so confident in that moment. I mean, I literally, in a matter of milliseconds, had my whole life planned out. I never imagined how quickly I would be robbed from that excitement… How fast it all would change.

How ironic to find true happiness amidst such anguish and disappointment. Now here I am with a precious baby boy and a man who I couldn't have dreamed of. Sometimes what seems to be right in the moment may not be right for the rest of the moments.

THE END

Also by Amy Gelsthorpe

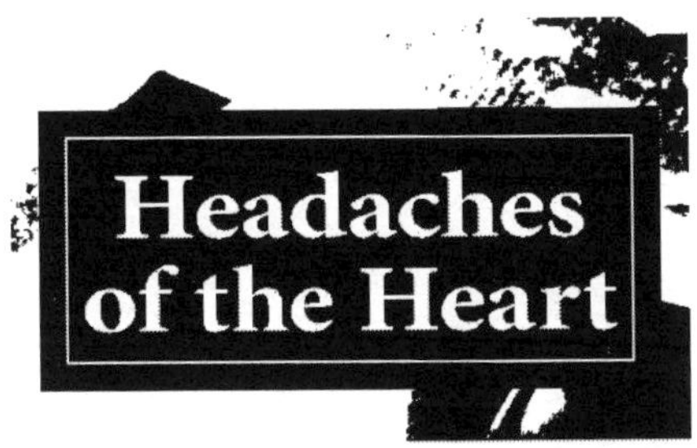

Amy Gelsthorpe

www.amygelsthorpe.com

www.facebook.com/AuthorAmyGelsthorpe

@amygelsthorpe

Made in the USA
Charleston, SC
11 November 2015